RICHMOND AND ELIZABETH

Richmond and Elizabeth

Brenda Honeyman

NEW ENGLISH LIBRARY
TIMES MIRROR

First published in Great Britain by Robert Hale in 1970

*

FIRST NEL EDITION OCTOBER 1971

*

NEL Books are published by
New English Library Limited from Barnard's Inn, Holborn, London, E.C.1.
Made and printed in Great Britain by Hunt Barnard Printing Ltd., Aylesbury, Bucks.

45000973 4

"We will unite the white rose and the red"

RICHARD III, Act V, Scene V

Prelude

In the year 1399, King Richard the second was deposed, and eventually murdered by his cousin, Henry of Bolingbroke, who usurped the crown as King Henry the fourth.

The childless Richard's acknowledged heir was his cousin, Roger Mortimer, grandson of Edward the third's third son, Lionel. The usurping Henry was the son of John of Gaunt, a younger son of that same monarch.

From this situation there arose, just over half a century later, the start of the bitter and bloody dynastic struggle, known to posterity as the Wars of the Roses.

Richard Plantagenet, Duke of York, direct descendant through his mother of Roger Mortimer, claimed the crown from his cousin, King Henry the sixth, the good, but partly insane grandson of Bolingbroke. York was driven to it by the unrelenting enmity of Henry's Queen, Margaret of Anjou, and was backed by his brother-in-law, the Earl of Salisbury, and Salisbury's eldest son, the Earl of Warwick.

The first blow was struck on May the twenty-second, 1455, and five years later, both York and Salisbury lost their lives at the battle of Wakefield.

Six months after his father's death, York's eldest son was crowned King Edward the fourth in Westminster Abbey.

At first, all went well, and this apparently easy-going young man of eighteen showed proper gratitude and respect for the architects of his victory, his mother's family of Neville, chief of whom was the mighty Earl of Warwick.

In the year 1464, however, while Warwick worked tirelessly to bring about a French alliance through Edward's marriage to Bona of Savoy, Edward secretly married Elizabeth Woodville, the widow of the Lancastrian Lord Grey; a woman five years his senior and already the mother of two sons.

This marriage estranged not only the Earl of Warwick, but also Edward's brother, George, Duke of Clarence. The King's younger brother, Richard, Duke of Gloucester, remained loyal in spite of his hatred of the Woodville family.

Eventually, in 1469, the Nevilles kidnapped the King and attempted to rule the country through their prisoner. When this failed, Warwick tried to adduce Edward's bastardy and put the Duke of Clarence, who had married the Earl's daughter, Isabel, on the throne in his brother's place. When this plan also foundered, Warwick, Clarence and their wives, together with Warwick's younger daughter, Anne, fled to France. Here, the Earl, completely changing his tactics, made peace with the exiled Margaret of Anjou and agreed to restore the imprisoned Henry the sixth to the throne. Anne Neville was betrothed to the son of Henry and Margaret, Edward of Lancaster.

In the autumn of 1470, Warwick and Clarence returned to England with men and money supplied by Louis the Eleventh of France. Partly through King Edward's own folly, he was out-generalled and caught in a trap. With the Duke of Gloucester and a handful of friends, he was forced to fly the country. He threw himself on the mercy of Duke Charles of Burgundy, the husband of his sister, Margaret.

Elizabeth Woodville and her three daughters sought the protection of Westminster sanctuary.

Part One

Elizabeth, Henry
1470–1485

1

A LITTLE girl sat before the smouldering fire in a small, cold room in Westminster sanctuary. Her name was Elizabeth and she was nearly five years old.

Since her birth and magnificent christening in the February of 1466, until just over a month ago. September in this year of 1470, she had been surrounded by all the pomp and ceremony attendant upon a Princess of England and heiress-presumptive to her father's throne. Now, her circumstances were drastically, painfully altered. She was bewildered: she could not understand what had happened and would have been inclined to believe that it was all a game, had not her mother been so hysterical. Her mother's outbursts frightened her.

Ladies in the Queen's condition, Mother Cobb assured Elizabeth, were often overwrought, particularly when they were as near their time as she was. 'And also,' the midwife had added, with a mournful, wheezy sigh, 'when they've had as much to put up with as Her Highness has endured during the past two years.'

Elizabeth glanced at her sisters who were playing amongst the rushes on the floor. Mary, a year younger than herself, was three; Cicely two. Mary, who was coughing badly, had been ordered by Mother Cobb to stay away from the little one. But Mary had a stubborn, defiant streak in her nature, inherited from their mother, and such a command was to invite her immediate opposition. Holding the baby by force, she was engaged in breathing into Cicely's mouth.

'You're not to do that,' Elizabeth admonished her, but without much hope of being attended to, Mary having small regard for a sister so near to her in age.

Elizabeth shrugged and hunched her knees against her chest for warmth. This first of November was bitterly cold. Food and fuel were both scarce for the royal refugees; and would have been even scarcer had not that ardent admirer of the Queen, Abbot Myling, sent in logs and furs and other comforts. There was a butcher, too, who lived close to the sanctuary, who smuggled beef and mutton to them once or twice a week, depending upon the vigilance of the Earl of Warwick's officers.

Richard Neville, Earl of Warwick, at present King Henry's Lieutenant of the Realm, was a confused figure to the young Elizabeth. First cousin to her father and his brothers, she knew that her uncle Gloucester still held Warwick in respect and affection; that her uncle Clarence was the Earl's son-in-law; and that her grandmother York regarded her nephew in the same light as she regarded all members of her family: whatever his shortcomings, one Neville was worth ten other men.

But Elizabeth's mother and her mother's mother, the Dowager Duchess of Bedford, hated the Earl with all the intensity of which two passionate-natured women were capable. A fact which, said the garrulous Mother Cobb, was hardly surprising, considering that only last year, during their brief ascendancy over the King, Warwick and Clarence had ordered the executions of the first Earl Rivers and his son, Sir John Woodville. These two deaths had left the Queen lacking a father and a brother; the Duchess a husband and a son. Such a loss would have been tragic in any family. To the devoted Woodvilles it was calamitous.

When the King had thrown off his enforced retirement and returned once more to Westminster, he had made no move to punish his brother or his cousin and the Queen had been to shrewd to press him to it. Only a fool would try to drive Edward the fourth along any path he had no wish to tread, and Elizabeth Woodville, former lady-in-waiting to Margaret of Anjou, had never been that.

She had raised herself to the throne of England, and maintained that position for six long years, in the teeth of all opposition, including that of her husband's intimidating mother, his two brothers and the formidable Neville family. She had made advantageous matches for all her beloved brothers and sisters; obtained lucrative posts for her cohorts of relations; and had even extended her bounty to the family of her first husband, Lord Grey. No; Elizabeth Woodville was certainly no fool, so she nursed her desire for revenge against Warwick and Clarence in secret. She was a woman who could bide her time.

Time, however, was running out for Elizabeth Woodville: fate seemed against Edward the fourth and all his supporters. Warwick reigned triumphant in London (for although the Earl had had the poor, mentally deranged Henry the sixth brought from the Tower and installed once again in the Palace of Westminster, there was no doubt in anyone's mind as to who was the true ruler of England).

'But what will happen when Margaret of Anjou and her

son arrive from France,' the elder Elizabeth had remarked significantly to the attentive midwife only this morning, 'is another story.'

For the present, however, Queen Margaret and her son, together with his wife, Anne Neville, and Anne's mother, the Countess of Warwick, appeared content to remain in France.

The Princess Elizabeth rolled over onto her stomach and stared into the caverns of the fire.

The century which lay behind her was one filled with fighting and blood-shed; with the shameful murder of Richard the second and the martial glory of Henry the fifth; with the factions and hatreds of a House divided against itself; with the glory of Thomas à Kempis and the pangs of cultural rebirth throughout the European continent.

In the century which lay ahead, Elizabeth's grand-daughter and namesake, Elizabeth of England, would prove that men had no monopoly of intelligence, intellect and political genius; while her great-grand-daughter, Mary of Scotland, would demonstrate that women would always be women, whether commoner or Queen. Yet another of her great-grand-daughters, the Lady Jane Grey, would die for her loyalty to that New Learning whose seeds were, even now, being sown across Europe; sent to the block by that one of Elizabeth's granddaughters whose devotion to the Old Faith would earn her the sobriquet 'Bloody Mary.'

But it was neither of the past nor of the future that the little girl was thinking at this moment, as she lay without moving, her fingers pushed into her ears to block out the screams and cries of her younger sisters. She was wondering when her father would come home; that fair-haired giant who stood well over six feet without his shoes and who, she dimly understood, was now an exile at the court of Burgundy. Elizabeth adored her father. She was even fond of her uncle Clarence who, instead of being at her father's side like her other royal uncle, Gloucester, and her mother's eldest brother, the new Earl Rivers, was here in London as a member of his father-in-law's government.

Elizabeth turned once more on to her back, staring at the ceiling. The warmth from the fire was making her tired and Mary and Cicely had stopped fighting at last. The streets were quiet, too; particularly so after the noise and clamour of a few weeks earlier, when the mob had run riot, mad with blood-lust as the hated Earl of Worcester had passed by on his way to execution. Elizabeth's eyelids fluttered down over the gentle, blue eyes, her fair lashes lying in golden half-moons against the tender, young skin of her cheeks. She heaved, a long, contented sigh.

Ten minutes later, Mother Cobb found her, sound asleep.

A little distance from the sanctuary, in the Palace of Westminster, a thirteen-year-old boy stood by the side of his uncle, Jasper Tudor, and listened with only half an ear to the testy exchange of words between him and the Earl of Warwick.

Henry Tudor knew that his uncle neither trusted nor liked this man who had been such an ardent supporter of York for the past fifteen years, and who now set himself up at the head of a Lancastrian government. Henry, eyeing the new Lieutenant of the King's Realm with a sapience far beyond his years, surmised that the Earl of Warwick had never been an ardent supporter of anyone or anything except himself. Richard Neville, thought Henry impatiently, was an impetuous fool, who would, if given enough rope, eventually hang himself. It was a pity that his hot-tempered uncle could not be brought to realise it.

The voices rose and fell, irritating Henry and distracting him from his thoughts; those secret thoughts that ran on and on inside his head and had nothing to do with what he said or did, or with the expression on his face. When was it, he wondered, that he had first learned to live this hidden life? Probably at the age of four, when he had been purchased by Lord and Lady Herbert for the princely sum of a thousand pounds.

For sold he had been, like any other of the spoils of war; and as being sold he regarded it, no matter how often he was told that it was the customary thing to happen. It might be normal for other, less important people, but in his veins ran the royal blood of both England and of France.

Now, here was his uncle demanding that Henry be restored to his father's old earldom of Richmond; and Warwick stalling because he had already promised the title to his son-in-law, the disgruntled Duke of Clarence. The colour was dangerously suffused in Jasper Tudor's face and Henry mentally curled his lip, all the while schooling his features to a look of injured innocence. Did his uncle really think that the earldom of Richmond held any lures for his nephew? And if Jasper had realised Henry's contempt, would he have understood it? Unlikely, thought Henry, as he hardly understood it, himself.

What did he want from life? He had no clear idea. Certainly not marriage with Maude Herbert, which, until a year ago, had seemed to be his fate. Maude Herbert! That fat little nobody! What did he want with her? He was not even sure that he liked women, not even the widowed Lady Herbert who had been so kind to him. He suspected, carefully analysing his every thought and action, that sex would play no very great part in his life, and that he would find it difficult to form a deep and lasting attachment to anyone. This might be some trait inherent in his character – although, coming as he did from strong-tempered and passionate people on both sides of his family, he doubted it – or it could be the result of his captive childhood. In either case, he was indifferent. Henry Tudor had early learned to accept himself as he was; to envy no one – no one, that was, with one exception.

In Richard, Duke of Gloucester, the eighteen-year-old brother of King Edward the fourth, Henry recognised a young man who had been born with similiar liabilities as himself. Richard Plantagenet was the small, dark member of a tall, fair family: Henry Tudor was insignificant amongst a mightier breed. Neither boy had been strong as a child, and each was of a reticent, almost puritanical disposition which made for uneasy relationships with those around them.

But the young Duke of Gloucester had overcome many of these disabilities, largely through the love and protection of that eldest brother whom he adored. By the time he had reached Henry's present age, Richard had been Admiral of England and become the trusted lieutenant of his King; had levied and marched with his troops; had sat on commissions of oyer and terminer. At seventeen, he had been Chief Justice of Wales, putting down rebellions with an ease and clemency which showed him to be a capable soldier and a merciful man. And now he was in Burgundy with his brother, working for Edward's restoration with all his ability and skill.

But what had happened to Henry Tudor? What opportunities had he had to prove his manhood or to fulfil his inchoate sense of destiny? He had spent eight years in Pembroke Castle as the petted foster-son of Lady Herbert and the prospective bridegroom of the odious, simpering Maude. He had been expected to show his gratitude; to smile and say thank-you, while Richard of Gloucester, that Plantagenet nearest to him in age, had shown him how life could – and should – be lived.

A deep resentment of this unknown cousin had taken root in Henry's mind and grown steadily over the years. It was a feeling no less profound because Henry resented his own resentment. He knew that such an emotion as envy was beneath him; it upset his rather cold and calculating nature and flawed that unemotional acceptance of himself which was so necessary to his peace of mind. Those who had been responsible for his childhood, he thought with a sudden surge of anger, had much to answer for.

He had been born in Pembroke Castle on January the twenty-eighth in the year 1457. His mother, who had been only fourteen years of age at the time of his birth, was Margaret Beaufort, great-grand-daughter of John of Gaunt and his mistress, Katherine Swynford. The Beauforts had been legitimatised by Richard the second, and Henry the fourth had confirmed their legitimacy, but had debarred them from ever claiming the crown. Yet, in spite of the patent, and the fact that Gaunt had eventually married his mistress, the taint of bastardy had lingered on.

Henry's father, Edmund Tudor, who had died two months before his only child was born, had also suffered from the slur of illegitimacy. Katherine of Valois, Princess of France and widow of King Henry the fifth, had lived in apparent seclusion after the death of her husband, her younger son, King Henry the sixth, being brought up by his royal uncles. But on her death, it was found that she had borne at least three children to her Clerk of the Wardrobe, Owen Tudor; Jasper, Edmund and another son who was now a monk at Westminster. Owen had sworn that he and Katherine had been married, but no proof had ever been forthcoming.

When Henry Tudor had been a year old, his widowed mother had married Sir Henry Stafford and relinquished her child into the care of her brother-in-law, Jasper. Those very early years in Pembroke Castle with his uncle and grandfather, Owen Tudor, had been happy ones, despite the fact that Jasper was often away fighting to keep his weak, and now insane half-brother on his throne.

Then, in February of 1461, Edward, the young Earl of March, had decisively defeated Jasper Tudor in battle at Mortimer's Cross. Jasper had fled to France; Henry's grandfather, Owen Tudor, had been captured and executed; and, in March, Henry the sixth had finally been deposed and Jasper's conqueror proclaimed King Edward the fourth in his stead. In September of the same year, the Yorkist Lord Herbert had been made Earl of Pembroke in place of Jasper Tudor, and had bought the wardship of the four-year-old Henry, and the right to dispose of him in marriage.

And so, Henry had lived for eight long, dull years with the Herberts, even staying on in Lady Herbert's care after the execution of her husband last year. (Lord Herbert had been captured during Warwick's rebellion and had suffered the same fate as Earl Rivers and his son.) Another eight uneventful years had appeared to stretch before the fretting and embittered young boy; perhaps a lifetime.

But then, suddenly, in the short space of twelve months, events occurred with amazing rapidity. And when Warwick had returned so triumphantly to England nine weeks ago, he had been accompanied by a number of the exiled Lancastrian lords, amongst whom was Jasper Tudor. The former Earl of Pembroke had immediately set out for Wales and taken his nephew once more into his custody. Together, they had travelled to London to await the arrival of Queen Margaret from France.

And that was how Henry Tudor came to be at Westminster on this miserable first of November in the year 1470, thinking his secret thoughts and praying that the long, dreary years of captivity were over for good.

2

ELIZABETH was warm again. More important still, she was once more clothed as a princess should be, in a velvet dress and fur-lined slippers.

Her father was home. He and his supporters had landed at Ravenspur, in Yorkshire, a month ago, in the cold, blustery days of mid-March, and had marched, almost unopposed, throughout the length of the country. Warwick was in Coventry and refused to come out; Jasper Tudor had returned to Wales; Queen Margaret was still in France; and Henry Percy, Earl of Northumberland, remained on his estates.

London had opened its gates to Edward yesterday, April the eleventh, Maundy Thursday, and the Yorkists had swarmed out of the sanctuaries to join Mayor Stokton and the rejoicing citizens in their exuberant demonstrations of welcome.

The Londoners had cheered themselves hoarse for the man whom they regarded as peculiarly their own King; big, strong, handsome and, above all, a shopkeeper of sorts like themselves; a man who loved trading and who spent freely amongst them; a man who, in adversity, had done the impossible by reaching his capital without the loss of a single man.

They had cheered, too, because the King was now the father

of that longed-for son; for a male heir to the Royal House of York had been born in sanctuary to Elizabeth Woodville on November the second, 1470, the day following Jasper and Henry Tudor's visit to Westminster.

And, finally, the people cheered because King Edward was accompanied not by one brother, but by two. Ten days ago, at Banbury, the Duke of Clarence had seized the opportunity to forswear the cause of Lancaster and return to his brother's side. The Earl of Warwick should be made to realise that he could not offer George of Clarence a crown and then abandon him for the half-witted Henry the sixth.

Elizabeth was seated now in her uncle Gloucester's apartments in Baynard's Castle, playing with his two bastard children; Katherine, who was three, and her brother, John, who was a year younger. Also present were Elizabeth's sisters and her cousin, John de la Pole, the Earl of Lincoln. Inside, it was noisy and warm; outside, it was bleak and the dismal tolling of the church bells denoted that it was Good Friday.

Her other uncle, George of Clarence, came in, unannounced, falling over the baby, John, who was sprawled just inside the door. While the young Duke of Gloucester rose, laughing, to greet his brother, the nurse picked up the screaming child and deposited him by the hearth with his cousins. Elizabeth rattled a fool's head on a stick to distract the little boy's attention, while the Earl of Lincoln put an arm around his small namesake and marched his wooden soldiers to and fro amongst the rushes.

John de la Pole, eldest son of the Duke and Duchess of Suffolk, was a tall, eager boy of eight, with a warmth and humour derived from his great-great-grandfather, Geoffrey Chaucer. He was his uncle Richard's favourite nephew and the Duke smiled at him now in acknowledgement of John's easy, good-natured ways.

George muttered an apology and moved towards the fire, spreading his hands to the blaze. His handsome face coarsening now as was his brother Edward's, was marred by a look of sullen discontent.

'I've been summoned to the War Council at the Tower,' he said. 'I take it that you have, too.' Richard nodded and George continued: 'Will Warwick come out and fight?'

'Reports say that he is already on the road.' Richard poured some wine into a silver-rimmed mazer and handed it to his brother. 'And in any case, he must be forced to fight. We know that Devonshire and Somerset have gone south to meet Margaret, which means that she must have at last left

France. It's vital that we settle accounts with Warwick before the Franco-Lancastrian army takes us in the rear.'

'And if – when – we beat Warwick, what will happen to him?'

'Do you care?'

The Duke of Clarence glanced quickly at his brother over his shoulder. 'He's my father-in-law.'

'Yes.' Richard's voice was harsh. 'But not mine.'

'No one's fault but your own.' George sank into a chair, pushing his long legs out in front of him, idly watching the ripples of light and shade made by the glow from the fire. 'You should have joined Warwick and me when we needed you. You could have married Anne Neville then. Now it's too late and she's the wife of Edward of Lancaster.'

Richard made no reply but his thin lips tightened until they were almost invisible.

George watched him in silence for a moment, then said with suppressed violence: 'Why didn't you join us, Diccon? You don't like the Woodvilles any more than the Nevilles do; any more than I do; any more than a hundred others I could name. Disregarding the swift, warning glance of his brother's eyes in the direction of their nieces, he went on: 'God's Body! That woman! Did you see the look on her face last night when she presented Edward with his heir? Like a cat that's licked the cream-pot clean. I could tell you something about her . . . an imposter. . . . She's not really. . . . ' He broke off abruptly, undergoing one of his lightning changes of mind and evidently deciding to keep his information to himself. Richard was relieved, but George had not yet finished. 'Did you see our mother's face? I've rarely seen her look so nauseated. And all the time that Woodville whore was preening herself and. . . . '

'For God's sake, shut-up, George!' Richard's fingers closed hard about his brother's arm and he nodded almost imperceptibly towards the children, who had stopped their games and were listening to their elders with unashamed interest.

The Duke of Clarence flushed and turned to the table, pouring himself another drink. Richard hoped that George had now come to the end of his diatribe, but the wine only served to inflame a temper which frustrated ambition and a general sense of ill-usage had made extremely short. Slamming the mazer down with a clatter that made everyone jump, George shouted: 'Elizabeth Woodville is not only a whore but a murderess!'

'George!'

'I haven't forgotten Desmond's two children, even if you have.'

The brothers stared into each other's eyes for a long moment. Then: 'No, I haven't forgotten,' Richard said at last.

A page came in. The King urgently requested the presence of the Dukes of Gloucester and of Clarence at the meeting at the Tower.

'We must go,' Richard said.

His daughter, Katherine, immediately got up and toddled over to his side, touching him cautiously and staring into his face with pouting lips and frowning brows, implying that she thought but poorly of of his constant desertions of her company for less compelling attractions. Her resemblance to her mother, the mistress who had died when John was born, caught Richard by the throat, and it was with a decidedly shaken laugh that he stooped to give Katherine a hug.

'I shall soon be back,' he promised.

He was as good as his word, but it was only to march out again the following day; northwards, in the direction of Barnet.

Pembroke Castle, first begun by Arnulph de Montgomery in the reign of William the second, stood massive and indestructible on its spur of limestone rock. Normally it was a grey and forbidding place, but on this warm spring evening of Sunday, May the fifth, even the enormous circular keep looked mellow in the light from the setting sun. The seagulls were thick on the horizon, wheeling and crying in the wind, tossed like pieces of paper against the darkening sky. A patch of silverweed lay by the wall of the courtyard, the bright yellow faces of the flowers peeping impudently through the tumble of hairy leaves. Maude Herbert, uttering an exclamation of delight, stooped to pick them.

'Oh look, Henry! Aren't they pretty?'

Henry Tudor, striding ahead, did not deign to reply. He found Maude a bore and privately branded her a nod-cock, an expression which was currently enjoying his favour. He stared with loathing at his surroundings and thought with bitterness that uncle Jasper had betrayed him.

When the news had reached Pembroke of the Earl of Warwick's defeat and death at Barnet and Margaret of Anjou's landing, on the same day, at Weymouth, Henry had assumed that he would be allowed to accompany his uncle when he rode out to meet his sister-in-law. For Queen Margaret, dissuaded by her advisers from marching on London, and terrified for the safety of her only child, the young Prince Edward of Lancaster, had struck westwards towards Bristol, hoping to join her Anglo-French forces with Jasper's Welsh retainers.

But Jasper had gone alone to meet her, leaving Henry once more to the care of Maude and Lady Herbert. The only consolation was that Henry, in his uncle's absence, was virtually the master, the ladies being merely dependants on Jasper Tudor's bounty. Even this thought, however, did not compensate for his uncle's decision to leave him at Pembroke. He was fourteen years old now and many boys had been blooded in battle by the time they had reached that age. Edward the fourth had seen his first fighting when a year younger, and Richard of Gloucester, although he had been involved in no major affray, had certainly seen some skirmishing.

And it was the young Duke of Gloucester who had been largely responsible for the recent victory of his side at Barnet; a fact which the Yorkist Lady Herbert, fond though she was of Henry, could not forbear to rub in.

'They say that he and his men fought their way out of a marshy pit and held the plateau above in the face of a terrible onslaught from Exeter's men and almost all of Warwick's reserves,' she had told Henry, pinching him under the chin and smiling a little at the closed, dark look on his face. She was a woman who could not resist the temptation to irritate, even when she knew that it would arouse anger in those whom she most wished to please.

Maude caught Henry up thrusting her arm through his and offering him the silverweed, quite unabashed when he roughly thrust her away. 'What were you thinking about?' she asked.

'Gloucester,' he answered curtly.

'The place or the Duke? If it's the first, I know nothing about it. If it's the second. . . . ' She broke off with an assumed, love-sick sigh. 'Would you fancy me as Duchess of Gloucester, Henry?'

'I wouldn't fancy you at all,' he snapped, with the simple brutality of youth, and she checked the impulse to spit at him.

Maude Herbert was a shrewd girl. She had been quite small when she had first realised that the contemptuous, patronising answer was often more effective than the direct and quarrelsome kind.

'Never mind, Henry,' she said with a smile reminiscent of her mother's. 'One day you may get the chance to prove that you are just as brave.'

Her words had an unexpected effect upon her companion. Henry stood still, looking unseeingly ahead. A frightening revelation had just been vouchsafed him, as he stared at a piece of moss-covered stone whose irregular shape presented the appearance of a stunted human hand. He had realised in that moment of blinding clarity, that he did not really want to fight: it had all been self-delusion; and the contemplation of violence made him feel physically ill.

He shook his head like a boy coming out of a dream and pushed the realisation down into the unexplored recesses of his mind; deep and still deeper until it could no longer reach the light of day or be reflected in the mirrors of his eyes.

Maude was regarding him curiously. She was just going to speak but the rattle of the drawbridge made her turn her head, forgetting what it was that she had been about to say. The next instant, the courtyard was filled with a ragged, exhausted, blood-stained band of men and Jasper Tudor was sliding wearily from his horse. The air rasped in his lungs.

Lady Herbert appeared in the doorway and he made her a mocking salute.

'You may take Pembroke back, madam,' he gasped. 'I shall have no need of it . . . for a while, at least.' He turned to Henry. 'Margaret's army was routed,' he went on, 'yesterday, at Tewkesbury. She has gone into hiding. Edward of Lancaster is dead.'

'And you?' queried Henry. Did anyone notice the hint of tears in his voice?

'France,' Jasper answered. 'One of my men has gone to Milford Haven to fix our passage.'

'Ours?' Henry's voice rose on a note of hope. Were his years of captivity and inactivity really over at last? Or did Jasper simply mean himself and his men?

'You're coming with me. That's why I'm here.'

Maude stood open-mouthed, while Lady Herbert was moved to protest.

'You surely won't take him into exile, my lord! A delicate boy like that!' Henry threw her a glance of hatred, but, oblivious, she continued: 'He can stay here as he has always done.'

Jasper wiped the sweat from his mouth. It was almost dark and a sharp breeze was blowing in from the sea, making the torch flames belly in the draught and spangling the men's beards with a fine salt spray. Jasper looked at Lady Herbert.

'I told you that Edward of Lancaster is dead. Killed on the field.'

'So?'

He smiled, grimly. 'If I were Edward of York,' he said,

'I don't think that I'd let the father outlive the son by many weeks.'

Lady Herbert digested this in slowly gathering wrath. 'If you mean what I believe you to mean. . . . '

Jasper laughed. 'Precisely! Edward is no fool and he won't waste this opportunity to stamp out Bolingbroke's line.'

'But what has that to do with the boy?' Lady Herbert demanded, putting a protective arm about Henry's shrinking shoulders.

Jasper said nothing, merely turning away to straighten his saddle. Lady Herbert watched him, a frown in her eyes. After a second or two, she tapped Jasper on the arm. 'If you're thinking that perhaps the bastard Beaufort line. . . . '

'They were granted a patent of legitimacy,' he put in, but she went on, unheeding.

' . . . might claim the throne, then remember that Henry of Bolingbroke debarred them from the succession.'

Jasper laughed again. 'Nevertheless, the boy is coming with me. He wants his heavy frieze cloak and a change of clothing. That will be sufficient.'

Lady Herbert sighed. She saw that he was adamant and, in any case, she had no power to prevent him. Until the victorious Yorkists arrived, he was still the master of Pembroke.

And it was with an unexpectedly heavy heart that she stood with Maude on the following morning, watching the ship slip its moorings and slide slowly out of the harbour. She was also extremely uneasy. She did not at all like the looks of the ship's Breton captain.

3

ELIZABETH covered her ears, as much against the squealing protests of Mary and Cicely as against the booming of the guns. Her father was still in the midlands, where he had gone after the battle of Tewkesbury, and it was her maternal uncle, Earl Rivers, who was directing the defences of London.

The cause of the trouble was the Bastard of Fauconberg. An illegitimate son of Elizabeth's great-uncle, Lord Fauconberg, the Bastard had, like his father before him, remained loyal to the House of Neville. On hearing the news of Barnet Field, he had arrived at Sandwich, roused those most bellicose of Englishmen, the men of Kent, and marched on London. Repelled at Aldgate and Bishopsgate by the angry citizens, the infuriated Bastard had ordered his ships to sail up the Thames and was now engaged in the bombardment of London bridge. The recently rebuilt gate at the Southwark end had just been fired, much to the secret delight of the two commanders, Earl Rivers and the Earl of Essex, both of whom realised that by this act the Bastard had irrevocably lost any remnants of support which he might have had amongst the Londoners.

Elizabeth Woodville, together with her mother, daughters and baby son, had taken refuge in the Tower, where she was fretfully awaiting news of Edward's return from Coventry.

The Duchess of Bedford, who still wore black in spite of the fact that the second anniversary of her husband's execution was fast approaching, smiled somewhat cynically at her daughter.

'You should have more faith in Anthony's ability as a commander,' she remarked. 'In the lists he is superb.'

'In the lists . . .' the Queen began impatiently, then saw the gleam of irony in her mother's eyes. She laughed reluctantly. 'Anthony's a dreamer. The only one of our family who is.'

The Duchess pursed her lips, considering her first-born. 'He's fatalistic and always has been since childhood. "What will be, will be" is Anthony's motto. Now that the Bastard has fired the bridge and brought the wrath of the Londoners gathering about his head, Anthony will be galvanized into new life. He will see that Fate is on his side.' Jacquetta slowly lowered herself into a chair. She felt so tired of late that she found it hard to cope with even the simple mechanics of everyday life. The shrill screams of her two youngest granddaughters, every time the guns sounded, irritated her beyond endurance and she rounded on them with a sharp admonition.

Elizabeth drew Cicely into her arms and nursed her as well as she could. She was too young as yet to admit openly to herself that she could dislike a member of her own flesh and blood, but she wished with all her might that it had been her grandmother York who had accompanied them into the Tower, and not her grandmother Bedford. But the intrepid Cicely Neville, snapping her gnarled fingers at the invaders and daring her nephew, the Bastard, to do his worst, remained in her own home, Baynard's Castle.

There was a sudden lull in the bombardment and the two

younger girls stopped crying. A silence settled over the room, so profound that Elizabeth felt that she had only to put out her hand to touch it. The May sunshine flooded through the high windows, filling the apartment with a golden transparency in which a myriad particles of mortar and brick dust whirled and gyrated, like dancers on the village greens in summer, performing their ancient and mystical rites which had origins far back in the mists of the druidical past.

Mary got up and tottered purposefully in the direction of her mother. Leaning her plump arms on the Queen's knees, she looked into the still beautiful face and asked earnestly: 'Whatsa whore?'

Little Elizabeth knew at once by the quick, furtive glance which passed between her mother and grandmother that it was a word that she and her sisters had no business to know. The Queen, taken off her guard, parried the insistently repeated enquiry in the time-honoured, parental fashion of counter-question. 'Why?'

'Ocken Clawence says you are one.'

'Indeed!' Elizabeth Woodville knew very well her brother-in-law's opinion of herself, but she flushed angrily, nevertheless.

'Whatsit mean?'

The Queen hesitated. If she told a direct lie, it might result in her daughter so addressing other ladies at the court, under the impression that she was paying them a compliment. Instead, Elizabeth Woodville resorted to that other time-honoured strategem: It is not a nice word: Do not repeat it: You shall know the meaning when you are older.

Mary was dissatisfied and tried again.

'What's a 'poster?'

The Queen was nonplussed and looked at her eldest daughter for enlightenment.

'I think she means an . . . an . . . *impostor*,' Elizabeth said, carefully recalling her uncle's exact words and wondering if this, too, was something that should not be repeated.

Apparently it was and far worse than the other, for her mother instantly sprang to her feet and began pacing the floor.

'Did uncle Clarence say that of me as well?'

Mary and Elizabeth nodded in unison. The Queen looked at her mother under suddenly frowning brows.

The Duchess shrugged. 'You've had your suspicions that he knew . . . Stillington. . . . ' Little Elizabeth, listening intently, could make nothing of these words.

'I wasn't sure.' Elizabeth Woodville moved to and fro, her amethyst coloured gown flowing against her body in ripples of violet and plum. She drove her fist into her palm, then paused, her clenched hands raised to her mouth. 'My children will never be safe while Clarence is alive,' she muttered.

Jacquetta smiled grimly. 'And never forget that he and Warwick ordered the executions of your father and brother. Warwick has paid his account.'

'I don't forget,' her daughter answered, 'but if Clarence knows. . . . It could prove of advantage. Edward will never avenge my relatives on his. I've known that for years. But if he thought the succession was in danger. . . .'

The Duchess nodded. 'Now that he has a son, he will be interested. Bring it to his notice, but not yet. At present, George is the lost sheep only just returned to the fold; the prodigal newly repentant and forgiven. But in time, Edward's pleasure in his company is bound to pall. Your eldest brother-in-law, my dear, is a man who cannot resist digging pits for himself to fall in. He continually underestimates Edward and judges him by his lazy, easy-going appearance. Clarence will be making trouble soon enough and then will be your chance.'

The Queen listened attentively, as the Woodville children had always done, to the astute, predatory woman who was her mother. Born of the royal House of Luxembourg, and wife for a short time to Henry the fifth's brother, the Duke of Bedford, Jacquetta had never allowed anything to stand in the path of her self-interest. Her life had been dedicated to getting her own way, and to her eldest daughter she had imparted the gift of patience; the ability to wait for years if necessary, to accomplish a design; and the gift of tenacity to see that purpose carried through to its conclusion.

The calm was split into a thousand fragments with the explosion of a gun and the roar of falling masonry. The smell of charred timbers and the crackle of burning wood, caused the children to run, shrieking, under a table. Elizabeth sat huddled with her hands once more over her ears, while the noise battered at her senses. But beneath the fear that consumed her, snippets of the afternoon's conversation kept drifting around in her head. Looking back on it in after years, she always felt that it was then, on that May afternoon of sunshine and terror, that she first became aware of her mother as a person, instead of the vague, fairy-tale presence that she had hitherto been.

And round and round in Elizabeth's mind there also ran the words of her uncle Clarence; for although she might not have the slightest notion of the meaning of the word 'impostor' and but the haziest idea of what the word 'whore' could mean, she knew beyond the shadow of a doubt all the implications attached to the word 'murderess.'

Henry stood on deck, his frieze cloak wrapped securely about him. The waves rose in sheets of black glass, glimmering with frost-green depths, and the foam flew thick in the air, settling on his shoulders like snow. Behind him, Jasper Tudor paced up and down, uneasiness written in every line of his prowling figure, but Henry neither enquired, nor did he care, why his uncle was so perturbed. He was too busy with his own thoughts.

He was free; free from Pembroke, free from the Herberts, and this, surely, was what he had always wanted. And yet, now, he was not so certain. Since that moment of self-revelation just under a week ago, he was beginning to know himself extremely well. He had come to realise that between the imagined vision of himself and the reality, there was a deep and yawning chasm; and with the acceptance of this fact, he had stepped across the border-line between childhood and maturity. He had always thought that he wanted to go adventuring, but now that the role of adventurer had been thrust upon him, he knew that what he most craved from life was security and a permanent place in the scheme of things. And a place, moreover, that would do justice to his descent from both Alfred and Charlemagne; that would acknowledge his close ties of kinship with both Edward the fourth of England and Louis the eleventh of France.

He knew also, that it was this that had always irked him; that he, who was so closely allied by blood to the two great royal Houses of Europe, Valois and Plantagenet, should have been treated throughout his life as a person of no account. But of what importance was he? Of what use, except as a royal ward to be bartered for money and lands? He realised now that his jealousy of Richard of Gloucester stemmed as much from the political power wielded by that young man, and from the love and esteem that his brothers and sisters accorded him, as from envy of his cousin's military prowess. Although many people had regarded the late Duke of York as rightful King of England, his children had no more been born princes than had Henry Tudor. Yet York's eldest son now occupied the throne, while his two other remaining sons were unequalled in importance. And for those who had eyes to see, it was obvious that whereas George of Clarence's power was as evanescent as dew on a summer's morning, Richard of Gloucester's was rooted deep in his King's affection and trust.

Had matters gone differently at Tewkesbury, however, it would be Henry Tudor who was now at Westminster at the beginning of what could have been a brilliant career in the service of his half-uncle, King Henry the sixth. That his career would have been highly successful Henry had no doubt, for he felt in himself the same stirrings of political genius that had made his cousin, Louis the eleventh of France, the cleverest king in Europe. And just as Louis, in his earlier years, had been tormented by the frustration of his exceptional talents, so Henry Tudor railed inwardly against a Fate which doomed him to a life of exile and inactivity at a foreign court.

Outwardly, however, he remained calm. The coast loomed on the horizon, a thin, dun-coloured line, lost every now and then in a flurry of rain and a froth of spume. The captain came towards them and Jasper caught him roughly by the cloak.

'Where is this?' he asked, his voice almost carried away by the wind.

The captain's eyes moved shiftily in his weather-beaten face.

'The storm has driven us off course,' he muttered defensively. 'This is Brest.'

Brittany! That perpetual thorn in the side of France; the home of those descendants of the old Celtic peoples of Britain, who had followed Maximus on his abortive expedition overseas in the dying years of Rome; people who were more akin to the Cornish and the Welsh than to their French neighbours. And what of Duke Francis? What would he do, Jasper wondered, with two such valuable political pawns as his nephew and himself? Would they be allowed to pass into France, or would they be held, unwilling 'guests' until such time as Francis decided how to use them?

As Jasper stepped ashore in the cold, clinging grey light of early morning, he knew the gravest misgivings.

4

THE Milanese ambassador laid down his pen and rubbed his hands together. He cursed viciously a climate that had you sweltering at the beginning of May and freezing in the middle of June. Then he re-read his last sentence, 'King Edward has had King Henry assassinated in the Tower,' and smiled.

He could not really be expected to quote Edward's official version of the event; that Henry had died of 'pure displeasure and melancholy' on hearing the news of Tewkesbury. Indeed, he could not be expected to believe it. Certainly no member of the Sforza family would give it a moment's credence.

The ambassador rose and went to the hearth where a small fire was burning. He had been one of the hundreds who had seen Henry's body as it had lain outside St Paul's the day following Edward's return to his capital, and he had been forced to admit that it was as neat an assassination as any he had witnessed in Italy. The face had been peaceful, the body unmarked as far as the eye could see. Stories had been current that pools of blood had mysteriously appeared and disappeared under the bier, but what public event was not attended by its crop of rumours and miraculous signs, particularly here in England? Surely no other people in the world were so well supplied with portents and prophecies.

Shouting and the braying of trumpets brought the ambassador out of his reverie and to the window, just in time to see Richard of Gloucester returning triumphantly from Sandwich, where the Bastard of Fauconberg and his men had submitted to the Duke's command. Here was a young man to watch, thought the ambassador; the greatest man in the kingdom after the King, and Edward's most trusted lieutenant. Honours had fallen thick and fast upon the young Duke these past few weeks – Great Chamberlain, Steward of the Duchy of Lancaster beyond Trent, Warden of the West Marches towards Scotland – and, with the honours, lands to make him one of the richest men in the country. All Warwick's estates in Cumberland and Yorkshire were now his, including Penrith, Middleham and Sheriff Hutton.

The ambassador stretched his leg and heard it crack. He longed for the Italian sun, for the strong, clear colours of his native land instead of the fragile, muted tones of this island.

The Duke's procession passed, the slim, lank-haired young man riding at its head. Rumour had it, reflected the ambassador, that the Duke was determined to marry Edward of Lancaster's widow, Anne Neville, and had obtained the King's permission to do so. In this case, rumour was probably correct, if the bad temper of the Duke of Clarence was anything to judge by. The lady in question was at present living in his household with her sister and, as long as she remained unwed, the larger part of the Neville inheritance would be claimed by her brother-in-law. Already enraged by the granting of part of Warwick's lands to Gloucester, Clarence was determined that there should be no legitimate excuse for granting him more.

The ambassador went back to his despatches. Time alone, he thought, would tell which of the brothers would win, but for the present, the contest would have to be suspended. In a few days, the Duke of Gloucester would ride north to the Border, where the Scots, taking every advantage of England's internal strife, had been raiding and harrying their neighbours.

The trumpets sounded and the minstrels struck up a light, tinkling tune. The doors were flung open to allow the King and his guest-of-honour, the Governor of Holland, who had been Edward's host during his late, enforced stay in Burgundy, to pass into the Queen's Windsor apartments.

A charmingly arranged scene met the eyes of the enraptured Gruthuyse. In the fire-and candle-light, Elizabeth Woodville and her ladies played at ninepins, while the five-years-old Princess Elizabeth stood at her mother's side.

'Enchanting! Enchanting!' breathed the Governor ecstatically, and sank to his knees. With an uprush of skirts, like a flock of birds taking wing, the Queen and her ladies swooped forward to greet him.

Elizabeth Woodville was wearing blue, the colour of marital fidelity and tonight, knowing that she was again pregnant, she was playing to the top of her bent the role of wife and mother – taking care, nevertheless, to flaunt her still impressive visible charms for the admiration of Gruthuyse. The Governor admired, worshipped and was her slave. The Queen's laughter, catching now and then in her throat on a note of triumphant excitement, floated through the room as she led the guest-of-honour into the main apartment and took his hand for the first dance.

The ladies stood expectant, their eyes on the King, but he said: 'I shall dance with the prettiest lady in the room,' and held out his hands to his little daughter. She came running, with a shy, upward giggle at her uncle Gloucester as she passed, but Richard, normally responsive to his niece's feminine wiles, hardly noticed her, preoccupied as he was with his own affairs.

After his return to London from the Border, where he had successfully repelled the invading Scots, Richard had discovered Anne Neville, the playmate of his childhood and the friend of his adolescence, concealed as a cook-maid at the Cross Hands inn in the city. She had been hidden there by Clarence, and Richard, having obtained her willing consent to their marriage, had immediately removed her to the sanctuary of

St Martin-le-Grand.

And there she still was, even though it was now September, for George was proving difficult, claiming guardianship over Anne and, in this capacity, prohibiting her proposed marriage with his brother. Edward, furious, had declared that Clarence must present proof of guardianship before the Royal Council, giving Richard right of reply. But Richard had no great faith in his verbal ability compared with that of his brother. It was ironic, the young Duke reflected bitterly, as he propped the wall and watched the dancers, that he should now be in precisely the same position as he had been in five years earlier, but that the brother who had then thwarted his wish to marry Anne should now support him, while the one who had first planted the seed of desire in his mind should now oppose him.

Edward, moving in time to the music and shortening his steps to match those of his daughter, was aware of his youngest brother's unhappiness and silently cursed. He found it hard to fathom George's ambivalent attitude towards Richard; small wonder, since George, himself, could never understand it. He might, the King thought, bowing sedately to little Elizabeth at the end of the dance, force Clarence to comply with his and Richard's wishes, but he was still fond of both his brothers. If a way out could be found without showing a dangerous preference for one over the other – he had done that once, years ago, and it had only caused trouble in the long run – then that way must be discovered. As he shared a late-night cup of hippocras with Gruthuyse, Edward determined to speak with George on the following day.

But Clarence proved elusive. Next morning, after hearing the Mass of Our Lady in the Royal Chapel and presenting his guest with a golden cup studded with precious gems and a piece of magical unicorn's horn, the King looked for his brothers in vain. Richard, he knew, rarely hunted and he had not expected to see him at the chase, but George was a keen sportsman and his absence, therefore, the more noticeable. As they galloped through the golden autumn landscape of Windsor Park, Edward turned to his cousin, the young Duke of Buckingham.

'A pity that Clarence couldn't be with us today,' he remarked and his bow at a venture found its mark.

Henry Stafford, like his kinsman, George of Clarence, had a nose for gossip, a passion for intrigue and the same uncanny instinct for unearthing other people's secrets. Acutely conscious of his own high heritage as a descendant of Edward the third, his Plantagenet pride was nevertheless tempered with Stafford shrewdness and he had long ago realised that he stood too far from the throne ever to be of dynastic importance. Instead, he liked to attach himself to anyone he considered to be the man of the moment and to picture himself as a powerful, though unseen, influence upon events. At present, he regarded the Duke of Gloucester as the coming man and, therefore, anything he knew to the detriment of George could only enhance Richard's prestige in the eyes of the King. His light eyelashes flickered momentarily before he answered.

'A pity, indeed, Your Grace. But no doubt his business in London was pressing.'

'In London?' The King spoke sharply.

'With the Archbishop! Of York,' Buckingham added by way of explanation, and had the satisfaction of seeing Edward's brows snap together in a frown.

The King had recently released Warwick's brother, George Neville, from the Tower, but he trusted him as little as he trusted that other George, his own brother. The two in collusion could mean nothing but mischief and the thought nagged at the back of his mind, spoiling a good day's sport.

Even so, he brought down six of the eight bucks which, at the day's end, were presented to Gruthuyse, together with Edward's own horse, buckhounds and velvet-covered crossbow, embossed with his royal arms. By now it was late and they returned to the castle and a banquet given by the Queen in her apartments.

The Duke of Gloucester had spent an unrewarding day, trying to marshal his facts and arguments for the Royal Council, and his eldest noticed how tired and miserable he looked as he took his place at the high table. He had neither the skill nor the panache of George who, in full rhetorical flight, could, as their mother was so fond of remarking, charm the birds from the trees.

The room was uncomfortably full – many of the Queen's gentlewomen and the servants of Gruthuyse had been banished to an ante-room – and the shrill chatter of the more important of the Queen's ladies, seated at a side table, set Richard's nerves on edge. Little Elizabeth, watching him intently, noticed how viciously he drove his knife into a pastry coffin filled with a mess of pork and pine-cones, and how the pungent smell of the spices – cinnamon, ginger and saffron – immediately made him retch.

Into a moment of silence came the voice of Gruthuyse, hushed and adoring, congratulating Elizabeth Woodville on her endowment of Queen's College at Oxford, and there was a smattering of sycophantic applause from her relations. The Queen modestly disclaimed – 'so little a thing' – but the flattering murmurs of praise were suddenly stilled.

'When you say Queens' . . .' George's voice, loud and harsh, shattered the rosy moment. Richard shook his head vehemently at his brother and Isabel Neville laid a restraining hand on her husband's arm, but as well did Canute try to turn back the waves. 'When you say Queens,' my Lord Governor, remember that the word is plural, as well as possessive. Margaret of Anjou endowed the college first.'

There was silence, during which Gruthuyse gobbled a few embarrassed words, only to be interrupted by the King. Carefully washing the remains of a fish tart from his hands, he enquired languidly: 'You found our cousin, the Archbishop, well, I trust, George?'

Richard's head jerked up. A torch guttered and went out. George's angry eyes searched the faces of the company, trying to guess who had known and revealed his secret. Buckingham studied the profile of his wife, Catherine Woodville, with apparent unconcern.

'My wife's uncle,' said George, stressing these three extenuating words, 'was very well. He sent his respects to Your Grace.'

Edward hesitated, then inclined his head, smiling. Gradually, a murmur here, a mutter there, the conversation drifted back like a rising wind, until the rush of sound once more beat about little Elizabeth's ears. During the dancing that followed, she noticed how her uncle Richard continually tried to speak to her uncle George and, later, as they followed Gruthuyse to his ceremonial bath, how he forced his way to his brother's side.

'Gruthuyse must have treated you all very well in Burgundy to merit this,' sneered George as the men passed through the first chamber, where the great bed was canopied in cloth-of-gold and ermine, and the walls hung with silk and linen.

Richard ignored this. 'Why did you visit George Neville?' he asked, clasping his brother's wrist in a vice-like grip.

'We had business to discuss and you're hurting my arm!' George petulantly tugged his wrist free. 'Too cold for my taste,' he went on as they entered the second bed-chamber. 'I've never liked white. But luxurious! Carpets, too! What did Gruthuyse do? Lend Edward a fortune and forgive him half of it?'

Richard again ignored the question. As he pushed by the feather-filled couch with its white net hangings, he said: 'George Neville can have no say concerning Anne's affairs.'

George stared at him for a moment. Then, as he preceded his brother into the third room, where the bath stood ready, he laughed.

'Anne! Anne! You think of nothing else! Our cousin and I had other things to talk about.' And he went forward to help the squires disrobe their guest.

Relieved on one point, but now deeply disturbed on another, Richard absent-mindedly helped himself from a plate of green ginger, before remembering his obligations and carrying it to Gruthuyse, who, wallowing in the scented waters of his sponge-lined tub, was sipping hippocras and exchanging bawdy stories with Lord Hastings and with George. Once again, Richard, standing apart, knew himself cut off from his fellow-men by that strong puritanical streak which ran, rock-hard, through his nature.

The February weather was bitter. Sir John Paston blew on his numbed fingers, sharpened his pen and started a letter to his brother.

'Brother, I commend myself to you and ask you to look up my *Temple of Glass*' – he was very fond of Lydgate's poem – 'and send it to me by return messenger.' There then followed some personal matters before Sir John continued: 'Yesterday, the King, the Queen, my lords of Clarence and Gloucester all went to Sheen, very much out of charity with one another. What will happen, no one can say.'

Sir John stopped, shivering, and threw another log on the fire. A pity, he reflected, that Clarence so obstinately opposed his brother's marriage. A pity, too, that the Royal Council had been confused by all the specious arguments advanced by the Duke of Clarence, and by the obvious preference of the King for the Duke of Gloucester, into suspending judgment on the case. That was worse than useless, as Sir John, a member of an extremely litigious family, knew well. He dipped his pen once more into the ink.

'The King entreats my lord of Clarence for my lord of Gloucester. Clarence, it is now reported, has finally agreed that his brother may have his sister-in-law, but that they shall share no more of the estates. So what will be the end of it all, I cannot imagine.'

Sir John paused, biting the end of his pen, but no further

tit-bits of court gossip occurring to him, he turned again to domestic affairs.

The icy air hung in the room like a tangible presence. Holy Mother, how cold it was!

5

THE year 1472 was drawing to its close when Henry Tudor accompanied Duke Francis and his court to St Servan, on the coast of Brittany.

Jasper's forebodings had been justified. For the last eighteen months he and his nephew had been virtually prisoners of Duke Francis and it seemed likely that they would remain so for some time to come. The wily Francis, in his never-ending struggle against his over-lord, King Louis the eleventh of France, had continual need of English support and, in the captive Tudors, he had seen a weapon to force Edward's hand.

The English King had approached him concerning the return of the fugitives as soon as he had known where they were; whilst Louis had made equally pressing overtures for their custody. The assassination of Henry the sixth and, with his death, the snuffing out of the legitimate Lancastrian line, had made Henry Tudor of enormous potential value to the French King. If one discounted his mother – and a woman had never yet sat on the English throne – Henry Tudor was now the chief representative of the senior Beaufort line and, as such, a threat to the House of York. Although Louis considered it highly unlikely that the Lancastrian supporters would rally to the bastard branch of old Gaunt's descendants, he could see, nevertheless, that Henry's presence in France could prove extremely irksome to King Edward. Duke Francis, however, refused to part with his guests and ensured that they were discreetly guarded day and night. While he had these two pawns on his board, he could manoeuvre both his Kings with greater ease.

And so Henry Tudor had passed from one captivity into another; had exchanged the Herberts for Duke Francis. Very soon, in a month or so, he would be sixteen years old. At that age, Richard of Gloucester had been the father of two children, an accredited soldier and a promising administrator. Now, only five years Henry's senior, he was a married man and a king in all but name. For after his marriage to Anne Neville in March, he had retired to Yorkshire and there Edward had created for his brother a palatinate where Richard's writ ran almost as authoritatively as the King's. In a few years time would Henry Tudor know such power? Or would he still be what he had been all his life, a petted and pampered prisoner?

Jasper glanced at his nephew as they rode side-by-side along the cliffs. A secret boy, Henry! Jasper never knew what thoughts lurked behind that thin, aesthetic face; no indication of Henry's feelings looked out from the small, blue eyes. That he was clever Jasper had no doubt, for the boy's mother, Margaret Beaufort, was considered to be one of the most learned women of her generation. But other than that, Jasper felt that he had no knowledge of his nephew and probably never would have. The boy turned inwards upon himself and confided in no one.

The older man sighed and looked back over his shoulder. A group of Duke Francis' men followed on horse-back at a discreet distance, laughing and talking amongst themselves, yet keeping an eye on the two figures riding ahead. Jasper shivered. He hated these dark, dank days of winter, when the sunlight disappeared and the ground was carpeted with sodden leaves; when the black, bare branches of the trees curved menacingly overhead, like the vaulting of some satanic chapel. They were days when the world, itself, seemed devoid of hope; without that prospect of re-birth, so essential to man and beast.

After a while, he slowed his pace, forcing Henry to do the same. Then, when another quick glance behind had assured him that their guardians had done likewise, he suddenly drove his spurs into his horse's flanks, gave Henry's mount a sharp tap with his whip and they were both galloping furiously across the turf, past brakes of wind-torn gorse and tangled thickets of briar. On the horizon, a ragged bank of clouds was fringed with amber, shedding a twilight glow over the winter scene.

Henry's heart was pounding against his ribs as he wondered if this were an attempt at escape. He felt sick with fright and despised himself utterly for the sensation. Then he realised that they were turning away from the sea, down a rough cart-track flanked by high hedges. A man appeared, materialising as though from nowhere, his face and clothes streaked with salt, and Jasper reined in.

'Christopher Urswick?' he asked in a low, urgent voice.

'From Dr John Morton?'

The man nodded, producing from inside his jacket a glove, which satisfied Jasper that he was indeed the messenger of Edward's Master of the Rolls. Henry knew the name of Dr John Morton. An ardent Lancastrian, Morton had fought for Henry the sixth as recently as Tewkesbury, but he was too brilliant and ambitious a politician to waste his talents in idle banishment. With the end of Lancaster, he had offered his services to York, and King Edward, who recognised and valued Morton's unique capabilities, had gladly taken him into the royal service and appointed him to his present position. But it appeared that Morton had not entirely forsaken his original loyalties and still kept in touch with his exiled friends across the Channel.

Jasper slid to the ground. 'What news?' he demanded. 'Quickly! We are followed and haven't much time.'

Urswick inclined his head. 'There's little enough to tell,' he said. 'Clarence is still in touch with the Earl of Oxford. There are rumours from France that the Earl might try a landing in England this coming summer.'

Jasper laughed. 'It will fail,' he prophesied, 'because, when it comes to the pinch, Clarence won't give Oxford any open support. What of Oxford's brother-in-law, George Neville?'

Urswick shook his head. 'He's still in the fortress at Hammes. Edward won't release him yet; not after he discovered that the Archbishop was again plotting with Clarence, back in March.'

Jasper nodded. 'It's highly unlikely,' he agreed. 'And without his brains to guide them, I give Oxford and Clarence even less chance of a successful insurrection.'

'So Dr Morton said. He told me that there would be no need to advise you to leave this particular affair well alone.'

The faint sound of distant shouting, borne on a rising wind, came to their ears. Jasper grasped Urswick's shoulder. 'You must go very soon. What other news?'

The man shrugged. 'The Queen's not well. Oh, nothing serious,' he added as he saw the look of hope spring into Jasper's eyes. 'She had a difficult labour earlier this year: then the baby girl died in July. And now her mother is dead.'

Jasper gave a spurt of laughter. 'Don't tell me that that old harridan, Bedford, is dead at last. There were few tears shed over her, I'll be bound. The Londoners hated her ever since she and her husband ransacked Sir Thomas Cooke's house while he was in prison.'

Urswick smiled. 'No, as you say, no tears except from the

Woodvilles. I hear rumours of trouble in the north. Henry Percy is objecting to the power of the Duke of Gloucester.'

Jasper pursed his lips. 'That was inevitable,' he remarked. 'The Earls of Northumberland have been lords of the north for centuries. Ah well! Every little disturbance helps to keep Edward busy.'

The thudding of horses' hooves sounded plainly now and Jasper swung himself back into the saddle. 'My thanks to your master and I shall look for you again in a few months' time. Go now! Hurry!'

The man disappeared as mysteriously as he had come. As Duke Francis' men turned into the track, they found the two fugitives seated astride their mounts, apparently lost in admiration of the rather uninspiring view.

The Castle of Nottingham was dismal in spite of the May sunshine outside. Lighted candles stood on the table so that the King and members of the Council could see more clearly the faces of the men before them.

Richard, Duke of Gloucester, and Henry Percy, Earl of Northumberland, were there to swear to a compact; an agreement by which Northumberland recognised Richard as the supreme authority in the north and by which Richard, in his turn, recognised the ancient rights and privileges of the Percys. It was a compact which Richard had been urging on his brother for the past year in order to clarify his position and to define his relationship with Hotspur's great-grandson.

Later, in the privacy of Edward's bed-chamber, watching his brother being undressed by his four Squires of the Body, Richard expressed satisfaction that the agreement had at last been completed. He was about to add something more, when his attention was arrested and held by the tallest of the squires and he raised his eyebrows in delicate enquiry. Edward laughed.

'Quite right, my dear Diccon.' He pulled the boy's hair, fair like his own. 'He couldn't be anyone else's, could he?' He grimaced ruefully. 'I'm finding it a job to provide for them all. All right when, like yourself, you have only two, but for men like me. . . . ' He broke off, shrugging, as two pages carried in his all-night, a loaf of bread and half a gallon of wine, which they placed on a table near the bed. 'And how is my new – and legitimate – nephew? And Anne?'

Richard hesitated and his hesitation told Edward more than the bright 'Both well!' with which he answered the question. The King could guess, without being told, that his delicate, sixteen-year-old sister-in-law had had a difficult labour and would only have more children at the risk of her own life. And he knew what that meant. Richard had never ceased blaming himself for the death, in childbirth, of his mistress: he would never endanger the life of the woman he loved. Edward doubted that he would turn elsewhere. 'Loyalty binds me' was not only his brother's motto, but his creed.

'Are you happy?' he asked, hating the trite question but compelled, nevertheless, to ask it.

Richard tipped his head back against his chair and smiled. 'I'm more than happy,' he said, 'I'm content.'

Contentment, Edward realised, was the elusive quality which hung about his brother like a cloak. In his two brief meetings with Richard during the past year – two parliamentary sessions, one last autumn, another early this spring of 1473 – the King had sensed the change which, until this moment, he had been unable to define. He knew the stirrings of envy.

'It's going to be a year for babies,' he remarked with an assumed lightness of tone. 'Your Edward, George's Margaret and my . . . what? My little Richard or yet another girl?' Thank God, at any rate, that Elizabeth was a healthy and prolific woman. Why should he be jealous of his brother? The answer, hovering at the back of his mind, was ruthlessly pushed down. 'You said that you have something to ask me. A request.'

'Two requests, both very important to Anne and myself.'

There was a silence, broken by the squires as they pulled out their truckle-beds from beneath the King's large one.

'Go on,' prompted Edward.

'I want leave to bring the Countess of Warwick out of Beaulieu sanctuary. She's been there ever since Barnet. Give me permission and I'll send Sir James Tyrrell immediately to fetch her.'

'You are offering her a home at Middleham?'

'Yes.'

'Your mother-in-law?' The King cocked an amused but questioning eyebrow.

'My cousin's wife and my very good friend! She was kind to me when I was an apprentice knight in Warwick's household.'

Edward said nothing for a moment. Then he asked: 'And the second request?'

'Let George Neville come back from Calais. He's been imprisoned there for over a year now. Let him come home.'

Loyalty bound Richard to all the Nevilles it seemed. Edward drummed his fingers thoughtfully on the arm of his chair, then sent a page for his chief clerk. 'I can't accede to your second request, Diccon. There's going to be trouble this year....'

'As Hogan predicted?'

'Hogan be damned! He's in the Tower and it will give me great pleasure to have his head if nothing happens. No greasy prophet is going to claim that I took any notice of his advice. But Oxford's hovering in the Channel and I don't trust our cousin, the Archbishop. However, your first request I will grant. I'll dictate the necessary order now. All the same, I warn you! Brother George won't like it.'

A month later, at the beginning of June, Sir John Paston wrote busily to his brother.

'The Countess of Warwick has been allowed out of Beauleu sanctuary and Sir James Tyrrell has taken her north, rumour has it with the King's permission. They say that the Duke of Clarence is not amenable to the arrangement,' – as euphemistic a statement as that worthy knight ever committed to paper. Not only was George not amenable, he was furious, and the walls of his London home reverberated with his anger.

'It's a ruse,' he shouted at Isabel, 'to ensure that Richard obtains the remainder of your mother's property. He may have agreed to take less than half of your father's estates in order to marry Anne, but he means to steal the Despenser-Beauchamp lands from under my very nose.' He noticed how pale his wife looked – the birth of their daughter had left her extremely weak – and he moderated his voice somewhat. 'But he won't get away with it. I shall see Edward as soon as he returns to London and demand that the whole question of the partitioning be fairly and justly considered.'

Isabel could only regard him helplessly, mesmerised, as were most people, by George's effrontery. She knew, none better, that while her husband demanded justice of the King, he had been, and was still, in consant communication with the outlawed Earl of Oxford. When the Earl had landed on the Essex coast a week earlier – in time to save not only the prophet Hogan's face but also his head – George had merely been lying low, waiting to see which way the cat would jump. But Oxford had been repelled and Isabel had breathed again.

Nevertheless, throughout that long, hot, plague-ridden summer, she lived in daily terror of some overt act of treason on the part of George. Clarence, however, showing unexpected acuity, saw a way of using his quarrel with his younger brother to advantage, loudly insisting that the assembling and arming of his retainers was to deal with Richard and had nothing to do with another obviously imminent invasion by Oxford and his troops. But, by the time that the Earl landed in Cornwall on September the thirtieth, George's private army had swollen to such alarming proportions that no one any longer believed his story, and the King urgently requested the Duke of Gloucester to come south, bringing his Yorkshire levies with him.

But Oxford was once more doomed to failure. In February of the year 1474, after a miserable and uncomfortable winter spent besieging St Michael's Mount, he threw in his hand and sued for peace.

'Which I shall grant,' Edward told his Council. 'I have accepted Oxford's surrender in return for his life.'

The Council members murmured assent. The snow lay thick outside and the Thames was frozen. The King's feet were numb; he felt bad-tempered and wanted nothing more than to retire to his own apartments. But there was still work to be done.

On either side of him sat his brothers; Richard annoyed at having been summoned yet again from his northern fastness, ostensibly for the christening of his new little nephew, Richard, Duke of York, but, in reality, to determine the division of his mother-in-law's estates; George sullen and morose, not only at the failure of all his plans, but because, by a recent Parliamentary Act of Resumption of Crown Lands, he had lost the great manor of Tutbury, while Richard had been exempted from the Act.

In view of this, it came as a complete surprise to George, as well as to most of the other Councillors present, when Edward now proposed giving Clarence the larger share of the Countess of Warwick's estates. Those persons like the Duke of Buckingham and Dr. John Morton, who had been willing to wager their last groat that the King had finally washed his hands of the Duke of Clarence, found themselves at a loss to explain Edward's sudden change of attitude.

But, by the spring of 1475, when, almost four years after his death, the final settlement of Warwick's and his wife's estates received Parliamentary sanction, most people, not only at court but throughout the country, knew the reason for Edward's leniency with George. The King needed the loyalty and support of every man who could raise an army. England was once more about to invade the realm of France.

6

At the age of nine, Elizabeth suddenly found herself thrust upon the stage of great events.

She had not been used to considering herself of much importance, not since the birth of Edward, Prince of Wales, when she was four years old, and especially not since the arrival of little Richard, Duke of York. She was, of course, surrounded by all the panoply of court existence; she lived a life hedged about by protocol and encompassed by a vast army of servants — estate officers, parkers, keepers and bailiffs; surveyors, huntsmen, butlers and sewers; cooks, scullions, squires and pages; henchmen, minstrels, cup-bearers and carvers. But this was a part of her world and in it she played very much the minor role compared with her two brothers.

Now, in this autumn of 1475, she found herself an object of interest and importance throughout the entire court, for it was her betrothal to the Dauphin of France that had been one of the major clauses in the treaty of Picquigny.

Edward had embarked for France in July with one of the finest armies an English king had ever taken into that country – or so said Phillippe de Commynes, the pet historian of Louis the eleventh. But Edward's heart had not been in the invasion; it was a war he had neither sought nor wanted. But like Henry the fifth before him, he had seen the force of his Councillors' representations that, in a renewed attack upon France, he might be able to dissipate the unrest at home. Moreover, the King, always sensitive to the climate of public opinion, had realised that his people wanted this war. The English had never forgiven the French for their humiliation and defeat thirty years earlier, when they had been driven from the land they had come to regard as their own. Furthermore, Edward knew that there was in his subjects an innate arrogance and restlessness which, combined, engendered in them a desire to break through the confines of their little island and impose their ideals and institutions on the other peoples of Europe.

The English had responded to the call to arms with alacrity. The men of Yorkshire alone, had reacted so eagerly to Richard of Gloucester's summons that he had been able to bring south three hundred more men than those for which he had indented. (And a grateful King had duly rewarded his brother with

Skpton Castle and the office of Sheriff of Cumberland.)

Not only men but money had been forthcoming – a sure sign of English enthusiasm – and for this, the reluctant King, himself, had been largely responsible. He had travelled the length and breadth of his kingdom and in each city he had summoned before him every man and woman who had property worth forty pounds or more. An Italian visitor to the court had written home in bewilderment that everyone had been made to give willingly. This had been done, the Italian had disclosed in a transport of admiration, by the King having given each person a great welcome and an invitation to contribute what he could. If the amount proffered had been considered sufficient, the Chief Notary had written down the name and amount. If, however, as had often been the case, it had been considered insufficient, Edward had suggested gently: 'Surely you can give a little more freely than that, when you are so rich. Many poorer people have given more,' and the blushing culprit had opened his pockets still wider.

But, in spite of men and money, Edward could not, in the end, bring himself to fight and upset the precarious balance of his economy. Louis, that other astute and careful monarch, had offered rosy terms for a peace treaty and, on August the twenty-ninth, the two Kings had met on the bridge at Picquigny. A favourable settlement had been reached with the result that Louis was to pay Edward a pension of fifty thousand crowns a year for life; a large number of English nobles, including Clarence, Lord Hastings, Lord Stanley and Dr John Morton, also received monetary inducements; and a contract of marriage between Elizabeth and the Dauphin was signed.

Thus it was the future Madame la Dauphine who, on a warm, late October afternoon sat on a window seat in her mother's private solar. The Queen, pregnant yet again, lay back in a chair while one of her ladies rubbed her swollen ankles. The fire was hot and the herbs strewn among the rushes gave off a faint, rather sickly fragrance, making her head throb.

'What are you watching?' she asked at length, her eyes on her daughter's intent, unmoving figure.

'Uncle Gloucester. He's leaving for Middleham.'

The Queen nodded, her mind suddenly focusing on the commotion outside, the previously indistinct babel of sound breaking up into separate and clearly defined noises; the neighing and stamping of impatient horses, the shouts and cries of the grooms and the men-at-arms.

'He'll be glad to go. He's been at outs with your father

since the treaty was signed. He didn't approve of it, you know. He said Edward had betrayed the people – or some such rubbish. Wouldn't take a penny from Louis and verbally castigated everyone who did. A very self-righteous young man,' the Queen finished waspishly; then added judicially: 'Not that he has ever done me any harm.'

Since the death of her mother, she had dropped into the habit of treating her eldest daughter as her coeval; making Elizabeth the recipient of confidences and comments which she might otherwise have withheld. That this might make the child old beyond her years, Elizabeth Woodville did not consider and she would have discounted the thought even if it had occurred to her.

'Who's the lady with father?' Elizabeth enquired and her mother laughed.

'There are so many,' was the indifferent answer, 'but if she has a remarkable head of hair, then it's probably Jane Shore, your father's latest . . . friend.'

The Queen smiled and her ladies sniggered. Elizabeth, uncertain why they were laughing, ignored them. After a moment, she asked: 'Who was the Lady Eleanor Butler?'

Glancing at her mother's face as she spoke, Elizabeth was amazed by what she saw there: it was as though she were looking at Elizabeth Woodville's death-mask. It was like a frozen parody of old age; every line, every wrinkle suddenly accentuated against the carefully whitened skin and every bone sharply outlined under the tautened flesh. After a long time the lips moved stiffly to form the one word: 'Why?'

'I've heard her spoken of,' Elizabeth muttered. She was frightened by the effect her words were having.

'When? By whom?' The almost immovable jaw worked once more up and down.

'I don't know. It's not important.'

Nor was it. It had been an idle question, idly asked. Elizabeth had no idea exactly where or when she had heard that particular name mentioned. A whisper here, a murmur there and she had been left with the vague imprint of a name upon her memory. That was all.

'Uncle Gloucester's going,' she said, desperately trying to divert her mother's attention. 'He's waving good-bye.'

The Queen did not answer. Then she lurched forward, moaning and clutching her stomach amid the cries and screams of her women. Three days later, on the second of November, she gave birth to another girl, the Princess Anne,

Royal Birth was followed by royal death. At the beginning of the following year, 1476, Anne, Duchess of Exeter and the King's eldest sister, died at the age of thirty-six.

The news reached Richard of Gloucester at his castle of Middleham as he and his family returned from the village where they had been watching the Plough Monday celebrations. Katherine and John had shouted and clapped as the villagers had danced through the street, dragging the plough behind them, but the three-year-old Edward, held in his father's arms, had watched listlessly with his large, dark-circled eyes. And as the Countess of Warwick lifted her grandson from Richard's horse – spurning irritably those servants who would have deprived her of this pleasure – he began to cry with fatigue.

John Kendall, Rickard's secretary, touched his master's shoulder, indicating the King's messenger. The sight of the black scarf tied about the man's arm made the Duke falter, the fear of death catching him by the throat, as his mind darted from Edward to George and back again to the King. But, after all, it was only Anne who was dead; that eldest sister who had drifted, ghost-like, along the periphery of his life, recognised, but almost unknown. Since Exeter's death she had been married again to a west-country knight, Sir Thomas St Leger – a marriage of choice, Richard wondered, or another attempt on the part of his brother to enlist the support of a Lancastrian nobleman?

Only Anne! And yet he was unaccountably moved by her death, and his wife discovered him that evening staring moodily into the fire instead of playing at cards or chess or listening to the musicians in the hall. She put her arms round his neck, not quite understanding his emotion, but willing to try, and it was this quiet acceptance of all his moods that Richard found her most endearing quality. He lifted his hand to her hair, aware that there was, as well as sympathy, a hint of coaxing in her embrace. He raised his eyes to hers smiling.

'What is it you want?' he asked.

She smiled in return, but hesitantly, smoothing his sleeve, streaking the dark velvet to a milky white.

'I've had a letter from my aunt of Oxford,' she said. 'She's still in sanctuary and neither the King nor George will do anything for her. Edward eventually let my uncle the Archbishop out of Hammes prison because you asked it. Perhaps if you requested this. . . ?' Her voice tailed off. Then, as Richard remained silent, she pleaded: 'She is your cousin; my father's sister.'

Richard looked into the face so close to his. At nineteen, Anne Neville was growing more beautiful; the dark hollows under the high cheek-bones were less pronounced and four years of happy, married life had erased the lost and frightened look of adolescence. She coughed less, especially at nights, and, as always, he felt that he must do anything he could to compensate her for the fact that he had helped Edward to destroy the once rich and powerful House of Neville.

'I can't bring your aunt out of sanctuary,' he said, 'but I can make her an annuity out of my own revenues.'

Anne's face brightened immediately, but there was another favour still to ask. Her fingers pressed his hand.

'John Neville's son! The King has deprived him of everything he has. Can you do nothing for him?'

'If Edward will grant me his wardship, I can find a place for him here. Will that satisfy you?'

She kissed him. The nurse brought in the children; Katherine eight years of age and very conscious of her twelve months seniority over her brother, John, who, in his turn, resented his sister's domineering ways, but was too placid to do anything about them; and the baby, Edward, whom both elder children adored, but regarded with a certain amount of awe as being different from themselves. They knew that he would one day inherit all their father's great titles and estates; that he was not, as they were, a bastard.

Watching them as they crowded round the fire, raising a controlling finger at his daughter, soothing John's ruffled feelings, lifting Edward on to his knees and smiling over the baby's head at his wife, Richard knew himself a whole man at last. The strife and divided loyalties of his youth were over. If the Woodvilles, architects of the Nevilles' destruction, still reigned supreme in London, there was no one else whom he loved that they could bring to ruin. Clarence, whatever his follies, they dared not touch while he enjoyed the protection of the King. And George had been quiet of late, giving Richard the chance to know the blessings of family peace.

The Duke of Gloucester visited London and the court as little as possible. He had delegated most of the work entailed by his offices of Constable and Admiral of England to that brilliant and capable jurist, Dr William Godyer, and, consequently, he was able to spend as much time as he could in his beloved, north country, moving between Middleham, Sheriff Hutton and Pontefract, as the exigencies of work and the cleansing of the sewers dictated. Raids by the Scots ensured regular visits to the Border and in March of 1476, both he and Henry Percy were forced to quell trouble much nearer home, in the city of York, itself.

Anne, greeting Richard on his return, cried out at the sight of his bandaged hand.

'It's nothing,' he said, kissing her, 'the merest scratch.'

'But what caused the riots?' Anne demanded, anxious for news. And Richard could only say to her what he had said to Northumberland: that, at the root of the trouble, were disappointed men who had been recruited for a French war that had never been fought.

In his bed-chamber, his squires relieved him of his travel-stained clothes and a page knelt by the hearth, bellows in hand. The Duke sent for John Kendall.

'Edward is furious about the riots,' he told Anne. 'I shall have difficulty in persuading him not to withdraw the city's charter. Moreover, the City Fathers want to sack their clerk, Thomas Yotten. He's been embezzling the funds, but, unfortunately, he has enlisted Northumberland's support. The Mayor has appealed to me to lay the case before Edward for arbitration.'

'Henry Percy won't like that,' Anne said, frowning. 'There's no doubt, I suppose, that Yotten has been taking the money?'

'None at all, I'm afraid. I saw the accounts, myself. Northumberland won't like my interference, as you say, but what can I do?'

So it was, a month later, having carefully enquired into the case, that the King confirmed Yotten's dismissal, to the great jubilation of the York City Fathers and to the fury of Northumberland. Henry Percy would never forget this slight to his authority, nor who was responsible for it. He notched up one more grudge against the Duke of Gloucester.

7

HENRY TUDOR stood, white-faced and silent, in the Council Chamber, while Duke Francis advanced, with a wealth of Gallic gesture, a number of specious arguments as to why he had finally acceded to Edward's request for Henry's return to England.

A little to the Duke's right stood Anthony Woodville, Earl

Rivers, brother to the Queen; his nephew, Thomas Grey, Marquis of Dorset, and Elizabeth Woodville's son; and William, Lord Hastings, life-long companion and boon-friend of the King.

To the Duke's left stood his Treasurer, Pierre Landois, whose expressive features indicated strong disapproval of his master's decision and suggested that his thoughts were much the same as Henry's: he considered Duke Francis' reasons to be nothing more than plausible excuses. Landois' assumption was that Edward had at last offered a satisfactory price and that Francis had reached the conclusion that Henry Tudor was no longer an asset. In this, the Treasurer violently disagreed with his master and intended to do what he could to change his mind, even at this advanced stage in the negotiations.

It seemed, however, that he was unsuccessful, for as May of 1476 drew to its close in a blaze of early sunshine, Henry set out with his escort to take ship at St Marlo. He appeared dejected and depressed; and indeed, dread as to his fate at Edward's hands was making him almost ill with terror. But beneath his fear and the inevitable self-contempt which accompanied it, another, entirely separate part of Henry's mind was busy noting every look and gesture of his three chief companions and, with amazing rapidity, commuting his observations into possible advantage for the future.

He sensed, rather than saw, that Hastings and Earl Rivers did not like each other and, from a word here and a look there, that their enmity was based on a common desire for the King's latest mistress, Jane Shore. Of the two men he preferred Hastings, who, though far too loud and brash for Henry's taste, displayed a single-minded devotion to his own self-interests which struck an answering chord in the younger man's mind. (Henry Tudor liked plain, straightforward men whose thoughts lay open to him at a glance. The other sort, the dreamers, the fatalists, men such as Anthony Woodville, were far more difficult to know and, just when you thought that you had mastered all the intricacies of their tortuous minds, they would confound you yet again by some totally unexpected action). In Dorset Henry took but a passing interest, dismissing him as of small account; a man who, in his twenty-six years, had done little or nothing but bask in his mother's reflected glory, grasping at wealth and power like a child cramming his mouth with sweetmeats; an immanent sense of insecurity making him greedy in his fear that the cornucopia might one day dry up.

Of the escort of men-at-arms, only the captain, a tall, swarthy man with the air of an adventurer and a definitely semitic cast of countenance, was worthy of Henry's notice. Careful enquiry elicited for Henry the information that the captain had indeed been born a Jew – a Portuguese Jew – and that he was called Edward Brampton. This, of course, was not his real name. When he had been baptised into the Christian faith, Edward the fourth had stood as his god-father and the man had returned the compliment by adopting Edward as his baptismal name. How or why he had chosen Brampton was not clear, but Henry considered it an unfortunate choice in so much that it had been a Thomas Brampton, a servant of the Crown, who had been hacked to death at the start of the peasants' revolt less than a hundred years earlier. Henry did not care for Brampton, but quickly perceived that this was a purely personal dislike. Brampton was ostentatiously a Yorkist supporter and, in particular, an ardent admirer of the young Duke of Gloucester, to whom he was obviously devoted.

In addition to all these emotions, Henry was experiencing a strong sense of outrage that he, Henry Tudor, should yet again have been bought and sold like a piece of merchandise. The years in Brittany, unlike the years at Pembroke, had given him a sense of his own importance, even though his role had only been a passive one. But now, it seemed that he had been of purely monetary value to Duke Francis and he was once more being tossed back to Edward, simply because the English King had at last raised his bargaining price. And he was filled with fury that Dorset, Rivers and Hastings should be witnesses to his humiliation.

By the time St Malo was reached, however, and Henry had glimpsed the painted sails of the ships between the sloping roofs of the houses, fear had subordinated all other feelings. The assassination of his half-uncle, Henry the sixth, had confirmed him in his opinion that, beneath the friendly and genial exterior, Edward the fourth was a ruthless man. This idea had been implanted in Henry's mind when very small, by the execution of his grandfather, Owen Tudor, at Edward's instigation after the battle of Mortimer's Cross. Owen had been old and of comparatively little importance, but Edward had revenged upon him the death of his own father and brother.

As he dismounted, Henry realised that his terror had transmitted itself to his body and he shook so violently that he could hardly stand. He had never experienced this before and it appalled him, but, try as he might, he could control neither the trembling of his limbs nor the chattering of his teeth. He saw the other men staring at him in open disbelief and heard

Dorset's high-pitched laugh that filled him with shame and mortification.

'It's all right, my dear fellow,' Earl Rivers said, laying his arm across Henry's shoulders, 'King Edward won't eat you.'

But, as always, that small portion of Henry's mind which continued to function whatever his physical or mental distress, came to his rescue. Through white lips Henry whispered: 'I'm ill! Please held me to bed.'

Anthony Woodville, immediately ashamed that he had attributed Henry's condition to fear, made arrangements for the young man to be accommodated at the inn, and there Henry remained for three days, pretending to be sick and hoping against hope for a miracle to happen.

The luck was with him. On the fourth morning, just as the impatient English lords were about to insist that he went aboard ship whatever his state of health, Pierre Landois arrived in St Malo with a heavily-armed escort. Duke Francis had changed his mind.

'Changed his mind?' roared Hastings, confronting Landois in the inn parlour. 'He can't! The agreement is signed.'

Landois took covert stock of the man before him. Then: 'Very true,' he said. 'If I might also have a word with Earl Rivers and the lord Dorset . . . perhaps . . . something might be arranged?' He rubbed his fingers together suggestively.

Hastings sneered. These foreigners were all the same, he thought: grease their palms and an Englishman could twist them around his little finger. As he agreed to have Landois rowed out to the flag-ship, no thought crossed his mind of the comfortable pension which he received annually from King Louis.

As soon as Hastings and Landois were safely aboard, the captain of the Breton guard, apparently bored by the whole proceedings, approached Edward Brampton. Conjuring up a Portuguese grandfather on his mother's side and addressing Brampton with the few words of Portuguese which he had picked up on his travels, he revealed the existence of a small tavern where the wines of the Iberian peninsula were sold for a moderate sum. Ten minutes later, he and Brampton were to be seen strolling arm-in-arm in the direction of a neighbouring street.

Their departure was the signal for action. With a speed that took the English men-at-arms completely by surprise, the Breton guard rushed the inn where Henry Tudor lay and carried him triumphantly into the sanctuary of a near-by church.

The news was conveyed to Earl Rivers on board ship. Landois, smiling into the stunned faces of the three men seated with him in the small and stuffy cabin, raised a white hand to stem the tide of bitter recriminations.

'My dear sirs,' he reproved them, preparing to take his leave, 'this has come about entirely through your own carelessness.' And with this taunt, Landois took his formal leave of the Englishmen and went up on deck.

Two months later, Elizabeth stood in the courtyard of Fotheringay Castle dressed from head to foot in black and carrying a lighted candle in her hand. On her right stood her grandmother, Cicely Neville, and on her left, her aunt, Elizabeth Plantagenet, Duchess of Suffolk, both similarly attired. Behind her, she could hear her sisters, Mary and Cicely, shuffling their feet and the subdued murmurs of the ladies-in-waiting.

It seemed to the ten-years-old child that they had been standing like this for hours. Her legs ached abominably and she longed to sit down, but a glance at Cicely Neville's upright figure made her feel ashamed. She wondered what her grandmother was thinking, on this solemn occasion, when she was being so forcibly reminded of the tragic past, and, on a sudden impulse, Elizabeth slipped her small, smooth hand into the hot, dry one of the older woman. For a brief moment, Cicely returned the pressure of her grand-daughter's fingers before placing Elizabeth's arm back at her side.

Cicely smiled to herself. She reflected that there could be few more satisfactory relationships than that between grandmother and grand-daughter – provided, of course, that one had the right grand-daughter. The relationship was close enough for each to understand and indulge those little oddities in the other which mother and daughter found so irksome; remote enough to ensure of their being parted before these foibles became irritating to either. Also, the greater gap between the ages seemed to make for a larger tolerance, most probably engendered, Cicely thought, by the fact that neither was directly responsible to, or for, the other.

Elizabeth surreptitiously rubbed her back. The hot July sunshine lay all about them and a ray of light glanced off the shield above the north gate. This shield showed the arms of England impaling those of León and Castile and had belonged, Elizabeth knew, to her great-great-grandfather, Edmund of Langley, who had married an Infanta of Spain. The black dress was hot and sticky and it seemed to Elizabeth that she had been dressed in mourning throughout the entire summer, although, in fact, it had only been for the past eight weeks. On June the eighth her cousin, George Neville, Archbishop of York, had died at Blyth and, in spite of the fact that Edward had secretly rejoiced at the demise of one of his most persistent enemies, he had ordered a brief period of mourning, partly because he knew that it would please his mother and partly out of deference to the Church. He had not looked askance, however, at anyone who had lapsed and worn colours, but today, of course, was different; an almost sacred occasion for the House of York, and amongst the group of ladies on the steps, there was nothing to be seen but the most funereal of robes.

A trumpet sounded from the battlements. As the last note died away, they were held for a moment in a bubble of silence, the flames from the candles and tapers pale echoes of the brilliant mid-summer sun. Then everything came to life. Hastings, as Lord Chamberlain, came out into the courtyard from the keep; that keep built in the shape of a fetterlock, one of the family badges of York. Servants and men-at-arms appeared almost as from nowhere and the quiet of the Northamptonshire countryside was shattered by the lowering of the double drawbridge across the inner and outer moats.

Now, through the aperture, Elizabeth could see the procession, a dark mass moving slowly against the back-drop of Milton woods; a sombre procession, swollen to three times its original size, as the people in their hundreds had left fields and cottages to join in its wake during the four day journey from Pontefract to Fotheringay.

At the head of the cortège came a hearse, bearing two sable-draped coffins under a cloth displaying the arms of England and France. Enormous candles in golden sconces burned on either side and on one of the coffins there lay a golden crown. Beside the hearse rode a knight carrying the banner of the long-dead Duke of York.

Elizabeth knew that the two caskets contained the disinterred remains of her grandfather York and her uncle Edmund, killed six years before her own birth at the ill-fated battle of Wakefield. For the past sixteen years they had been buried at Pontefract: now her father had determined to honour his dead with a splendid re-burial in the collegiate chapel at Fotheringay. As the hearse rumbled into the courtyard, the choristers and chapel-children began chanting the offices for the dead and Elizabeth instinctively drew nearer to her grand-mother. How did *she* feel after all these years, being faced with the mortal remains, however magnificently shrouded, of her husband and second eldest son?

Behind the coffins rode the King and his two brothers, and, behind them again, all the lords and nobles of the realm. Elizabeth caught sight of her maternal uncles; Earl Rivers, still in disgrace over the fiasco at St Malo; Lionel Woodville, Bishop of Salisbury; Edward and Richard Woodville, riding side-by-side with their brother-in-law, the Duke of Buckingham, and Lord John Howard. And her aunt's husband, the Duke of Suffolk, was there also, looking more surly than ever now that his old enemy, the Duke of Norfolk, was dead and he no longer had anyone to fight with.

The King and his brothers dismounted. With tears running down their faces, they advanced and kissed the coffins, doing special obeisance to their father as the man who should have been, had death not intervened, King of England. The coffins were then carried into the church, the Duke's being placed in the choir, Edmund's in the Lady Chapel.

Now it was Elizabeth's turn. At a signal from her grandmother, she took from Lord Hastings several large purses filled with money and began distributing it amongst the people who had followed the hearse and were now crowding into the courtyard. It was the first time she had ever taken active part at an official function and she felt extremely nervous. It was not the people who frightened her, for she was used to them. Whenever she travelled abroad they would crowd about her, staring and cheering and even, at times, being downright rude. She did not care about that for she realised that, underlying their rough remarks, was a genuine affection such as they felt for her father. And she had always listened to Edward's advice.

'The man who wishes to rule England,' he had once told her, 'will let the English rule him. They have an independence of mind which will never subdued by force. Only a fool will ever believe that he has mastered the Saxon race. Just when they seem most quiescent, they will rise up again. And when they are at their most slanderous, they are at their most affectionate. Oh! Not to foreigners! They hate foreigners and will be rude to them for the sheer pleasure of it. But when they abuse their own, that often betokens esteem.'

So the people did not worry her, although today they stood silent, in solemn, serried ranks, only their eyes moving greedily from side to side, watching and waiting for the moment when the Mass penny would be pressed into their itching, filthy palms. Elizabeth was more afraid that she would do something to disgrace herself, or that Mary and Cicely, who were assisting her, would start to giggle. Mary was irrepressible and only a delicate constitution prevented her from doing all the outrageous things that Cicely helped her to plan.

But at last the ceremony was over, for the time being at least, although there would be more people forcing their way in tomorrow – and the next day, and the next.

The funeral rites continued for three days and it was on the third day, as the two coffins, now swathed in cloth-of-gold, were lowered to their final resting places in the vaults, that Elizabeth made two discoveries about herself that were to have a profound effect upon her life.

The first concerned Dr John Morton, recently made Bishop of Ely. That she did not like him came to Elizabeth in a sudden, inexplicable moment of revulsion as he brushed against her and turned, with one of his beautiful, graceful gestures; to apologise. The other concerned her uncle of Gloucester. In that self-same moment, she caught his eye and he half smiled at her, his face very pale above his sable-trimmed suit, for he had shared the all-night vigil with his brothers. And Elizabeth felt the first stirrings of a love that had nothing to do with the normal affection of a niece for her uncle.

8

AFTER the interment, some ten thousand people were wined and dined in the pavilions of black and purple silk which had been especially erected in Fotheringay courtyard. In the royal tent, the press of overheated bodies was greater than anywhere else and had it not been for her cousin, the Earl of Lincoln, Elizabeth doubted if she and her sisters would have tasted so much as a mouthful of food. As it was, John de la Pole, now a tall, well-built young man of thirteen, with very little in his pleasant, open countenance to suggest that he was the son of the choleric Suffolk, forced his way to and fro through the crowds to bring his little cousins an endless supply of dainties; roast heron and cygnet, boiled brawn, fish tarts and a large selection of pastry 'coffins' filled with anything and everything from fried pork and cinnamon to a melange of cream, honey and saffron. By the time that Mary and Cicely had rounded off this repast with rosewater-junkets and sugared violets, they were both forced to retire precipitately to the open air and the ministrations of their nurse; leaving Elizabeth and the Earl of Lincoln to enjoy a laugh at their expense.

Lincoln turned away to speak to his father and Elizabeth edged nearer the tent opening, through which wafted a small breeze, bringing, besides the inevitable smells of the kitchens and sewers, a faint reminder of the meadows and woods beyond. Elizabeth took a deep breath and closed her eyes, escaping into that inner sanctuary of the imagination which had been her refuge and strength since childhood. She had been very small when she had first discovered that, no matter what went on around and outside her, there was an inner life, a world of the spirit, that belonged to her alone; the inviolable, the immortal part of her that no one could ever destroy. She was vaguely aware that not everyone was conscious of, or, indeed, needed, this private existence. It had been the sudden recognition of her uncle Gloucester as a kindred spirit which had so stirred her emotions in the chapel that morning: there had been something in his face, a lost, withdrawn expression, to which her heart had immediately responded.

A woman's well-modulated voice sounded just behind her. 'My dear Bishop,' it said, 'three hundred years ago, Adelard of Bath was promulgating the theory that to accept authority for authority's sake, and in defiance of reason, was nothing but the action of an insensate brute.'

Elizabeth turned her head and found herself looking into the sharp, clever features of her grandmother's cousin, Margaret Beaufort. At thirty-three, Margaret was acknowledged as one of the most erudite women of her age and had recently married her third husband, that wealthy and powerful widower, Lord Stanley. Elizabeth knew that Margaret's only child, born when she was fourteen years old, was that same Henry Tudor whose escape at St Malo had so enraged King Edward and brought the vials of his wrath pouring about the unfortunate Anthony Woodville's head.

In answer to Lady Stanley came the soft, unctuous tones of the Bishop of Ely. 'I could not agree more. To imagine that everything can be settled by recourse to authority is, as you say, absurd. But governing bodies, such as the Church and the Law and the Nobility, will they ever see it that way?' John Morton's hands, smooth and white – like slugs, thought Elizabeth with a shudder – were spread with a hopeless shrug. 'The stronger men's critical faculties grow, and the greater their desire for participation in controlling their own destinies, the more refractory will our established institutions become –

especially the Church.'

'You bit the hand that feeds you, my lord.' Margaret Beaufort sounded grim. She was an extremely pious woman and, while she was secretly flattered to find the admired and brilliant Morton so much in accord with herself, she nevertheless disliked hearing a churchman belittle the Church.

John Morton merely smiled. He was not a man to betray his own opinions for the sake of others' approval, however much he might desire that approbation. 'Our institutions live too much in the past,' he said. 'The code of chivalry is dead. It is useless to offer people ideals when what they need are practical solutions to the problems of every-day life and the processes of developing thought.' He dropped his voice almost to a whisper, unaware of the child just beside him. 'To say to a people: I am the King, therefore I am right: love me! is no longer possible. Your first husband's half-brother, King Henry the sixth, found that out to his cost. King Edward knows it, so we may hope that he passes the knowledge on to his sons.' Elizabeth saw the Bishop nod towards her uncle Gloucester, who had just appeared inside the tent. 'And there is a man who would never comprehend it, not if he lived to be as old as Methusalah.'

Elizabeth had understood practically nothing of this conversation, but she did realise from the Bishop's last remark that he did not like Richard. This at once strengthened the affection that Elizabeth felt for her uncle and she struggled towards him through the crowd on a sudden, overpowering impulse to get to his side. But, almost immediately, he had gone again, busy about some business of his own. He had not noticed her and Elizabeth felt near to tears.

And, a day or so later, as she watched him ride out of Fotheringay on his way home to the north, she felt a sense of desolation entirely new to her and which she was utterly at a loss to explain.

As the Duke of Gloucester rode home to Middleham, his thoughts were of his deceased father and brother. He found it difficult to recall the faces of those long-dead men. Edmund's was lost to him for ever, an oval blur under a thatch of light-brown hair. But he could remember his father's moustaches drooping over the corners of a mouth which would open on a sudden roar of laughter; the blue eyes wrinkled at the corners; the strong head on the thick neck which Margaret of Anjou had ordered to be severed from his lifeless body and crowned with a paper crown. (She, at least, would trouble them no more. A grudging Louis had at last ransomed her and she was now a prisoner on one of her father's estates.)

Summer gave place to autumn. Tenants who were being evicted from their land thronged the Duke of Gloucester's courts to obtain redress against the landlords, men anxious to convert arable into pastureland. With his fellow councillors, lawyers and Justices of the Assize, Richard spent the rapidly shortening days immersed in the work of alleviating economic hardship, hearing complaints and endeavouring to mete out justice. In the evenings, he entertained his friends and neighbours in the great hall, or sat quietly with Anne, her mother and his children, finding his deepest pleasure in their company.

Winter closed in and by Christmas Day snow threatened. Leafless trees were etched against a leaden-grey sky. Easy enough for John to imagine them hobgoblins, without Katherine grimacing and flapping her arms as they walked in procession to hear the Boy-Bishop preach his sermon. But John soon forgot his fears in the feasting and mumming that followed, screaming with laughter at the antics of Francis Lovell, his father's closest friend, as the Lord of Misrule.

The boar's head was carried the length of the room to the high table. But as guests and servants, tenants and retainers cheered themselves hoarse, and as Richard smiled at Anne and the three excited children beside him, an exhausted messenger, wearing the livery of the Duke of Clarence, rode painfully across the drawbridge, a black scarf fluttering from his numbed left arm.

The year was ending as it had begun, in death. Isabel of Clarence had died in childbirth three days earlier.

It was to be a time of death. As the year 1477, opened, blanketing Europe in snow, Edward the fourth's brother-in-law, Charles, Duke of Burgundy, was killed whilst besieging Nancy. As he had lived, so he was buried, with the utmost pomp and panache. His conqueror, the Duke of Lorraine, came to the funeral dressed as one of the Nine Worthies, a golden beard flowing to his waist, and prayed long and extremely loudly by the coffin for a full quarter of an hour. But Charles' death was to have far-reaching consequences, for he had only one child to inherit the richest and most powerful apanage in western Europe; Mary, the daughter of his first marriage and now the greatest heiress of the civilised world.

In Brittany, these events were followed with the closest interest, and, as the bitterly cold weather receded and March came in, bringing the milder, damper days, John Morton sent his messenger across the Channel, taking Jasper the latest news. Duke Francis, while still honouring his pledge to Edward to keep watch upon the Tudors, turned a blind eye to these meetings, provided that they were conducted with the outward semblance of secrecy. And so, although Jasper knew full well that his conversation with Christopher Urswick would be uninterrupted by any of his Breton companions, he nevertheless chose a morning of thick fog for the rendezvous, thus giving the escort every excuse for losing his nephew and himself in the narrow, winding streets of Rennes.

They rode slowly. The torches, held aloft by unseen hands, hissed and flared in the encircling fog, their jets of red-gold flame Promethean fire, stolen from the haunts of the gods. The lanterns gave a more subtle light, glimmering through the mist with the sparkle of gems veiled by a clinging silk gauze. Henry loved days such as this; loved the silence and secrecy of a world enveloped in obscurity.

His uncle, riding beside him, could not see the boy's face, but could sense his contentment. How desperately he wished that Henry were less of an introvert, more open and far more confiding, only Jasper knew. His opinion of his nephew he kept to himself and spoke of him to other people with a respect that bordered on reverence. And, indeed, Jasper was not without sympathy for his brother's only child, for he realised that for Henry to have spent nearly all his life in virtual captivity, must almost certainly result in his turning inwards upon himself. That Henry trusted no one, not even his devoted uncle, was a direct consequence of his having been surrounded throughout his twenty years by people who, however fond of him they might be, were, of necessity, spies for someone else. Having lived his life, thought Jasper, knowing that every movement, every expression would be observed and reported and commented upon, it would have been remarkable had Henry been other than he was.

But however secretive he was in most ways, there was one thing that Henry made abundantly clear: when it came to politics he was an extremely astute young man, quick to grasp all the implications of any situation.

His voice sounded now through the mist. 'Edward will be in difficulties. King Louis will almost certainly make an attempt to annexe Burgundy now that Duke Charles is dead. Duke Francis told me, himself, that this has long been a dream of Louis.'

'And so?' prompted Jasper, after a pause. He felt the movement as Henry shrugged his shoulders.

'And so, Edward, as Burgundy's old and loyal ally, should go to Mary's aid. Indeed, England's wool trade is so bound up with that of the Flemish weavers that she dare not risk Burgundy's being overrun by France. But. . . .'

'But?'

Henry laughed. 'My dear uncle Jasper, you know as well as I do what the "but" is.'

'I like to hear you talk. It makes a change and it shows me that your understanding of foreign affairs is all that it should be.'

Henry laughed again, but this time it was a far more mirthful sound. Jasper made a mental note that his nephew was not averse to flattery, if not too obviously used.

'Well then,' Henry continued, 'the "but", as you are already aware, is that if Edward joins Burgundy in open warfare against Louis, Louis will certainly seize on it as a pretext to stop Edward's pension. Immediately! And the loss of fifty thousand crowns a year could prove an embarrassment to Edward – or so I should imagine.'

Jasper grunted. 'And to the rest of his nobles who benefited under the Picquigny treaty. Including,' Jasper added with a sly grin, 'our friend, John Morton.'

'But not Richard of Gloucester.' Henry's voice sounded so furiously in Jasper's ear that he jumped. 'One of the righteous who refused a French bribe.'

Jasper turned his head curiously, but although the fog was lifting a little, it was still impossible to see Henry's face clearly. However, his tone had been sufficient and it was the first indication Jasper had had of his nephew's dislike of the Duke of Gloucester. The older man was thoughtful. As far as he knew, the two cousins had never met and, except that one was a scion of the victorious House of York and the other of the ill-fated House of Lancaster, there seemed no explanation of Henry's obvious bitterness against his young kinsman.

There was no time for further speculation, however. They were opposite the cathedral. Jasper caught at Henry's bridle and forced his horse to enter a noisome alley which ran alongside it. Here they dismounted and entered the church by a side door.

A surprise awaited Jasper, for Christopher Urswick was not alone. He introduced his companion as one, Reginald Bray, who came from Margaret Beaufort. Jasper grimaced to himself. So his quondam sister-in-law was going to dabble in a little intrigue, was she? Well, she was an abnormally clever woman and it could do them no harm to have her on their side. It might, indeed, do Henry a great deal of good to know that his mother was at last interesting herself in his affairs.

Urswick's voice was low and rapid and he spoke as though he were mentally looking over his shoulder. Not all Jasper's assurances that Duke Francis was fully aware of these meetings, and even took a benign interest in them, could put Urswick at his ease.

Much of what he told them, they knew already, but, suddenly, there was an interesting twist to the story. It appeared that Duke Charles' death had resulted in difficulties for Edward which no one had foreseen.

'It was at a Council meeting, last month.' Urswick dropped his voice still lower. 'The Duke of Clarence proposed that, as he was now a widower, he should marry Mary of Burgundy.'

'In fact it was not merely a proposal,' Reginald Bray put in. 'The Duke, it seems, had already written to his sister, the Dowager Duchess of Burgundy on the subject. She is apparently very eager for a match between her brother and step-daughter.'

'What happened then?'

'King Edward was furious, as you may imagine. He might have forgiven brother George for his disaffection in the past, but he doesn't trust him. He certainly won't have him ruler of Burgundy with all that wealth and power at his back. He's wise enough to realise that in those circumstances, it probably would not be long before Clarence made another bid for the English crown.'

'What then?'

Urswick smiled. 'King Edward played his trump card. He didn't forbid his brother to offer for Mary, but he put up his brother-in-law, Earl Rivers, as the official English candidate for the lady's hand.'

A smothered explosion of laughter broke from Jasper. 'Superb!' he exclaimed. 'I don't like the man, but I must admit that as a statesman he commands my admiration. George of Clarence won't vie for favours with a Woodville.'

'Precisely.' Reginald Bray smiled. 'Even Dr Morton says that it's an honour to serve such a man.'

'My lord Bishop,' said Urswick reprovingly, giving Morton his title, 'says that Clarence is very embittered and talks openly of revenge. He's making wild accusations of witchcraft, not only against the Queen, but also the King; refusing to eat anything while he's in London before it has first been tasted for poison. My lord says to wait upon events. Anything might happen.'

And anything might, thought Jasper as he and Henry rode away into the fog. The situation in England was now interesting in the extreme and as explosive as a barrel of gunpowder.

9

ELIZABETH sat in her father's apartments, playing chess. It was not often that she had this honour and she should have been enjoying herself, but she was not. Edward's attention to the game was half-hearted and his thoughts clearly elsewhere. Something of his depression of spirits communicated itself to his daughter and she sighed. Through the window, above the roofs of the houses, she could see a ragged fringe of trees topping the dun-coloured hills and an oyster sky, scored with the palest pink. Fragile clouds drifted like wood-smoke just above the horizon.

There was a sharp, autumnal chill in the air and the mists rose dankly from the Thames, permeating every corner of Westminster Palace. But they were not responsible for the air of gloom, the low-voiced whispers, the furtive glances that made discordant the life of the court. It was more than the dying cadences of a year whose chief note had been that of death. The Duke of Clarence was now a state prisoner, confined to the felons' quarters of the Tower.

Elizabeth slid an ivory pawn across the board and her father responded with an equally haphazard move. As the afternoon wore on, a storm blew up, long, straight spears of rain slapping into the courtyard below, fragmenting into a thousand drops that danced and spattered on the age-worn stones.

The door was flung open by a startled page and her uncle Gloucester appeared, unannounced, the water spangling his heavy cloak making the fire splutter as he advanced into the room. Elizabeth's heart gave a little lift, as always when she saw him, and she was almost glad of the terrible circumstances which had brought him to London from his northern home.

Edward got up from the table with the quick, jerky movements of a man about to ward off something unpleasant, upsetting the chess-board and scattering the men to lie like red and white flowers among the rushes on the floor. He snatched up a folio, golden tassles bobbing against the blue silk binding, and began to talk in the hurried way people had – or so Elizabeth had noticed – when they wished to prevent the discussion of an unwelcome subject.

'You should look at this, Diccon,' he said. 'Stories by an Italian called Boccaccio.'

'I've read them,' his brother replied shortly. 'They're very entertaining.'

The King was momentarily diverted. For a young man who had pondered the writings of the Yorkshire mystic, Richard Rolle, perused Thomas à Kempis, and even studied the lollard Bible of William Wycliffe, the Decameron was not the sort of book one expected Richard to have read, let alone to have enjoyed. Edward's remark had been made purely to avert another fruitless argument with the Duke and he reflected that this youngest brother of his was not always predictable; somewhere, Richard concealed a vein of humour not immediately apparent, even to those who knew him best.

Seeing the Duke's mouth open to speak, Edward intervened once more, trying another tack. 'I know what you've come to see me about. The letter from the York City Fathers about the weir in the river Aire . . . ah! . . . Goldale garth! That's it! I suggest that when you return home, you set about having all illegal fishgarths destroyed, using my authority if necessary. Have the whole business thoroughly investigated this time. Set up a commission of enquiry and get Northumberland to appoint some representatives as well as your own. Hastings' brother, Ralph, would be a good man to have, and Sir William Redeman and. . . .[2]

Richard's voice cut impatiently across the King's. 'Yes, I daresay,' he said, 'but that's not what I've come to see you about. I have just been to the Moor Gate to see the city walls being rebuilt. The Mayor, Ralph Josselyn, was there and he told me that Robert Stillington has also been committed to the Tower. Why?'

'Why?' repeated Edward, defensively.

'Yes, why? I know quite well that the Bishop of Bath and Wells has been close friends with our brother for a number of years now. I don't know the reason, nor have I ever wanted to. Since childhood I have always thought it best to leave George's affairs well alone if I wished to stay out of trouble. But now. . . . '

'Even now,' the King interrupted harshly, 'you would do well to leave George's affairs well alone.'

Richard flung off the wet cloak and moved closer to the fire, laying his hand on his brother's arm. He had not noticed Elizabeth and Edward had forgotten her presence. She knew that she ought to slip away, but she did not want to. This glimpse into the adult world, particularly into the tragedy that now beset her family, fascinated her and she drew further back into the shadow of the wall.

'Edward,' her uncle implored, shaking her father's arm, 'what do you intend? What am I going to tell our mother? Can you imagine what it's like, staying in her house, eating her food and not being able to offer her as much as a crumb of comfort in return? Let me reassure her that you mean no harm to George; that you only mean to frighten him.'

Edward turned away and Elizabeth noted a peculiarly hard expression in his eyes. For no apparent reason, from far in the distant past, she could hear her mother's voice. 'My children will never be safe while Clarence is alive.' And there also came the echo of grandmother Bedford: 'You've had your suspicions that he knew . . . Stillington. . . .'

'Why should you and our mother treat me as the criminal?' Edward demanded petulantly of the Duke. 'Over the years, George has betrayed me, flouted my authority, plotted against me, tried, even, to seize my crown. And always I've forgiven him.'

'But not forgotten,' Richard said.

The King turned on him in a blaze of anger. 'God's Body! Did you expect me to do that as well? Look at what George had done this year alone. First, he proposes himself for Mary of Burgundy behind my back and when I scotch that plan, he screams abuse. Even now, when Mary has married Maximilian, and made it abundantly clear that the Hapsburg was always her choice, George continues to believe that I ruined his chances, mouthing his obscenities about witchcraft and sorcery.' Edward poured some wine into a mazer and gulped it furiously. A gust of wind made the fire smoke, leaving a trail of grey vapour that wreathed and coiled about the hearth for a while, before vanishing like a ghost in the dawn. Edward continued: 'And then, not content with that, he usurps my royal prerogative and has two of his late wife's servants summarily executed on the unproven charge that they poisoned Isabel – presumably at my in-laws' instigation.'

'And you,' Richard responded accusingly, 'promptly had one of George's servants hanged, despite his protests of innocence. You're like two children, smashing each other's toys, only a great deal more dangerous.' Richard slammed his hand down on the table. 'Do you think that I'm a fool, Edward? You haven't suddenly decided to arrest George because he has merely continued to do the sort of things that he has done all his life. There's something else behind all this. Something George has threatened you with that I know nothing about. Something to do with Stillington.'

There was a sudden silence. The two brothers faced each other, both breathing hard and it was almost, Elizabeth thought, as though her father were trying to communicate something to her uncle; trying to tell him something without putting it into words. Then Edward opened his mouth slowly, putting out his hand....

At that instant, Elizabeth sneezed. The smoke from the fire had been tickling the back of her nose and now jerked her head forward on a sudden explosion of sound. Both men jumped and turned, Richard in surprise, Edward with a smothered exclamation of dismay. Elizabeth, blushing and curtseying, slid towards the door and out into the draughty corridor.

But inside the room the spell had been broken, and Richard realised that whatever it was that his brother had been about to impart, would never be told to him now. The moment had passed, slipping away, dream-like, into the limbo of the might-have-been.

On the fifteenth of January in the following year, 1478, Richard, the four-year-old Duke of York, was married to the Lady Anne Mowbray, sole heiress of the late Duke of Norfolk. The Duke of Clarence still rotted in prison and no one knew what the King's intentions were towards him.

The wedding day dawned clear and frosty. The dim interior of St Stephen's Chapel was ablaze with candles, the walls glowing with the rich reds and greens, purples and blues of the tapestries. Near the high altar, a golden canopy had been set up and beneath it stood the Queen and her four daughters, awaiting the bridegroom and his five-year-old bride. Elizabeth, clutching the hand of the baby, Anne, turned every now and then to direct a quelling stare at Mary and Cicely, who showed a deplorable tendency to shuffle their feet and cough and admire each other's dresses in high-pitched, penetrating whispers.

She, herself, wore a charming new dress of blue velvet edged with ermine, but, child-like, thought that it compared but poorly with her mother's resplendent creation in violet cloth-of-gold. Glancing around, she could see the Duchess of Norfolk peering anxiously towards the door; her aunt, Elizabeth Plantagenet, muttering something to her husband, which caused Suffolk's heavy features to crease into an unexpected grin; her eldest half-brother, the Marquis of Dorset, and his wife; her younger half-brother, Sir Richard Grey; Henry, Duke of Buckingham, magnificent in silver and green, talking to Lord John Howard, a cousin of the Mowbrays; and all the other members of that dazzling congregation who impatiently awaited the young bridegroom.

Elizabeth was fond of little Richard. Generally, he was a pleasant-tempered, undemanding child, but he had the temper of his Plantagenet father, whom he strongly resembled. Her other brother, the Prince of Wales, Elizabeth knew hardly at all. Since the age of two, he had had his own household in Ludlow Castle, on the borders of Wales. Such things as she heard, suggested that he was a clever and precocious six-year-old, more a Woodville in looks than anything else.

There was a shout from outside. The bridegroom had arrived, accompanied by the Duke and Duchess of Gloucester and attended by the little Earl of Warwick, Clarence's son. That the two boys looked rather alike was commented upon by various people in the crowds, amongst whom was an organ-builder from Oxford, who remarked on the similarity to the priest by his side.

Richard Simons nodded disinterestedly. Then, more because he felt that his companion expected a reply than for any other reason, he said jokingly: 'If it comes to that, Tom, they both look a bit like your little Lambert.'

Thomas Simnel laughed and, as the bridegroom's procession disappeared inside the church, turned his head to look for the bride's.

To a fanfare of trumpets, Anne Mowbray arrived at last, escorted by the King, and with Earl Rivers and the Earl of Lincoln walking one on each side of them. As she approached the altar, she looked at her small bridegroom, and he at her, with blighting indifference. She obediently put a fat, dimpled hand into his, there was a surge of music and the Nuptial Mass had begun.

When it was over, Richard of Gloucester moved forward to escort the new Duchess of York to the palace for the wedding feast. Her hand felt damp in his and he noticed that there was an unhealthy pallor about the plump little face turned so enquiringly up to his. She seemed eager to leave the church, pulling on his arm, but she waited patiently enough by his side while he paused to throw gold to the crowds. She even plunged her own tiny fists into the bowls and managed to heave some of the coins in their direction. And as she walked back to the palace, trotting beside her new uncle, the crowds cheering themselves hoarse, Richard was forcibly reminded of a remark that George had once made. 'Give the English a child or an animal and the fools will run mad with joy.'

But it seemed that the Duke of Clarence's jibes were to be heard no more in Westminster. Three hours later, as the wedding banquet drew to its close with the serving of spiced wines and sugared fruits; as the bride sat sleepily staring into space; and as the overwrought bridegroom gave vent to his feelings in a truly royal bout of Plantagenet rage, the King announced that his brother, George, would be brought to trial the following day.

The climax of the extremely lavish wedding festivities came on Thursday, the twenty-second of January, with a tournament held in the courtyard near Westminster Abbey. The royal family and the foreign ambassadors sat beneath the embroidered canopy of their box, with Anne Mowbray High Princess of the Feast. Elizabeth, relegated today to a subordinate place, was one of the council of ladies who helped her sister-in-law to judge the competitions and award the insignias of gold. The 'Party Within,' headed by the Marquis of Dorset broke lances, clashed swords and vied in the opulence of their costumes with the 'Party Without,' led by that champion jouster, Earl Rivers.

But Elizabeth's thoughts were elsewhere. The day after the wedding, her uncle Clarence had been tried and condemned to death in Westminster Hall and her uncle Gloucester had turned his back on the court. Not that he had returned to the north: he and his wife still lingered on in grandmother York's London home, Baynard's Castle, but they attended no more festivities and their chairs were ostentatiously empty today. As long as Clarence lived, Elizabeth knew that Richard would not leave the capital, although, like him, she could not really believe that her father would order the execution of his own brother. But most distressing of all to an eleven-year-old child, were the whispers, the half-heard snatches of conversation, the sudden silences, all of which suggested that the Woodvilles were determined on Clarence's death. Only last night, Elizabeth had overheard a remark of Buckingham's, made to her aunt, Catherine Woodville.

'Your sister,' he had said nastily, 'will murder George just as she once did the Earl of Desmond. And it will be in the same way, by execution: but murder, nonetheless.'

But Buckingham's prophecy was to prove false in one respect: the Duke of Clarence was never brought to the block and the headsman's axe. In the middle of February, on one of those short, twilight days of wind and sleet, George Plantagenet died in the Tower.

10

DUKE FRANCIS was incredulous.

'A butt of malmsey!' he exclaimed. 'Drowned in a butt of malmsey? The King's brother?'

'That is the story,' said Jasper, picking the meat from between his teeth and spitting it into the rushes.

Duke Francis, delicately trifling with his fried pork and onions (which had been stewed to perfection in a good beef broth with pepper, cinnamon and cloves), shut his eyes against the offensive sight. There were times, he thought distastefully, when one was reminded that although Jasper was the grandson of a King of France on his mother's side, his paternal grandfather had been nothing but a Welsh brewer before he became butler to the Bishop of Bangor. And it was this, as much as his amused disgust at the manner of Clarence's death, that prompted Francis to turn to Henry and say: 'What a barbarous lot you English are, to be sure.'

Henry flushed: he was fully aware of the Duke's thoughts. It was one of his captor's most irritating habits that not only did he refuse to acknowledge any difference between the Welsh and English races, but that anything which displeased him was immediately attributed to Henry's Anglo-Saxon blood. Oddly enough, it was this thin strain, inherited from his mother, that Henry most valued, for it was that which gave him his claim – such as it was – to the English throne; and of late, he had begun to think more and more about his doubtful inheritance of his. This was partly due to his uncle Jasper, and partly to his new secretary, Richard Fox.

Fox, whom he could see at one of the lower tables, was a man of some thirty years of age; the son of an English yeoman, who had studied law at Magdalen College and, later, taken a degree in Canon Law at Paris University, where he had also been ordained. From there, he had travelled into Brittany to offer his services to Henry Tudor. That a man of such considerable talents, who might have made a brilliant career for himself at home, should elect to join an exile of doubtful lineage – the bar sinister shadowed Henry's ancestry on both the spear and distaff sides – had given the two Tudors considerable food for thought. Henry was thinking about it now, as he smiled politely at Duke Francis' jibe and dabbled his fingers in the silver bowl provided for his use.

Duke Francis continued: 'You should really consider the proposition I made that you should marry my daughter, Anne. You would then have the satisfaction of knowing yourself allied to a civilised people.'

'The Lady Anne is a little young for my nephew, don't you think?' Jasper put in drily, pausing from the enjoyable task of picking his nose. 'At less than a year old, she is more than twenty years his junior.'

'But how pleasant,' Francis replied, averting his gaze, 'for when your nephew reaches forty, he will have the pleasure of a virginal young wife – if he can manage anything then, of course.'

There was a ripple of laughter from all those within earshot, but the astute Pierre Landois was not smiling. He would have liked to have made the jest a reality, for he had become increasingly aware this past year that Henry Tudor might one day be somebody in the world. The Treasurer could not have said, if asked, what made him feel this way. Henry, on the face of it, was a penniless exile; a young man doomed to a bleak and precarious future, never sure who was his friend and who is enemy; uncertain whether, this time next year, he would be in Brittany, France or handed over to Edward of England. But Landois, like a dog tracking a buried bone, following the scent of his political nose, knew that many people in England were beginning to take note of this unadventurous, rather uninspiring, but sagacious youth who had lived for seven years as the unwilling guest of the Duke of Brittany. Deep in his bones, the Treasurer felt that an alliance with Henry Tudor might well profit the Duchy in the future struggle against France.

Later, while Duke Francis held court in the great hall and was entertained by a motet especially composed by his Master of Music for the choir-children to sing, Henry and Richard Fox strolled in the dreary gardens. A rising wind whispered through the branches of the trees, setting them rattling and shaking, skeletons performing the Dance of Death. The distant hills stood ghost-like on the horizon and, now and then, a small twig, black and brittle in the February cold, drifted sadly to the ground.

The two men said little at first. Fox had soon realised that his new master was a singularly uncommunicative young man and that it was best to let him inaugurate the topic of conversation. When Henry did at last speak, his secretary was not altogether surprised at the trend of his thoughts.

'When King Henry the fourth confirmed my great-grandfather Beaufort's patent of legitimacy, had he any right to add the qualifying clause *excepta dignitate regali*?'

'Offhand,' Fox replied, thrusting out a judicious underlip, 'I cannot say definitely, but I should doubt it. One understands his reasons for doing it, of course. He had recently taken the crown by force from his cousin and his possession of it was extremely insecure. He had enough to do defending himself from King Richard's adherents without the possible aspirations of a brace of ambitious half-brothers.'

Henry was silent for a moment. Then: 'The stigma of bastardy still attaches itself to my great-grandfather,' he remarked slowly; almost, thought Fox, as though he were reproaching some unseen presence. The secretary hastened to reassure his master.

'There is no doubt that he and his brothers and sisters were born to Lady Swynford before she married John of Gaunt. But there is no doubt, either, that after the wedding, King Richard the second, in order to please his uncle, legitimatised the Beaufort children.'

There was another silence, more protracted than before. Somewhere a bird was singing, a sad little reminder of summer's faded glory. Henry said, carefully choosing his words: 'Now that Henry the fourth's line has been completely wiped out. . . .'

He looked sideways at Fox, raising his thin eyebrows. The secretary shrugged and waved his hands.

'Then you, as the direct male descendant of the eldest Beaufort, could be regarded as . . . King of England.'

Henry shook his head. '*Lancastrian* King of England,' he corrected. 'In the vexed matter of primogeniture, the Yorkists will always have the prior claim.' His voice had risen on a sharp and bitter note and he turned abruptly on his heel. 'I am cold and I want to go in.'

The year 1478 slipped uneventfully into history. The escape, in August, of the Earl of Oxford from the fortress of Hammes into France was the only happening worthy of comment. As the cold mists of November swirled low over the Thames Valley, young William Paston, writing from Eton, found his news restricted to a demand for extra clothing and an urgent request that his brother pay his debts; followed by the eternal cry of the schoolboy: 'Please may I come up to London and have some fun?'

A humid winter brought in its wake the inevitable increase in disease and 1479 was ushered in with such a terrible bout of plague, that King Edward again secured a papal dispensation for himself and his courtiers to eat meat on all fast days, in order to keep up their strength.

In February, another daughter, the Princess Katherine, was born to the King and Queen, and Elizabeth celebrated her thirteenth birthday. On her father's orders, she was now openly addressed as Madame la Dauphine and was shrewd enough to see this as an indication of Edward's growing apprehension over his friendship with France. Maximilian and Mary were doing badly in their struggle against Louis, and the annexation of Burgundy could mean the French King's repudiation of the Treaty of Picquigny.

There was a restlessness everywhere. It was as though people were seeking for something as yet undefined and unrecognised. At the Sign of the Red Pale in Westminster Yard, the former merchant, William Caxton, printed his books and, at the beginning of 1480, published *Descriptions of England*. In their new quest for knowledge, Englishmen bought the book at the workshop door, sometimes still wet from the presses.

The Church, too, was changing. The Inspector General of the Cluniac Monasteries in England declared that it was not only the buildings which were falling into decay, but the observance of religion, also. An austere, pious man, he could not be expected to understand that his fellow countrymen's indifference to Rome was deep-rooted and had its origins in the essence of the Englishman's nature.

In May, an expedition set out from Bristol; a ship of eighty tons, owned by one John Jay and under the skilled command of the Welshman, Thomas Lloyd. The intention was to find the Island of Brazil, reputed to lie somewhere in the turbulent waters of the Atlantic ocean.

Yes, it was true indeed, thought Elizabeth, as she stared into the sunlit courtyard and waited patiently while her women shaved her eyebrows and fixed her high gauze head-dress; there was a feeling of change in the very air. It was as though men's spirits were opening like flowers in the sun, after centuries in the dark bowels of the earth.

She adjusted the long sleeves of her gown, viewed herself quickly in the mirror and went down to the great hall where her family were already assembling to welcome her aunt Margaret, the Dowager Duchess of Burgundy.

Margaret Plantagenet, who had left her native land fourteen years earlier to become the wife of Charles of Burgundy, was now a tall, full-bosomed woman of thirty-four.

Lord Hastings, viewing her majestic arrival in company with the Mayor of London, was moved to remark unkindly to his neighbour that the Rose of York had become somewhat overblown. Her brother, Richard of Gloucester, noting her strong resemblance to the King, wondered if there had been any truth in her late husband's assertion that he had married the greatest whore in Europe. Elizabeth Woodville, eyeing her sister-in-law's taut stomach muscles with envy, reflected bitterly on Margaret's childless state, while she was pregnant yet again. Cicely Neville, watching her daughter through narrowed eyes, thought that this sixth-born child of hers had grown into an unfulfilled and discontented woman. And the Princess Elizabeth wondered why it was that some members of her family were so positively healthy, while others, like her sister Mary, so early fell a prey to that wasting cough known as the English disease.

But it was the King, moving forward to kiss his sister with every outward appearance of pleasure, who was most wary. Ever since the death of George of Clarence, he had been an uneasy and unhappy man. His mother, while doing him public homage, in private refused to speak to him. His elder sister, the Duchess of Suffolk, was a little reserved in her manner; almost, he thought bitterly, as though she were afraid of him. And his brother, Richard, deeply embittered but always loyal, had, as usual, transferred the blame and, therefore, his hatred, from Edward to the Woodvilles. There was no doubt either, that George had been Margaret's favourite brother and her reactions on meeting one whom many people regarded as Clarence's murderer, were difficult to predict.

Edward need not have worried, however. With every advancing year, Margaret had come to identify herself more with the House of York than with any particular member of it. Her consequence in the country of her adoption rested more on her being the sister of England's King than the widow of Charles of Burgundy, and she was fully aware of this fact. Moreover, she had come determined to enjoy herself and recriminations for George's death was the thing farthest from her thoughts. Instead, she thanked her eldest brother prettily for the magnificent guard-of-honour which he had sent to Dover to meet her, and for the escort of his brother-in-law, Sir Edward Woodville, who had proved a most entertaining companion.

In consequence, the weeks she spent in England were extremely happy ones and among the many guests who were entertained at Cold Harbour House – put entirely at Margaret's disposal by the King – were her young nieces, to whom she imparted a great deal of worldly wisdom and, occasionally, snippets of information which Elizabeth, at least, found interesting.

One of these came through a casual remark of the Princess, as, on a clear, golden morning in early July, she idly watched her aunt's voluptuous figure being eased into a new gown of purple velvet, heavily embroidered with suns and white roses. The subject under discussion was the two-year-old marriage of the Duke of York and his little bride, Anne Mowbray.

'I get the impression,' Elizabeth confided, 'that my mother doesn't like her. I don't know why.'

Margaret ran her hands down over her hips and, turning slowly before the mirror of polished metal, answered abstractedly: 'Oh, I daresay she likes the child all right. It's her mother, the Duchess, that Elizabeth can't stand. Do you think this makes me look a trifle broad?'

'No, not at all,' Elizabeth replied mendaciously. 'Why doesn't my mother like the Duchess of Norfolk?'

Margaret pursed her lips in dissatisfaction at her own appearance. 'Mmm? Oh, I don't know. Because she doesn't like the Talbots, I suppose. The Duchess is rather militant: takes after her father, old Talbot of Shrewsbury. You must have heard of him. He was a great general in the French wars. And then,' Margaret added, turning to smile conspiratorially at her niece, 'the other daughter, Eleanor, was a . . . a friend of your father at one time.'

'Eleanor?'

'Eleanor Butler was her married name. I recall that Edward was very enamoured in that direction just after he became King.'

'And what happened to her?'

'I don't really know. After a while she retired from court and what then became of her, I've never discovered. And now, my dear child, I shall beg you to accompany me while I receive one of those tedious deputations, of welcome, this time from the Fishmonger's Guild.'

This and many other official duties occupied the Dowager-Duchess during her London stay. It was not, as she commented acidly to the Burgundian ambassador, one continual round of hunting and feasting, picnicking and dancing as, no doubt, her step-daughter and that Hapsburg husband of hers imagined. Also, she was expected to visit those Flemings and Hollanders living either permanently or temporarily in the English capital; a task which she performed gracefully if not enthusiastically, meeting, amongst others, a certain John and Clara Warbeck from Tournai. This couple had lodged for a while with the Bramptons and Mrs Brampton was particularly fond of the Warbeck's little son, Peter.

But there was, nevertheless, plenty of time for the pleasures of life and Edward did not stint his sister's entertainments. It was with deepest regret that the Duchess at last departed for Burgundy at the end of September, taking with her, as a mark of her brother's esteem, a pillion cushion of blue and gold velvet, a dozen of Edward's best horses and as much duty-free wool as she could buy.

Her nieces were among those who were saddest to see her go and one of them would never see her again. In the May of the following year, 1481, six months after Elizabeth Woodville had given birth to her last child, another girl named Bridget, the Princess Mary died at Greenwich Palace, aged fourteen.

11

THE death of the sister nearest her in age did not have so profound an effect upon Elizabeth as it might have done. The extrovert Cicely had always been Mary's partner, while the quiet and more reserved Elizabeth had fallen naturally into the role of older sister. Her betrothal to the Dauphin of France had had the result of making her seem even more remote to her two immediate juniors, and although Cicely had also recently been affianced to the Duke of Albany, no one could pretend that the prospective alliance with the King of Scotland's brother was in any way of commensurable importance.

What did affect Elizabeth, however, was the depth of her father's grief and the realisation that Mary had been Edward's favourite daughter. Never before had Elizabeth questioned her lifelong conviction that she was her father's best-loved child and it came, therefore, as a sudden, bitter and humiliating blow to find that this was not so. And it was at this crucial stage in her adolescent development that she accompanied her parents to Nottingham in the autumn of that year, for a meeting with her uncle Gloucester.

For more than twelve months now, the Scots had been raiding over the Border and along the northern marches, egged on by Louis of France, (always happy to fish in the troubled waters of Anglo-Scottish relationships), and led by their cultured, artistic and homosexual King, James the third. Neither the stormy internal politics of Scotland, with the nobles violently opposing the King's low-born favourites and the Duke of Albany treating secretly with England in an effort to seize his brother's crown, nor the fact that Lord John Howard had, that summer, smashed their fleet in the Firth of Forth, seemed to deter the Scots. And it was concerning a full-scale war against their northern neighbour that Edward and Richard met at Nottingham Castle in the October of 1481.

For Elizabeth, this particular encounter with her uncle was a revelation; a crystallising of all those undefined feelings which she had experienced in the past and not really understood. At her first sight of him in the gloomy great hall, a slight figure surrounded by all the pomp of the greatest man in England bar the King, she knew without any further doubt that she loved him; not with the ties of family affection, but with passion; as a woman should love a man – but not her father's brother! That she might be placing him on the pedestal from which Edward has so recently toppled naturally did not occur to her. She only knew that when he was near, when he smiled or spoke to her, she felt a sense of protection and a stirring of the blood such as she had never known before. The fact that, as a serious young man of twenty-eight, Richard only now and then remembered her existence, merely added to his fascination in the eyes of a fifteen-year-old girl.

The Duke, anxious to complete arrangements and return home to Middleham as soon as possible, would have continued discussions on logistics even at the table, had not his brother forcibly interrupted him.

'For God's sake, Diccon!' he exclaimed, laughing, 'at least let me eat my food in peace. And take that worried frown off your face.' He surveyed his brother critically. 'It does nothing for your appearance and only emphasises the fact that you have a rather heavy jaw.'

Elizabeth, watching her uncle closely, saw a faint flush tinge the sallow skin: then he smiled. 'That only goes to show how alike we really are,' he retorted and the awkward moment passed.

'I seem to recall,' William Hastings put in, addressing the King, 'that the Duke of Gloucester was once referred to as the handsomest man in the room, excepting, of course, Your Grace.'

Edward was amused. 'Who said so?' he enquired, signing to a server to re-fill his plate with cheese-cakes.

A malicious expression had crept into the Lord Chamberlain's face and he did not answer immediately. Then he said: 'I believe it was the Countess of Desmond.'

It seemed to Elizabeth that there was an unaccountable silence following these words. She was aware also of a sudden stillness; in her mother's hands, poised like winged birds above her empty dish; in her father's slack mouth, half-open as though frozen in mid-speech; in her uncle's clenched fists and thin, immobile mouth; and in the generally arrested movements which had turned the high table into the court of Polydectes gazing upon the face of the Medusa.

Here again, with the name of Desmond as with that of Eleanor Butler, Elizabeth sensed a mystery, and, in each case, observation told her that her mother was deeply involved. Her feelings for her mother were not profound: Elizabeth Woodville's obsessive affection for her brothers and sisters precluded any intense relationship with her children. But Elizabeth was fond enough of her mother to wish her untouched by the many scandals of the court.

It was her uncle, pushing his lank hair away from his face with a quick, jerky movement of one hand, who released them all from the spell cast by Hastings' words. Ignoring his brother's injunction, he dragged their thoughts back to the impending war with a request that the men of York be exempted from the new tax, levied to pay for the cost of arms. As her father acquiesced, Elizabeth saw the glances of dislike directed at Richard by Lord Stanley and Henry Percy. Here, she thought, were two men who bitterly resented the power of the King's Lieutenant and General in the North.

Richard's growing influence with the men of Yorkshire and Westmorland, territory where, for generations, the Percys had held supreme sway, increased the enmity which the Earl of Northumberland felt for the Duke of Gloucester. This was in no way abated when, in January of the following year, the York City Fathers appealed to the King's brother, and not to

Hotspur's great-grandson, to settle their latest dispute.

Richard, waiting for his secretary to show the deputation into his presence-chamber at Middleham, thought ruefully that he was about to antagonise Henry Percy yet again. He had done it too often, and had said as much to Edward when they had met at Nottingham. But: 'Pooh! Northumberland!' was all that the King had deigned to reply. It was not, however a sentiment to which the Duke could subscribe and as he signed to John Kendall to admit the aldermen, he wondered how much the present trouble at York owed to his rival.

He moved to the table and sat down, the pallor of his face accentuated by his black clothes. Like the rest of his household and family, he was in mourning for the Duchess of York – Anne Mowbray – who had died the preceding November at the age of nine. The little body had been carried from Greenwich on a sable-draped barge, surrounded by tapers and candles, to its resting place in the Chapel of St Erasmus. Throughout her short life, Anne Mowbray had been of the first importance; sole heiress of the Norfolk estates, daughter-in-law of the King. But to Richard she remained a tired little girl with a resignation and patience beyond her years.

He was roused from these thoughts by the entrance of the Councillors, who, after respectful greetings, appealed for his intervention in the hotly contested result of the York mayoral election. This had been held on St Blaise's day and had been a fight between one, Richard York, and a great favourite of the Duke's, Thomas Wrangwysh.

'There is no doubt that the result was close, my lord.' Heads nodded agreement, bobbing like so many Hallowe'en apples. 'But there's no doubt either that York was the winner. But Wrangwysh's supporters won't have it and Wrangwysh, himself. . . . '

Alderman Tong lapsed into silence, loth to say more about one who was a personal friend of Richard. Miles Metcalfe, the City Recorder, was not going to leave it at that, however.

'He's a nice enough man, Your Grace, and will some day make a very good Mayor – but only when he is properly elected. And that's not just yet! Richard York is the winner, as Alderman Tong here has said, but no amount of talking will convince Thomas Wrangwysh, and he's out to make trouble. We know we can speak plainly to Your Grace and that personal prejudice won't weigh with you as it might with so many.'

There was a grunt of agreement from the rest of the deputation and Richard half smiled. 'Thank you,' he said, 'and if Richard York was indeed the winner, I shall certainly uphold his election. I shall write at once to the King. But I also suggest that, as soon as the weather breaks, you gentlemen go personally to London and state your case before His Grace. Take certificates from the magistrate with you – but I don't need to tell you what to do.'

'And in the meantime?' Alderman Tong was anxious: riots could so easily get out of hand.

'Let Robert Amyas continue in office,' Richard advised; then saw by their faces that there was still something more to be said. 'What else?' he prompted gently, with a lift of his brows.

Miles Metcalfe sucked his teeth; another man wiped his nose on the back of his hand; yet another spat on the floor. Finally, Alderman Tong said: 'It's about some of the rioters, my lord. We've clapped them in prison, right enough, and there's no doubt they'll deserve what's coming to them. But . . . well. . . . They're mostly young and foolish and. . . .'

'And you feel that a little clemency wouldn't be amiss, is that it?'

There was a hopeful shuffle and faces began to brighten.

'You have my permission to release them, but warn them that next time I might not be in such a good mood.'

Frowns lifted into smiles and the Aldermen went on their way rejoicing.

And, later that same year, in the summer, the city of York was able to prove its gratitude to the Duke by a warm and moving display of affection. On June the eighteenth, when, at five o'clock in the morning, Richard rode wearily into the city with the Duke of Albany, on his way to the Border to begin the planned offensive against Scotland, he was greeted at the Micklegate Bar by the Mayor and Corporation and all the craftsmen of York. He was presented with ten gallons of wine, two pikes, two tenches and six breams. For, as Richard York, now firmly established as Mayor, confided later to the Duke: 'We didn't want any Scotsman underrating your lordship's position in this city.'

'It was a fine display,' Richard said appreciatively, suppressing the amusement in his voice.

'That was only to be expected, Your Grace,' York answered with enthusiasm, adding ingenuously: 'Especially as every Alderman who absented himself would have been fined a shilling and every other defaulter six pennies.'

A muscle twitched at the corner of Richard's mouth, but he pressed the Mayor's hand in gratitude and rode on to the House of the Augustinian Friars. He was well aware how strongly his countrymen detested their Scots neighbours – 'those children of iniquity' as they called them – and it was not without a certain relish that he recounted to Albany the story of John Harrignton, Clerk to the city of York. Harrington had been so shunned because of the slanderous report that he came from over the Border, that he had been forced to obtain testimonials from at least three reputable people that he was 'no false Scot'. Albany smiled thinly and, taking the allusion more personally than had been intended, flushed to the roots of his rather sparse hair. Looking at him, Richard felt sorry for his niece, Cicely, who was promised to Albany in marriage.

The following morning, they set out once more for the Border.

Autumn laid its golden hand on Brittany, turning the trees to flame, ragged banners, flaunting aloft against the mellow, peach-bloom skies; searing the hills with brakes of dead, burnt-out gorse.

Henry Tudor felt that life was at its lowest ebb for him. The future seemed to hold nothing but years of exile and captivity: no glorious destiny awaited him as he had once imagined that it might. The House of York appeared firmly established upon England's throne and Edward's recent unpopularity, caused by increased taxation, had been redeemed for him by his brother's resounding victory over the Scots. Berwick was once more in English hands and there had been great rejoicing throughout the country. Even in Calais, the Captain had ordered a triumphal procession and the lighting of bonfires; while in London, the people had sung Te Deums and danced in the streets. The name of Richard of Gloucester was on everyone's lips and the King had published the text of the letter which he had despatched to Pope Sixtus the fourth.

'Thank God,' he had written, 'the Bestower of all good things, for the support which I have had from my dearly beloved brother, Richard of Gloucester, who has proved to the world that he would be sufficient of himself to bring retribution to the entire land of Scotland.'

In fact, Richard's retribution had stopped short of razing the city of Edinburgh to the ground, a forbearance that had made him unpopular with some of his more bloodthirsty compatriots.

For the Lancastrians, both at home and abroad, the one ray of hope was that Edward's foreign policy was proving to be built on sand. Mary of Burgundy had died earlier that year after a fall from her horse, but the widowed Maximilian was fighting on. He was no match for the French, however, and Burgundy had gone, Artois was overrun and now Louis was snatching at Holland and Flanders. Edward had vacillated, wondering whether to risk losing his pension from Louis by supporting Maximilian, or to trust that the Burgundians would repel the French without English aid. Now, it appeared to the politically discerning, like Henry Tudor, that the English King would lose, whatever the outcome. A victorious Louis would see no need to keep Edward sweet once England's main European ally lay prostrate at his feet.

But Edward Plantagenet had proved in the past an able and cunning man. He was only forty years old and Henry had no doubt that he would manage to regain his grip on affairs of state. As a King he was popular; as a man he was loved. Even John Morton found it a pleasure to serve him.

What possible future was there, then, for a young man whose inheritance was of the bastard branch of Lancaster? As the chill blasts of winter whipped through the streets of Rennes, and as the lowering clouds heralded the first falls of snow, Henry Tudor gave way to such a black despair that he was to carry the scar on his spirit until the day of his death.

12

ELIZABETH was no longer the future Dauphine of France. In the December of 1482, Louis and Maximilian signed the Treaty of Arras, one of the terms being that the Dauphin should marry Mary of Burgundy's daughter. It was a blow at the pride and prestige of both England and Edward, and one from which the latter at least, would never recover.

Throughout the winter and bitterly cold spring, Elizabeth, the Queen and the entire court watched the King in growing apprehension. It seemed, as the Earl of Lincoln remarked to his brother, Edmund de la Pole, as though their uncle had lost the will to live. The flesh sagged on the once handsome face and the splendid physique, the tireless vigour, gave place to a paunchy figure and flagging energy.

At Easter, however, Edward seemed to revive and insisted on riding as far as Islington to see the Easter hocking. On the first day, the women hocked, chasing and catching the men of the village and tying them up until they had paid the required forfeit. On Tuesday, it was the men's turn to do the same, and the King laughed louder than anyone at some of the forfeits demanded. And afterwards, he went fishing, cheerfully paying his toll every time the royal party came to a chain stretched across the road – another Easter custom and one that was both popular and profitable.

Eight days later, he was dead. On the morning of April the ninth, Elizabeth, Cicely and Anne were roused from their sleep and hurried to their father's bedchamber. As they entered, they were joined by the young Duke of York, who clutched nervously at his eldest sister's hand. There were people everywhere, crowding the ante-chambers, pressing about the great bed. The flickering candles cast distorted shadows and made grotesque patterns on the walls and ceiling. The low mutter of voices, blending with the sound of stifled sobs and the chanting of the priests, made a continuous sussuration like the swish of the sea upon sand. Over all, hung the scent of the aromatic tapers mingling with the sickly-sweet smell of death.

Edward was propped up on his pillows. He had received Extreme Unction and made his confession. His eyes, the only moving things in what was now a hideous travesty of his face, searched the throng about him, looking for someone he could not find.

'Diccon,' he muttered at last and it was his mother who bent over him, imperiously silencing the others with a glance.

'Richard is not here. He is in the north, at Middleham.'

'At Middleham,' the King repeated stupidly. Then he seemed to make a great effort, pulling his mind back from the borders of Eternity and forcing himself into the present.

'I leave my country . . . and my son. . . . ' He gasped for breath, then continued: ' . . . in the charge of my beloved . . . brother . . . Richard of Gloucester . . . My will states this clearly. Lord Stanley,' the bloodshot eyes were raised to Henry Tudor's step-father, 'I have also . . . named you executor of my will . . . in place . . . in place of the Queen.' There was a slight gasp, but Edward pressed on, unheeding, for he was a man who had seen the Everlasting Gates lift up their heads. 'Hastings, give me . . . your hand. Now you, Dorset.' His friend and his eldest step-son placed their hands in his and he made a feeble effort to join them. 'There must be . . . an end . . . to enmity. Leave Jane Shore . . . to God. Make friends.'

As the last words trailed into silence on a rush of foam-flecked breath, Edward the fourth turned on his side. Two minutes later he died.

Anne Neville and her mother, the Countess of Warwick, accompanied the grief-stricken Duke of Gloucester as far as York. Here, they participated in the Requiem Mass in the Minster, praying for the repose of the dead King's soul, and watched Richard, on behalf of the new King, his nephew, administer the oath of fealty to the magistrates. Then they saw him start south with his two hundred men, before returning to the House of the Augustinian Friars for the night.

'You are very quiet,' Anne remarked to her mother, as they sat over their evening meal and the Countess sighed.

'You and little Edward are all I have left,' she answered, 'and I'm afraid for the future.' Her hands shook and she dropped the orange she was holding. It rolled, a rich ball of colour, across the table.

'Afraid? Why should you be afraid?' Anne asked gently and it was a moment or two before the Countess replied.

'Because Richard is such a ruthless young man,' she said at last.

Anne laid down her knife in amazement. 'What do you mean?' she queried and her voice rose on a note of indignation.

Her mother smiled faintly. 'My child, I love Richard like the son I never had. Not just because he gave me a home with you and my grandson, but for himself. I have loved him from the very first day that he came to us as a child at Middleham.' The gnarled fingers pushed the retrieved orange around her plate. 'But consider the facts, my dear. All his life, Richard has remained loyal to his brother, and, through Edward, to the Woodvilles, whom he hates. He fought and helped to destroy your father and your uncles, whom he dearly loved. Only a man of immense willpower could have done that. Until this week, that willpower was directed solely against himself, forcing himself to bow to the dictates of his conscience. But now, for the very first time, his brother's death has set him free.'

A candle guttered, sending up a fragile, quivering column of smoke. Anne shifted uneasily in her chair. 'You think he might now seek to destroy the Woodvilles?' She knew only too well that George's death, and, above all, the manner of it, had awakened a side of Richard's nature hitherto dormant.

'Perhaps!' The Countess stretched out her hand to her

daughter. 'But my prayers will be for you both, now, as always.'

A thin, persistent drizzle turned the dust to mud and made this last night of April in the year 1483 extremely cold. The torches guttered in the wind and clouds of dust rose from the workmen's picks as they hacked through the wall of the sanctuary. Servants, shivering inside their soaking garments and pushing the hair back from rain-blinded eyes, came and went, hauling crates of tapestries, boxes of silver and gold plate, jewels, furs and furniture across the courtyard from Westminster Palace. Directing the operation and hindering everyone in her blind panic, Elizabeth Woodville turned now and then to consult with her eldest son, the Marquis of Dorset, in no less of a sweat of fear than his mother. Elizabeth, holding the two-year-old Bridget in her arms and comforting as best she could Cicely, Katherine, Richard and Anne, tried to clarify her confused and racing thoughts.

It was a mere ten days since she had stood beside her father's bier in St George's Chapel at Windsor; since, still shocked and disbelieving, she had seen the black-draped coffin lowered into the vault and sprinkled earth upon it as it went. But even then, confused and grieving as she had been, she was aware of an undercurrent of urgency amongst her mother's family. Her brother, now King Edward the fifth, was at Ludlow with her uncle, Earl Rivers, and her half-brother, Sir Richard Grey, had been despatched to meet them on the road.

'Tell your uncle,' she had heard her mother say, 'that he and the King must get to London before Richard of Gloucester arrives.'

But the Duke had moved too swiftly. He had overtaken the royal party at Stony Stratford and, apprised of events in London by his cousin, the Duke of Buckingham, had arrested both Earl Rivers and Sir Richard Grey, only that very morning. And events in London, thought Elizabeth, even allowing for her decided partiality for her uncle, had justified his actions. Not only had the Woodvilles tried to suborn the Council, seize the person of the King and sent Sir Edward Woodville to France with a large part of the royal treasure, but Elizabeth suspected that they had also plotted either to imprison or kill the Protector, himself. But why, she did not know. Nor, try as she might, could she think of a reason.

The news of the arrests, received an hour ago, had had the effect of making her mother and eldest step-brother rush for sanctuary and now, at midnight, Elizabeth watched as their crates of plunder were dragged through the gaping hole torn in the sanctuary wall. As they, themselves, stepped into the comparative warmth of a small, bleak room, the Queen Dowager suddenly gave way to her overwrought emotions and, sinking down among the rushes, burst into tears.

Before Elizabeth could go to her mother's side, a shadow darkened the aperture and her uncle Lionel, Bishop of Salisbury, came in, accompanied by Thomas Rotheram, Archbishop of York and Chancellor of England. The latter seemed dazed, partly by sleep and partly by the turn of events, and presented the appearance of a man who did not know on which side of the fence he ought to land. His eyes, blinking in the torchlight, reflected his indecision whether to come down in favour of the Woodvilles or the Protector.

'I have just been awakened by a messenger from Lord Hastings,' he said, patting Elizabeth Woodville's shoulder in what he assumed was a comforting manner. 'He knows of the arrests of your son and brother and is, of course, jubilant. He sent word to the Protector at Middleham and holds himself in some sort responsible for Gloucester's swift arrival at Northampton.'

Elizabeth Woodville forgot the presence of her children and swore. 'Hastings has always worked against my family,' she spat. 'He hates us!'

Lionel Woodville nodded. 'But he also hopes for a great position in the new government,' he said, adding with a smile: 'Let us trust that he will not be disappointed.'

'What do you mean?' demanded his sister.

'From what I hear, the Duke of Buckingham has stolen a march on our Lord Chamberlain. While Hastings busies himself on Richard's behalf in London, Henry Stafford is making himself indespensable at the Protector's side.' The Bishop rubbed his nose. 'And if Hastings finds his nose out of joint, who can predict what might happen?'

'You think – ' Dorset began eagerly, but his uncle flung up his hands.

'I think nothing, my dear Thomas. I shall merely wait and see.'

'But what of Edward?' The Queen Dowager asked, anxious for her son.

'It seems that he stays with the Protector in Northampton until London is quieter.'

'If any thing happens to him,' cried Rotheram, 'I shall crown the Duke of York,' but Elizabeth Woodville was not listening. Her eldest daughter heard her say to her brother in an urgent undertone: 'Where's Stillington?'

'Here in London,' was the muffled reply.

'Will he say anything?'

'God knows! We must pray that he decides not to do so.' Lionel saw his niece looking at him and turned hurriedly away.

Rotheram had produced a leather bag on a string and was pressing it into Elizabeth Woodville's hands.

'The Great Seal,' he muttered. 'Keep it for me until I decide. . . . '

Even Lionel Woodville was shocked. 'You cannot!' he exclaimed. 'No Chancellor has the right to dispose of the Seal.'

'I'll be back tomorrow. But for now. . . . As you say . . . anything might happen.'

Dominic Mancini was an Italian from Milan, who had been living in England for almost a year. He would soon have to leave, for, having come for twelve weeks, he had stayed for twelve months. He would be very loth to go, for the island and its people fascinated him, and he had made up his mind that he most certainly would not do so until the present fluid and interesting state of English politics had resolved itself.

The arrival in London, in May, of the Protector and the little Edward the fifth had not meant the end of the troubles attendant upon the late King's death. The Duke of Buckingham, elevated to a position of power second only to that of Gloucester's, had antagonised many people, not least of whom were Hastings, Lord Stanley, Archbishop Rotheram and John Morton. Banding together in a conspiracy to overthrow the Protector, they had been betrayed by Hastings' lawyer, William Catesby, who had become whole-heartedly Richard's man. And, a few days ago, on Friday, June the thirteenth, during a Council meeting at the Tower, the four men had been arrested and the ringleader, Hastings, beheaded without trial.

Dominic Mancini was finding it increasingly difficult to understand the character of the Protector. The summary execution of the Lord Chamberlain argued a ruthlessness totally at odds with Richard's subsequent actions. The Duke had been at great pains to ensure that Hastings should not be attainted and thus forfeit his lands to the crown. These had been scrupulously restored to Hastings' widow and her husband's body interred with due respect in St George's Chapel at Windsor. (It had been Edward's wish that he and his friend should be buried near to one another.)

But even more puzzling to the Italian was the proclamation

issued by the Protector immediately after the execution, when Mayor Shaa had galloped by on his way to the Tower and the citizens had stormed into the streets, trying to sort out the facts.

That Hastings had been detected in an act of treason for which he had paid the penalty, so much Mancini could understand. Indeed, the speedy nature of the punishment would have appealed to his master, Ludovico Sforza. But what the Italian could not comprehend were the various riders at the end of the proclamation; riders to the effect that Hastings had been an evil influence on Edward the fourth; that he had lured the King into a vicious ways of living; and that, the very night before his death, the Lord Chamberlain had slept with Jane Shore. Such arguments and their ready acceptance by many of the people, suggested a kind of puritanism which Mancini had encountered nowhere else in Europe.

But the excitement of this eventful summer was not yet over. On June the sixteenth, the little Duke of York came out of sanctuary at the request of the Council, to join his brother in the royal apartments in the Tower. The coronation date was set and all arrangements going forward smoothly, when Mancini, in common with all Englishmen, was staggered by the news that Edward the fifth was no longer King of England and that the crown had been offered by the Lords Spiritual and Temporal to his uncle, the Duke of Gloucester.

The Italian, sweating out the long, hot days in the plague-ridden London streets, had, like his informants, to sift rumour from fact; a molehill of fact from a mountain of speculation. For Mancini, this was easier than for the emotionally involved natives, and the bare bones of the matter he recorded briefly on paper for his own satisfaction.

'The Bishop of Bath and Wells, Robert Stillington, has declared that King Edward the fourth was already troth-plighted in marriage to the Lady Eleanor Butler at the time of his wedding to Dame Elizabeth Woodville,' Quite feasible, thought Mancini, when one remembered that equally secret marriage of Edward and Elizabeth Woodville. 'In the eyes of the Church – or so it is claimed – such a plighting is as binding as marriage and the offspring of any subsequent union are illegitimate unless the previous contract is rendered void. Therefore, all the late King's children by the Queen Dowager have been proclaimed bastards and Edward's brother will be crowned instead, as King Richard the third.'

But although the majority of magnates would, or so Mancini guessed, be thankful to be ruled by a man instead of a boy, and were no doubt grateful for the pretext to crown the Duke instead of his nephew, there were still many dissenting voices; many who thought that the matter should have been more carefully considered; many who had hoped to seize power under the child-like King, Edward the fifth, and who now saw their plans baulked by the coronation of Richard the third.

13

It was Sunday, the sixth of July, 1483. It was the day of Richard's coronation. His bare feet padded softly along the roll of red cloth as he walked in solemn procession from Westminster Hall to the Abbey.

First, went the Sergeant-at-arms and the heralds, their tabards a blaze of colour under the overcast skies; then the royal musicians, trumpets and clarions blaring above the clamour of the crowds. A stray shaft of sunlight turned the great, golden cross, preceding the lines of priests, abbots and bishops, into liquid fire. The Bishop of Rochester followed and behind him walked the reluctant Cardinal Archbishop of Canterbury.

It was with the most profound misgivings that Thomas Bourchier had finally consented to bear his part in today's proceedings. In his heart of hearts, he could not but feel that he was crowning and consecrating an unlawful King. Even if the story of the pre-contract were true – and there was only Stillington's word for it – he could not be sure that it offered sufficient grounds for the deposing of Edward's son. He knew only too well that any number of marriage contracts were lightly made by young noble men and women, only to be as lightly broken. As a good Christian and an eminent churchman he deplored the practice, but if all children of subsequent unions were to be declared illegitimate, there would be more bastards in the country even than there were at present. The Archbishop felt that today's coronation was one of expediency; and expediency had nothing to do with God.

Percy of Northumberland came next, carrying Curtana, the pointless sword of mercy. Behind him, all three abreast, walked Lord Stanley – restored to favour after his part in the Hastings plot – with the Constable's mace; the King's brother-in-law, the Duke of Suffolk, holding the sceptre; and Suffolk's eldest son, the Earl of Lincoln, cupping the orb in his long, slender hands. And, following them, came Lord John Howard, newly created Duke of Norfolk, to whom had fallen the honour of bearing the crown.

John Howard, a man as kind and clutured as he was brave, had four great passions in life; Colchester oysters, music, drama and the sea. The first he indulged in moderation. For the second, he kept his household harpers, bagpipers and singers, and greeted with enthusiasm the itinerant companies of musicians who roamed the countryside each summer. The wandering bands of mummers and players were equally sure of a welcome, but it was the sea that claimed most of his heart. An ardent supporter of the Yorkist cause ever since the battle of Towton, he had done Edward good service, harrying French shipping, fighting the vessels of the Hanseatic League and destroying the Scottish fleet in the Firth of Forth. He had also done valuable diplomatic duty at the court of King Louis. His mother had been a Mowbray – daughter of that Duke exiled by Richard the second – and now that her line was extinct, what more natural than that the dukedom should be given to the Howards?

His son, the Earl of Surrey, carrying the sheathed sword of state, immediately preceded the King, who moved slowly under the rich, jewelled canopy held by the Barons of the Cinque Ports. Beyond them, to Richard's left, walked Francis Lovell with the civil sword of justice, accompanied by the Bishop of Bath and Wells (Stillington's face was serene, Richard was thankful to note: no prickings of conscience there. The Bishop evidently believed implicitly in the rightness of what he had done.) To the King's right, the Earl of Kent carried the ecclesiastical sword of justice, followed by the Bishop of Durham. Holding Richard's train in one hand, and the white wand of High Steward in the other, Buckingham brought the King's procession to a magnificent close.

For the next few minutes, the people in the crowds took the opportunity to cough, spit, hail acquaintances or relieve themselves hurriedly against the nearest wall. Then they were once more cheering themselves hoarse as the Queen's procession came into view.

Viscount Lisle appeared first, carrying the cross with the dove; the Earl of Wiltshire came next, with the Queen's crown; and William Herbert, the Earl of Huntingdon, bore her sceptre.

William Herbert was happy. Under his shirt, he could feel the piece of embroidered ribbon given to him last night by the Lady Katherine Plantagenet. It was the first tangible sign he had received that the King's bastard daughter returned his affection. Moreover, Richard had smiled his approval. William was suddenly hopeful that his suit might yet be successful.

The Queen, walking between the Bishops of Exeter and Norwich, was thinking of her father. If only the Earl of Warwick could have lived, what a glorious moment this would have been for him: his old enemies, the Woodvilles in disgrace; Anthony Woodville and Sir Richard Grey executed two days ago at Pontefract; a young man whom he had always loved as his King; and, most important of all, the summit of his ambitions, one of his daughters as Queen. With an effort, Anne suppressed a sudden bout of coughing and told herself that her tiredness was due solely to the weight of her clothes. Her jewel-encrusted gown was certainly very heavy, but her furred mantle was supported in the capable hands of her distant kinswoman, Lady Stanley.

Margaret Beaufort, who had been successively a Tudor, a Stafford and was now a Stanley, still preferred, like the Queen Dowager, to be known by her maiden name. A woman of forty, with a long, narrow face, thin lips and rather cold, staring eyes, she was renowned for her scholastic ability, (and it was this brilliance of intellect and subtlety of mind which were to be her two most important legacies to her great-granddaughter, Elizabeth of England). As she walked now in the procession, her mind's eye saw quite a different scene, in which her only child, Henry Tudor, moved in the central position. Only that morning, her man-of-affairs, Reginald Bray, had returned from Brittany with the news that, in view of the developments in England, Duke Francis was willing to give her son enough ships and men to mount an autumn invasion. Furthermore, Henry had finally, if grudgingly, agreed with his mother's insistent demands that he offer for the hand of the Princess Elizabeth, still in sanctuary with her mother and sisters.

It was also rumoured, and Margaret's sharp ears were always attuned to current gossip, that the King intended to release John Morton from prison and place him in Buckingham's custody. If this should prove true, then it was a situation, knowing the characters of the Bishop and the Duke as well as she did, which could surely be turned to advantage.

Behind Margaret Beaufort, in splendid isolation, walked the King's eldest sister, the Duchess of Suffolk. Odd, Elizabeth reflected, that little Richard, whom nobody had taken much account of as a child, should now be wearing the crown. But, like her mother, she considered it only right. She had always despised the Woodvilles and her deposed nephew meant nothing to her. Besides, it was of more consequence to be the King's sister than his aunt. Writing from Burgundy, Margaret had also been delighted to hear of the turn of events, for, like all her family, she blamed the Woodvilles for the death of her favourite brother, George.

The new Duchess of Norfolk headed a line of twenty peeresses and the tail of the procession was brought up by a host of knights and gentlemen. As the last of them disappeared into the Abbey, the choir broke into the *Te Deum*.

In the secluded world of the sanctuary, Elizabeth lived again the life she had known, and dimly remembered, thirteen years earlier. But the rigours of the body were as nothing compared with the shock to her mind. That Richard, the man she loved, should have proclaimed her and her brothers and sisters bastards, and seized the crown of England for himself, had at first numbed her senses. But gradually, as feeling had returned with acceptance of the facts, she had known an almost suicidal despair. She felt cut off from her sisters: she could not join them in reviling her uncle: she drifted from day to day in a black world of her own.

At first, her inner belief that Stillington's story was true and that she and the other children were indeed illegitimate, only added to the pain. As the days passed, however, and her tired mind began to search for ways to cast off its burden of hopelessness, she snatched at this growing conviction as a means of vindicating Richard and her immense affection for him.

Her mother's refusal to say anything on the subject of the late Lady Eleanor Butler, did nothing to detract from Elizabeth's now whole-hearted acceptance of the Bishop's testimony, made before the Royal Council. She recalled her conversation with her aunt Margaret of Burgundy and that earlier exchange of words between her father and her uncle Gloucester. Fragments of it haunted her waking thoughts . . . 'Stillington has also been committed to the Tower' . . . 'the Bishop of Bath and Wells has been friends with our brother' . . . 'You would do well to let George's affairs well alone.'

Had her uncle of Clarence known the secret of his brother's pre-contract? And was that why he had had to die? If so, then it was her mother's family who had worked on the King to bring it about. It explained, also, her mother's stoic acceptance of the news that her eldest brother and second eldest son had been executed.

'A tooth for a tooth,' she had said to Elizabeth, staring at her with tearless eyes and standing so still that her daughter had, for a fleeting moment, feared for her reason.

And on this baking-hot August afternoon, while the stench of the river filled the tiny room, and the noises of the London streets drifted about their ears, Elizabeth Woodville sat by the open window in the same motionless fashion that had become so customary with her these past few weeks.

Elizabeth was more than ever aware of the change in her mother. The Queen Dowager was no longer the selfish, self-willed, predatory woman whom her eldest daughter knew so well; a creature indifferent to the feelings of others, meeting life head-on, defiant and contemptuous of people weaker than herself. It was, thought Elizabeth, as though her mother were awaiting some calamity which she alone could foresee and was powerless to prevent.

'Do you think Thomas has reached France yet?' Elizabeth asked, hoping to distract the Queen's mind from its sombre reflections. A week or so earlier, her oldest half-brother, the Marquis of Dorset, had escaped from the sanctuary and fled to Brittany to join the growing host of exiled Lancastrians and disaffected Yorkists gathering about Henry Tudor.

The Queen roused herself from her fit of abstraction and nodded. 'I heard yesterday that he is safe.'

Elizabeth was just going to reply, when a knock on the door was followed by the information that Sir Robert Brackenbury, Constable of the Tower, wished to be admitted. Elizabeth saw her mother's hands clench and her whole body stiffen. In some obscure way, she knew that the thing which her mother feared was about to come upon them.

Sir Robert Brackenbury, that courteous, upright man known to everyone as 'Honest Rob' or 'Gentle Brackenbury,' came in heavily, his eyes dark-rimmed in his parchment-coloured face. He took the Queen Dowager's hand and held it in his own, his lips forming words, but the sound choking in his throat. Elizabeth Woodville stared at him, mesmerised by her own terror.

At last, Brackenbury spoke, his words falling like stones into the silent pool of the room. 'Your sons,' he said, 'the lords Edward and Richard Plantagenet . . . they are dead.'

Elizabeth was on her feet with a cry of disbelief, of protest, of . . . she did not know what. But her mother, clinging desperately to the Constable's hand, merely whispered: 'Nemesis!'

From the distance came the cry: 'Pans for sale!' and the clattering of pots as a pewterer passed on his way. Sunlight caught the ruby buttons on Brackenbury's doublet, striking out crimson sparks. A vein began to pulse in Elizabeth Woodville's neck.

'How are they dead?' her daughter asked fiercely, and the next moment reeled as though from a physical blow as Brackenbury whispered: 'They were murdered two nights ago, in the Tower.'

'By what authority? On whose orders?' Elizabeth had flung up a hand, as though, thought the Constable, she were warding off some spectre which she was afraid to see. How like her father she was! Tall, fair and splendid; very much as Edward had looked when he, too, had been seventeen.

'By no one's authority.'

'Not the King's?'

'No! No!' cried Brackenbury, distressed. 'His Grace, who is at present in York, had sent Sir James Tyrrell to collect the lords Edward and Richard, to take them to his castle of Sheriff Hutton in Yorkshire. The Duke of Clarence's son and daughter are there. It was the King's intention to keep their lordships with their cousins.'

Elizabeth sat down, relief flooding through her. She should not have doubted Richard, even for a second.

'What happened?' Elizabeth Woodville asked listlessly.

'It was Catesby . . . William Catesby, the lawyer, and Sir Richard Ratcliffe. They asked for admittance . . . on legal business, so Catesby said. I allowed it. I did not dream. . . . ' Brackenbury rubbed his eyes with the back of his hand, like a child trying to shake off a nightmare. 'They are both trusted men of His Grace. Afterwards . . . Catesby sent for me. The boys were dead. He – Catesby – said that the bodies were to be put on display at St Paul's. The plague is very rife. They were to have died from the plague.' The Constable shivered. 'At first, I thought . . . as you. . . . But when I asked for King Richard's authority, they had none. No token; no credence; nothing! So then, I knew . . . .'

'But whey did they do it?' demanded Elizabeth, trying to absorb the hideous fact.

Brackenbury shrugged. 'They are both devoted to the King. I suppose they thought to make him safe.'

'Does the King know?'

'Sir James Tyrrell has gone back to York. He had to take the vestments for the Prince of Wales' investiture next month in York Minster. He will tell His Grace. I shall await his orders.'

'And in the meantime?' Elizabeth Woodville's voice seemed to come from a long way off.

'In the meantime, I shall say nothing and *beg* Your Highness to do likewise.'

After a while, Brackenbury went, leaving them to their grief. The shouts of the watermen, as they vied with each other for passengers, sounded loudly in the quiet. The fetid air quivered outside the window, glazing the grey buildings in the courtyard with a lustrous shimmer of heat.

Elizabeth rose and went towards her mother, uncertain, holding out a hand which was ignored. Elizabeth Woodville sat rocking herself to and fro, dry-eyed, staring unseeingly at the rushes on the floor. Suddenly she raised her head and looked at her daughter, speaking in a low, monotonous tone, as though she were reciting something in the confessional.

'A long time ago,' she said, 'before you were born, the Earl of Desmond came to this country from Ireland. It was at the time of my coronation and I was . . . very pleased with myself.' The bloodless lips were stretched into a brief, self-comprehending smile. 'Your father, at a public picnic, asked Desmond what he thought of me. The Earl, unfortunately, was one of those people who are honest to the point of rudeness. He told Edward to his face that he should have married a foreign princess who could have secured him military alliances. When I heard, I was furious. All my family swore revenge.' She gave a little laugh that choked in her throat. 'It seems so . . . so childish now. But my revenge wasn't childish. Several years later, when the Earl of Worcester went to Ireland as Lieutenant, he arraigned Desmond for me on some trumped-up charge and had him executed. I stole Edward's signet to seal the warrant and forged his signature. But matters went further than I intended. . . . Two of Desmond's children were murdered. Oh, don't shrink from me. That's one thing, at least, that I've learned in my life. Never judge other people. They have motives as compelling as your own. And one other thing, also, I've learned. Fate repays in kind.'

14

HENRY TUDOR stood with his uncle Jasper on the deck of his ship and stared landwards towards the unwalled town of Poole. The fag-end of a November gale whipped their cloaks about their shoulders and the spray whitened the raging sea to resemble the distant chalk hills of the Dorsetshire coast.

On October the thirty-first, Henry had left Paimpol with fifteen ships and five thousand men of Duke Francis' providing. But, within twenty-four hours, the entire fleet had been scattered by one of the terrible storms at present scourging the coastal regions of Europe. Only two ships remained to him and the anticipation of defeat on this, his first military adventure, and the prospect of returning to Brittany a humiliated failure, had deepened the lines of age on his never very youthful face and made him more taciturn than ever.

He glanced at the rows of what were obviously troops lining Poole harbour and at the small boat containing his envoys, which, even now, was rowing swiftly towards the safety of the parent ship. As the two messengers came aboard, he turned to face them with raised eyebrows.

'Well?'

The taller of the two, a young man of twenty-one, some five years younger than Henry himself, pursed his lips dubiously before replying. Edmund Dudley had been trained as a lawyer and possessed, as well as a shrewd brain, an instinct for trouble which was now to stand his master in good stead.

'The captain of the troops which your lordship can see, says that Buckingham's rebellion has been successful and that Richard of Gloucester has been irrevocably defeated. They invite you and your uncle ashore.'

'Then why wait?' demanded Jasper, but Henry did not move. He stayed looking at Edmund Dudley.

'And what do you think?'

'I think, my lord, that they are lying: that it's nothing more than a trap to lure you into their clutches . . . and from there to the Tower.'

'Nonsense!' exclaimed Jasper. 'Why should you think so?'

Dudley shrugged. 'A feeling; something to do with . . . oh, I don't know . . . the way their eyes don't meet mine when they speak.'

Jasper made a derisive gesture and the men about Henry

stirred impatiently. Apart from Henry, only Richard Empson, himself a lawyer, seemed to find Dudley's suspicions at all reasonable.

Henry stared thoughtfully at the waves slapping against the prow of the ship. He had had very little good fortune in his life, but, as though to compensate him for this, he had always had luck on his side during the most critical moments of his career. He had, over the years, come to believe in this luck with an almost religious fervour and he never ignored those signs which Fate was kind enough to provide. He felt now that Dudley's intuition was one of those pointers and although it might mean his eventual return to captivity in Brittany, such a contingency was preferable to the headsman's axe on Tower Green. He would not, therefore, ignore the lawyer's warning.

'We sail on,' he ordered, turning a blind eye to his uncle's dismayed face and a deaf ear to the murmurs of disgust amongst his immediate companions. He waited only until the anchor had been weighed before returning to the small, stuffy cabin that was his sanctuary against the outside world. He was in no mood for recriminations or reproaches, least of all for advice: he simply wanted to think.

The news that Richard of Gloucester had deposed his nephew and usurped the crown, had reached Brittany at the end of June. At first, Henry's emotion had been one of incredulous delight to think that his cousin was indeed as perfidious as Henry had always thought him. The story of the precontract, however, had quickly dispelled this elation; for whatever Henry might say in public, in private he considered, as did many others, that it was likely to be true. And if that were so, it gave to the man for whom Henry had always had an unreasoning hatred, the right, as well as the ability, to take the crown of England for himself. The agony of jealousy which this reflection had roused in Henry had made him physically ill, an object of concern to his baffled attendants and doctors, who could diagnose no cause for his malady.

At the end of August, while the court of Brittany was plunged in mourning for the death of Francis' arch-enemy, Louis the eleventh of France, Reginald Bray had arrived with the news that disaffected Yorkists under the leadership of the Woodvilles, were planning a rebellion on behalf of the deposed King Edward the fifth.

'But, my lords,' he had told the two Tudors, 'the Duke of Buckingham, with whom, as you know, the Bishop of Ely is living under house-arrest, has told Dr Morton that he believes the two princes to have been put to death.'

Further enquiries, eagerly made by Henry and Jasper, had elicited the information that Buckingham was not certain of this fact: he only knew that Catesby and Sir Richard Ratcliffe had been urging the King to this course since the coronation, and that Richard had not definitely prohibited the deed. However flimsy a basis this might seem for the Duke's suspicions that the murders had actually been committed, it had been sufficient to embroil him in Morton's plans to raise the country on behalf of Henry Tudor.

By disseminating the story of the princes' probable murder, the Bishop had fused the Yorkist rebellion with his own, and Buckingham, the darling of his cousin, King Richard, had agreed to arm his Welsh tenants and retainers. Whether the various risings in the south and west of England had been successful, Henry did not know. But if Dudley's suspicions were correct, they had not been. Nor was Henry in a position to effect a landing, with most of his forces either drowned or washed up on the coast of France.

On November the eighth, as Henry's two remaining ships stood off Plymouth Sound, one of Morton's men put out from Cawsand and was rowed to the flagship. He was dishevelled, tired and the bearer of bad news.

'All has miscarried,' he told them. 'Buckingham's rebellion failed completely and the Duke, himself, was executed a week ago at Salisbury.' The man licked his cracked lips and shivered. 'My master has gone into hiding in the fen country and hopes soon to join your lordships in Brittany.'

'And the other risings?' Jasper demanded, a desperate gleam of hope still in his eyes.

But this faded as the man replied: 'All have failed. Richard is at Exeter even now and Sir Thomas St Leger has been beheaded. The Duke of Norfolk has easily put down the Woodvilles' rebellion in the east. The country is undoubtedly loyal to the King – for the present!'

'My mother?' Henry enquired.

'So far as I know my lord, safe. Her husband, Lord Stanley, took no part – no overt part, that is – in the affair and she has been put into his custody. Some of her lands are forfeit. Nothing more! I should advise your lordships to return to Brittany as soon as maybe.'

So, it was over. The great adventure has drown to its humiliating close. Henry Tudor had been humbled by Richard of Gloucester and by the loyalty to their new king of the English people. But worse than this, mingling with his bitter shame and frustration, was the sense of relief that flooded through Henry that there would now be no fighting – for the present, at least.

Just over a month later, on Christmas Day, Henry stood in Rennes cathedral before the high altar. He had just sworn a solemn oath to marry the eldest daughter of King Edward the fourth, the Princess Elizabeth.

His mind was in a turmoil. The fact that he had never seen, and knew nothing of, the seventeen-year-old girl whom he had vowed to make his wife, weighed little with him. One woman was as good as another to Henry, for, as he had long ago suspected, his sexual appetite was small. The thing which really angered him about his promise was that it was necessary at all. For, by their insistence upon it, even his most ardent supporters, such as his uncle and his mother, betrayed their belief that his claim to the English throne could not stand alone; that the right of kingship by the law of primogeniture, truly belonged to the House of York and that only his marriage to Elizabeth could ensure the claims of his children, by their descent from the Plantagenet line. Most infuriating of all, he knew that they were right. Inside his thin, still form, there burned a rage so fierce that he needed all his self-control to prevent himself from screaming aloud.

The music swelled and the light of the candles was reflected back from the golden cross and glimmered in rainbow hues across the vestment of the priests. The congregation shuffled and whispered and, out of the corner of his eye, Henry could see that latest addition to his growing court, the Marquis of Dorset. As the Princess Elizabeth's half-brother, he had been given a place of prominence, but to Henry, he would always be the man who had witnessed his degradation at St Malo. The other two, Lord Hastings and Earl Rivers, were dead, gone to the block on Richard of Gloucester's orders, but Thomas Grey remained. Henry's lip curled. If Dorset looked for special favours as Henry's prospective brother-in-law, he would be disappointed. No man who could bungle a simple job as he had done, would ever command Henry Tudor's respect or confidence.

On Henry's other side, Duke Francis was inattentive, busy with his own troubled thoughts. King Richard of England was proving a worthy adversary and in the battles for naval supremacy in the Channel, the Bretons were faring badly. That accomplished sailor, the Duke of Norfolk, was directing his master's ships with all the skill for which he was noted, and too many Breton vessels had gone captive into English harbours. Hand over Henry Tudor, said Richard's envoys, and a peace could be arranged. Francis looked sideways at the young man who had turned to face his followers, and bit his underlip consideringly.

Henry stared at the men before him and came to a sudden decision. He might have been forced to swear marriage with Elizabeth, but if he ever did obtain the English crown, there should be no doubt as to who was the sovereign. He would never, he vowed secretly to himself, acknowledge any indebtedness for his position to the House of York and neither should anyone else. His followers should start now as he meant them to continue.

With an imperious gesture, he motioned Jasper to his side, whispering in his uncle's ear. A moment or so later, every Englishman in the cathedral was startled by the order to kneel and acclaim Henry Tudor as though he were indeed already a king.

The wood was dank; the ground slippery with midsummer rain; the horses churning up the mud around their restless hooves. With trembling fingers, made clumsy as much by fear as by the chill June weather, Henry tore off his clothes and stood naked and trembling in the damp air.

'Hurry!' he ordered his companion, who was still struggling with recalcitrant laces, and snatched the man's flaxen shirt from his fumbling hands. Within ten minutes, he, who six months earlier had been hailed like a king, was mounting his horse dressed in the garments of his servant.

'Your lordship will be all right?' the man queried doubtfully, and upon Henry's muttered assurance, hurled himself into the saddle, urging his master to waste no time. After a hasty embrace, the two young men parted, Henry riding for the Franco-Breton border, his servant returning more slowly to Vannes, keeping up for as long as possible the pretence that he was Henry Tudor.

Henry's fortunes were once more on the wane. In March, news had reached Brittany that Elizabeth Woodville had come to an agreement with King Richard. In return for his public assurance that no harm would come to her daughters, she had allowed the five former Princesses to leave Westminster sanctuary. Later, she, herself, had retired to one of her estates with a comfortable pension.

Worse was to follow. At the beginning of June, John Morton had sent word from Flanders, where he had found refuge, that Duke Francis was about to sign a treaty of peace with the usurper. At first, the two Tudors refused to believe it, but on June the eighth, the English King had signed a truce with Brittany against France; a codicil promising a thousand English archers to support Brittany in exchange for Henry Tudor, self-styled Earl of Richmond.

Duke Francis was suffering from temporary insanity and Pierre Landois, therefore, had conducted the negotiations on his master's behalf.

'We are not prepared,' he had told the English envoys, 'to hand over Henry and Jasper Tudor to your custody.' The English had argued, but it had been no more than they had expected: much too cautious, this Breton Treasurer, not to keep the bird in his hand. 'Nevertheless,' Landois had continued, 'my master will agree to place uncle and nephew in strict confinement and refuse them all aid against King Richard.' The English had accepted the terms.

A desperate situation called for a desperate remedy. A move must be made before the treaty was ratified. Neither Tudor was any longer resigned to exile and partial captivity. the schism in the Yorkist ranks caused by Richard's usurpation of the throne, and made even deeper by the rumours of his nephews' deaths, had presented them at last with the dazzling and wholly unexpected opportunity of seizing the English crown. What had been an improbability while England lay united under Edward the fourth, had now become a possibility in a land divided under Richard the third. Duke Francis had thought so and had supported the Tudors in their bid for power. But their ignominious failure and the growing need for English assistance against France had changed his and Landois' minds.

'We must escape,' Jasper had said. 'It will be dangerous, but we can no longer afford to delay. Given time, the English will adapt to Richard of Gloucester and accept him. We must invade again next year or forget it for ever.'

Once more, luck was with Henry Tudor. Because of his health, Duke Francis moved to one of his castles near the Angevin border. With Landois' permission, the English exiles also moved, to Vannes. A few days ago, Jasper Tudor and a party of companions had set out, ostensibly with a petition for Duke Francis. Then, as they neared the border, they had ridden south and gained the safety of Anjou before the startled Bretons had had time to divine their intentions.

Now, it was Henry's turn. It had been an essential part of the plan that he and his uncle did not escape together, for if he had travelled with Jasper, the Breton guards would have been more alert. No one had suspected that the elder man would leave the younger behind.

This morning, Henry had left with one servant to visit a sick friend – or so he had said. Again, suspicion was lulled because his court of exiles (and there were now many of them) was left at Vannes.

Riding wildly for the border, dressed in his servant's clothes and expecting at any moment to hear the sounds of pursuit, Henry felt sick with apprehension and dread. Instinct alone guided him as he twisted and turned and doubled back on his tracks, for his conscious mind was taken up by his fear; and behind the fear, the familiar feeling compound of self-contempt and bitter resentment, that he should be put to such shifts.

Suddenly, a group of horsemen loomed ahead, dark shapes in the gathering dusk. His breath rattled in his throat and, as they surrounded him, catching at his plunging horse, their faces merged together in a blood-red mist, and he fell from the saddle with a queer little grunt.

'You're safe! You're safe!' Jasper's voice said urgently in his ear, then was lost in a roaring like the tide.

It was a mere half-hour later that the frustrated Breton guards arrived at the border town so recently left by their quarry. Fortune had yet again proved herself Henry Tudor's most potent ally.

15

Elizabeth moved gently in time to the music, the dress of white cloth-of-gold swaying with the rhythm of her body. She danced well, as did her uncle who partnered her, and they were the cynosure of every eye in the room.

It was Christmas, Richard's second as King; Elizabeth's first at court since Edward's death. Last year she had been in sanctuary and she could not help contrasting her present state with the comparative penury which she had then endured. Now, she wore a magnificent gown, a replica of that worn by her aunt, the Queen; and, except that she was no longer addressed as Princess, accorded as much deference as she had enjoyed in her father's lifetime. She was dancing with the man she loved; she adored Christmas with its singing and miming and plays; she was nineteen and probably the loveliest woman at court. She should have been happy: she was not.

The reason for her misery was not far to seek. Her passion for Richard was now so deeply rooted that it was a part of her very being; her moods responding to his as though they were one and the same person. And the King was a man torn apart by grief. Eight months before, in April of this year of 1484, his only legitimate son, Edward, Prince of Wales, had died at the age of twelve. Anne Neville, always delicate and racked by the 'English disease,' had never recovered from the shock. She was slowly dying, and it needed only a glance at her emaciated form, where she still sat at the high table, to know that the end could not be many months away.

Elizabeth's hand touched her uncle's as they came together in the dance. She ached to comfort him, but could not, because he did not really see her. They talked, but desultorily; commonplaces that tripped off their tongues but had no meaning in their hearts. He canvassed her opinion of his choice of representatives at the Vatican – Thomas Langton, Bishop of St David's, and Dr John Sherwood, Bishop-elect of Durham. Did she think that these two men would do their country justice amongst the brilliance of the papal court?

'They should,' she answered, watching the way his eyes flickered every now and then towards Anne. 'They are very clever men, although I know nothing about the new Pope and what he may be like.'

Richard laughed, but the sound was empty. 'Innocent the eighth,' he said. 'Giovanni Batista Ciba! Innocent! What made him choose that name, I wonder? He openly acknowledges sixteen bastards. A weak man, by what I hear, chosen because Cardinals Borgia and Barbo could neither command the necessary majority.'

The moved apart in a widening circle, then drew close again, palm to palm. Her eyes devoured him, but she knew that she was not even in his thoughts.

'They say Rome is very lax now,' she remarked, desperately trying to hold his attention.

'So I believe. There are murders committed there almost every hour. More than anywhere else in the world! And criminals escape by bribing papal officials.' He laughed again, his sudden sense of humour spurting up like a fountain through his gloom. 'Cardinal Borgia is reported as having said that God does not want the death of sinners, but only that they may be fined and the money used to the greater glory of His Church.'

He saw Elizabeth's shocked face and smiled. 'It will need a stronger Pope than Innocent to control men such as Rodrigo Borgia.'

But in the following April, a month after the death of Queen Anne, it seemed as though His Holiness might prove a more forceful man than Richard of England thought him. Workmen in Rome unearthed a statue, later identified as Julia, the daughter of Claudius; a reminder of the carefree, pagan world. It was greeted with such extravagant acclaim, being set up in the Capitol and adored by thousands, that, one night, Innocent ordered it to be secretly re-buried, seeing in the frenzied worship accorded it, a threat to the one true faith. It was symptomatic, he said of the restlessness and the desire for change which was afflicting the whole of civilisation.

While good churchmen everywhere trembled for the future of mankind, Lancastrians trembled for the future of their dynasty.

The death of Anne Neville on March the sixteenth, had brought a crop of rumours in its wake concerning Richard and his niece. Reginald Bray, despatched hot-foot to France by an agitated Margaret Beaufort, reported that the English court was in daily expectation of the King's envoy being sent to Rome to seek a dispensation for his marriage with Elizabeth.

'It would be incestuous,' said Jasper hopefully.

'But not unknown,' Edmund Dudley answered dismally. 'Dispensations have been granted to blood uncle and niece.'

Henry said nothing. He felt both uneasiness and relief; uneasiness because, if the marriage did take place, Richard, at thirty-two, might be expected to father new heirs for the House of York; relief because, if by some miracle he did invade England successfully and wrest the crown from his cousin, he would be free to reject Elizabeth and so feel himself King in his own right, and not in that of his wife.

But Jasper was despondent. 'Whom else could you marry?' he asked gloomily.

'Maude Herbert,' his nephew flung at him, and laughed at Jasper's look of outraged astonishment.

But by mid-summer, the English exiles were able to breathe freely once again. King Richard, it seemed, had had no intention of marrying his niece and had publicly denounced all such stories as baseless lies in the hall of St John at Clerkenwell. Elizabeth was sent to Sheriff Hutton, where Richard had already installed her younger sisters, along with Clarence's two children, the Earl of Warwick and Margaret Plantagenet.

Everything was now in train for the Tudors' invasion. King Charles the eighth of France, advised by his eldest sister and Regent, the Lady of Beaujeu, had promised men and ships, and Duke Francis, recovering his sanity, had allowed Henry's followers to leave Brittany and rejoin their master in France.

'What's done, is done,' he had remarked to Landois, 'and if you ask me, we're well rid of them all.'

Landois was inclined to agree. King Richard had been two years upon his throne and was, moreover, one of the most capable soldiers of his age. It seemed unlikely that Henry Tudor had any hope of dislodging him now, and the Treasurer felt that whoever backed Henry in the future, was pouring men and money into a lost cause. He did not want it to be Breton men and Breton money.

'I hear,' he confided to Francis, 'that the Lady of Beaujeu has emptied the Normandy gaols to make up her promised quota of soldiers.' He grinned. 'Hardly a move which denotes confidence in the success of our late guests.'

Similar sentiments were prevalent in England. Very few people, including Henry Tudor's step-father, Lord Stanley, and his brother, Sir William, really felt that the projected invasion stood any chance of succeeding. Only the King, lost in a world of misery and regret, had serious doubts as to the outcome.

Richard was now terribly alone. Of those remaining who were dear to him, his daughter was in Wales, married to William Herbert; his son, John, he had sent with his cousins to Sheriff Hutton; his mother had retired to her manor of Berkhampstead and the life of a recluse; and of his sisters, Margaret was in Burgundy, Elizabeth occupied with her own affairs.

In the summer, Richard left London for Nottingham, pausing on the way to pay a short visit to the home of his lifelong friend, Francis Lovell.

Minster Lovell, built by the Viscount's grandfather, stood on the banks of the Windrush, south of Wychwood Forest, and on the site of a Benedictine Priory. For three days, Richard was able to indulge his new-found passion for hunting, and, with Francis Lovell and Robert Percy beside him, recapture the days of his youth when the three of them had been apprentice Knights in Warwick's household at Middleham.

They laughed together, rode together and, together, explored the secret vault that lay somewhere beneath the great banqueting hall. The Viscount showed his friends the mechanism which worked the concealed entrance.

'The lock is faulty,' he said. 'I must have it mended.'

Robert Percy smiled. 'You told me that two years ago, when I was last here. Make certain that you have it done this time, or one day you may find yourself locked in here for ever.'

They all laughed and went out to their waiting horses. Later, Lovell and Percy were amongst the concourse of nobles who accompanied Richard to Nottingham Castle. Watching them, liking to have them near, Richard was glad to know that he could count upon the loyalty of one Percy, at least. For of Northumberland's intentions he was extremely doubtful. Too much enmity lay between him and the man who had always resented the esteem and affection which the King enjoyed in the north.

On August the seventh, Henry landed at Milford Haven. The south coast of England had proved itself hostile in the past and Henry would not risk its shores again. Instead, he had decided to place his life in the hands of his grandfather's countrymen.

His instinct was well-founded. Wales was undergoing one of its periodic spasms of extreme nationalism; this time an expression of the general restlessness and longing for change. The Welsh chieftains flocked to meet him, seeing in Henry, not a semi-foreign young man of English and French, as well as Welsh blood, but a reincarnation of the great Celtic heroes of the past.

Henry, on the other hand, hearing the strange, sad music of the harps and the voices raised in singing, had never been more conscious of his alien ancestry; never before realised to what extent his strain of Welsh blood had been thinned by his French and English. These chieftains from the mountains, with their lean, wolfish faces, were men of another age; direct descendants of those vanished British Princes – Emrys and Arthur, Conan and Cuneglas – who had made that last abortive stand against the encroaching hordes of Saxons.

Long, long ago, the forbears of these men had ranged this island from Cumberland – whose name still bore witness to the fighting force of the Cymry – to the primeval hills of Cornwall. The chieftains stood now in the flickering light of the torches, held in thrall by the unearthly music which, for centuries, had been both their salvation and their downfall; listening to those wild, faery melodies that spoke to them of the light on the mountains and the dark caverns of the moon; that took them beyond the stars and showed them the timeless spaces of eternity. A thousand years ago, the doomed Celtic peoples of this land had been held powerless by those self-same visions, while the Saxons, without the imagination to know when they were beaten, or to desire more of life than a piece of land, cattle and children playing at the hearth, had inexorably forced them further and further west until they had vanished into the last stronghold of the mountains.

As Henry, in the dying rays of the sun, stooped to kiss the ground, and signed to his followers to break into the more orthodox music of the psalm *Judica me Deus,* he could not help wondering how reliable were these new-found adherents of his. And as camp was struck for the night and he heard the screams and scufflings amongst his gaol-bird Frenchmen, he wondered miserably what real chance he stood of taking his cousin's crown.

This sense of insecurity found relief in the issuing of peremptory summonses to all his probable supporters and in the signing of these documents 'By the King's hand.' He also derived some comfort in branding Richard as 'Usurper and Traitor,' but his uncertainty was in no way assuaged by the ambiguous replies received from both the Stanleys and from Northumberland.

'We may count on their support if we win,' he said resentfully to his uncle. 'If not . . . we may whistle for it.'

Jasper agreed, his face drawn with strain and worry. They had been joined by the Earl of Oxford and Rhys ap Thomas, but they needed the might of the Stanleys if they were to be assured of victory.

'Your step-father says that Richard holds his son as hostage and he dare not risk an open breach with him.'

'Perhaps,' retorted Henry savagely, 'but that excuse doesn't apply to his brother.'

He foresaw a long struggle. Even if, by a stroke of luck, he should win his first encounter with Richard, there was small possibility of Richard's being killed. He would surely live to fight another day, and if the Stanleys and Percy still delayed, uncertain of the final outcome, Henry Tudor's position could become precarious indeed.

As his motley host advanced and crossed the border into England, he could not sleep and his main preoccupation was to keep open an escape route to the sea. He ate little and jumped at every shout. Jasper could only marvel at the driving ambition and invincible will-power which forced this most unadventurous of adventurers along his chosen path. Henry would, thought his uncle, make an admirable King, for his single-mindedness of purpose might well lead a country to greatness.

By the time they reached the neighbourhood of Leicester, word reached them that Richard was rapidly advancing and determined to give battle.

Reginald Bray, who brought the information, added: 'My spies report that for some reason best known to himself, he is set upon fighting at once. Norfolk and all his generals are urging him to wait for the levies from Yorkshire which are still upon the road, but he takes no notice.'

'Northumberland?' queried Jasper.

'Is with the Usurper, but, like the Stanleys, will wait upon events.'

'Are my step-father and his brother with my cousin?' asked Henry.

'They are on the march and will probably be on the battle-field – wherever that may be.' Bray shrugged. 'The rest is up to Fate.'

'Or luck,' murmured Henry, placing his faith in his old comrade.

And his faith, as always, was justified. For on the morning of Monday, August the twenty-second, a hot, cloudless day that turned the ground into a parched wasteland and shrouded the fields about Market Bosworth in a veil of shimmering heat, Henry Tudor became, against all odds and expectation, King of England.

The Duke of Norfolk fell early in the battle and Richard, in what seemed to his enemies, to be a burst of suicidal fury, stormed into the heart of their lines. Most of his close friends and supporters who rode with him were killed. Only Francis Lovell and William Catesby escaped, but the latter was later captured.

For one terrible moment, it seemed that all would be lost. Richard was within a few feet of Henry, fighting with the strength and courage of ten men. He felled the huge William Brandon, Henry's standard-bearer, with a single blow from his axe, all the time yelling 'Treason!' at the top of his voice. Henry recoiled. He could see his cousin's awful figure advancing upon him, the eyes gleaming in a passion of hate through his vizor, and a fear such as he had never experienced in his life had him in its grip. He could not move: the taste of death was in his mouth. . . .

Then it was over. The Stanleys and Northumberland had moved at last, throwing in their lot with the Tudors. A few minutes later, Richard was dead and Sir William Stanley had picked up the jewelled circlet which, becoming dislodged from the dead King's helmet, had rolled into a bush. With a flourish, Sir William placed it on Henry Tudor's head and knelt to kiss his hand.

But the eyes of King Henry the seventh were veiled. He would never forget that if only the Stanleys had come to his assistance sooner, he would have been spared a moment which, in its terror and humiliation, would haunt him for the rest of his days.

Interlude

BOSWORTH FIELD, far from being the landmark in English history which it appeared to be to posterity, seemed to the Englishman of 1485 nothing more than another battle in that struggle for the crown which had begun as long ago as 1455. The man-in-the-street 'stood amazed' at the news of King Richard's defeat, but accepted with stoicism or indifference this latest change in the country's government.

Only in the north did men resist the new authority with every means at their disposal. When, a week after Bosworth, Bishop Stillington was brought captive into the city of York on his way to London and life-long imprisonment in the Tower, the City Fathers refused to allow him to be taken on his way until he had rested for four or five days. Later in the same year, they successfully obstructed Henry's attempt to oust Miles Metcalfe from the office of Recorder and put his own man in Metcalfe's place. Early in the following year, 1486, when the death of Miles left the post vacant, the men of York again foiled the King's attempt to fill it, electing instead John Vavasour, who had been one of Richard's officers and a member of his ducal council.

Other Englishmen, however, were far more apathetic, although they were moved to protest against one of Henry's first Acts of Parliament; the attainder of the late King and all those who had fought for him at Bosworth. This Act was only made possible by dating the beginning of Henry's reign from August the twenty first, 1485; in other words, from the day before the battle. The people were horrified and the Croyland Chronicler wrote: 'Dear God! What security can any King find in the future, on the day of battle, if he cannot be supported by his subjects?'

Of Richard's close friends and advisers who survived the field, Francis Lovell went into hiding; Catesby, grovelling for mercy to Lord Stanley and his brother, was executed the following week; whilst an attempt to conciliate the Earl of Lincoln was made by making him a member of the Council, together with his father, the Duke of Suffolk. The young Earl of Warwick was brought from Sheriff Hutton and imprisoned in the Tower, while Richard's bastard son, John, was granted a pension and allowed, temporarily, to live in peace.

Elizabeth, herself, was also brought to London, Lord Willoughby having been sent to Yorkshire immediately after the battle to conduct her south. Henry, however, seemed curiously reluctant to marry her and it was not until the January of 1486 that this event took place, nearly three months after the King's coronation, which he had enjoyed in solitary splendour.

Henry's supporters received their just rewards. In 1486, John Morton became Chancellor and, on the death of Thomas Bourchier, Archbishop of Canterbury. Jasper Tudor was made Duke of Bedford and a member of the Council, along with Empson and Dudley, Lord Stanley and his son, Lord Strange, and Stanley's brother, Sir William. The latter also enriched himself by seizing most of the late King's lands, thus making himself, most unwisely, one of the richest men in England. Elizabeth Woodville was restored to her estates.

At Easter, 1486, news reached Henry during his country-wide progress, that Humphrey and Thomas Stafford were fomenting rebellion in and around Worcester, while Francis Lovell was rousing the men of the north. With Jasper Tudor in command, both insurrections were swiftly crushed. Lovell fled abroad, to Burgundy and the Dowager Duchess Margaret, who was more than eager to avenge the death of her brother and the overthrow of her House.

The new Queen, meanwhile, had quickly become pregnant and, as September of 1486 approached, she and her mother went to Winchester for the confinement.

Part Two

Elizabeth and Henry
1486–1503

16

It was September and one long, golden day succeeded another. The haze of late summer clouded the Hampshire valleys and hung over the thickly-wooded hills in a shimmering veil. Only the faint yellowing of the leaves and a sudden sharp bite in the air, night and morning, hinted that autumn was not too far away. And at Winchester, Elizabeth awaited the coming of her first baby.

Winchester had been specifically chosen by the New King for the birthplace of his eldest child because it was the ancient capital of England. It had been the chief city of Alfred – the only one of its kings to whom the Anglo-Saxon race had ever appended the epithet 'the Great' – and, even further back in time, it had had associations with the best known of those princes from whome Henry claimed descent; Arthur, the Amherawdyr of Britain. And if the child were a boy, he, too, was to be called Arthur.

In the Queen's apartments in Winchester Castle, it was stifling. All the doors were shut, the curtains and hangings pulled, and a fire burned on the hearth. For Elizabeth was expecting her labour to start at any time and was confined now to a strictly all-female world. No man, not even her physician, was allowed to cross her threshold and any male intrepid or foolish enough to try, would soon have been ejected by her scandalised ladies and jealous midwives.

Elizabeth her body running with sweat, her hands idly plucking at some embroidery in her lap, was making desultory conversation with her aunt, Catherine Woodville, widow of the executed Henry of Buckingham and now the wife of Jasper Tudor. One of the small consolations brought to Catherine by her second marriage had been that she bore her mother's old title, Duchess of Bedford. Glancing at her niece, she wondered what were the thoughts behind that impassive countenance. She had a sudden picture of Elizabeth, a gay, impulsive child of five, running to dance with her father all those years ago at Windsor, when the court had celebrated the arrival of the Signeur de la Gruthuyse. A quiet child, thought Catherine, but with a vivacity, a spontaneity, a seemingly unquenchable spark of life that had never been entirely hidden beneath her sedate demeanour.

That her niece would have grown into a passionate-natured woman, Catherine would have been ready to swear. She was so like her father in looks that it had appeared inevitable. And in Elizabeth's late teens, there had been a sudden flowering, a certain look, which had indicated to the elder woman's experienced eye that her niece had at last fallen in love. But, try as she would, Catherine had been unable to discover the object of Elizabeth's affections. Two years ago, after the death of Queen Anne and during the subsequent months, the suspicion that King Richard had become the object of his niece's devotion had flitted across the Duchess' mind, only to be dismissed. It seemed to her improbable that a girl of eighteen could have fallen in love with a man of thirty-two, who was also her father's brother. It would be an incestuous love, to say the least. Moreover, Catherine Woodville could not believe that, in those circumstances, Richard would have rejected Elizabeth. She would have liked to probe a little, but something in her niece's face forbade it. These days, Elizabeth neither gave, nor invited, confidences. Perhaps she was wise: these days it was foolish to say too much about either the late King or his reign.

Instead: 'I hear my royal nephew is to improve the navy,' Catherine remarked and Elizabeth inclined her head.

'So I believe. The men of Bristol complained so much to Henry during his visit in the summer about the decline of their trade and the general decay of the harbour, that he decided to look into the entire question of shipping. He has given the Bristolians permission to build a number of new vessels.'

Catherine Woodville shifted her position. Dear God! How bored she was! What a pass things had come to when one was reduced to discussing the state of the port of Bristol with one's niece. Whatever had happened to the gossip and scandal of King Edward's time? What had become of the gaiety, the intrigue and the clandestine affairs? The disgruntled Catherine had no hesitation in attributing the air of piety and gloom which now hung like a pall over the English court, to the King's mother, the austere Margaret Beaufort.

For Henry, meeting his mother for the first time since infancy, had succumbed to her rather elusive charm and formed what he, himself, had always thought impossible; a profound and lasting attachment for another human being. It was in deference to her will that he had eventually married Elizabeth of York, a contingency he had determined, if at all possible, to avoid. It was on her advice that he had persuaded the Pope and the monks of Canterbury to accept John Morton as the new Primate of all England. And it was so that she might once more enjoy the status of Countess, that he had elevated her husband, Lord Stanley, to the earldom of Derby.

What Elizabeth thought of the daily increasing domination of her mother-in-law, Catherine Woodville did not know, but she was under no illusion as to her eldest sister's feelings. The Queen Dowager might have been restored to her estates by her son-in-law, but she made no secret of her dissatisfaction at the lack of power wielded by her daughter. She was foremost amongst those who protested because Elizabeth had not yet been crowned; first of those who made it obvious that they considered Henry to be King only in right of his wife.

Catherine Woodville was of the opinion that her sister, although so astute in some ways, was inclined to be rash in others, and for some months past she had been afraid for the Queen Dowager's future.

'Where is your mother?' she now asked abruptly of her niece.

Elizabeth shrugged. 'With some priest or other from Oxford.' Then she added, seeing Catherine's look of amazed enquiry: 'He was most insistent that she should see him.'

Elizabeth Woodville went slowly along the gloomy corridors and down the twisting staircases of Winchester Castle. Even on a warm day such as this, the rushes lifted and whispered in a hundred little draughts and the grim, grey walls were damp to the touch. As she turned the corner and hesitated before entering a small ante-chamber that led off the main hall, she was aware of two young men standing close at hand. The elder was John de la Pole, Earl of Lincoln, and the younger, although his face was in shadow, was also immediately recognisable. At seventeen, John of Gloucester bore too close a resemblance to his dead father for anyone to mistake his royal ancestry. Elizabeth Woodville shivered as she wondered how long it would be before his fatal likeness brought about his destruction. Perhaps, after all, his sister, Katherine, who had died in childbirth a month or so before Bosworth Field, had had the better part.

The Queen Dowager pushed open the door and entered the ante-chamber. At once, a tall, thin man in priest's garb rose from a joint-stool and made her a low bow. Elizabeth Woodville raised haughty eyebrows.

'You wished to see me? The matter is pressing, I understand.'

'Pressing and private.'

The widowed Queen was intrigued. But: 'I don't even know your name,' she pointed out.

'Richard Simons, and Your Grace's very humble servant.'

'Yes.' Elizabeth Woodville pursed her lips. There was something a little too humble in this obsequious young man's manner. She noticed, too, that his breath smelt unpleasantly as he drew close to her.

'I must know for certain, Your Grace. Are your two sons dead?'

There was a terrible silence which, together with Elizabeth Woodville's white face and shaking hands, answered the priest's question only too well. But he had to make sure.

'Why do you wish to know?' she whispered at last.

'Because — ' and his hands fluttered pale and menacingly against his clerical gown – 'there have been so many rumours, so many conflicting stories, both before and since August of last year.'

'And if I tell you that they are both . . . alive?'

The Queen Dowager saw at once by the look on her companion's face that this was not what he wanted to hear, and realised by the sharpened tone in which he repeated the word 'Both?' that he desired for one, but not two of her sons to be alive. It followed, therefore, that it must be for Edward's death that he wished, for a younger brother could never prove an embarrassment to an elder in his claim to the throne. And Elizabeth Woodville had small doubt by now that the priest was involved in a conspiracy against her son-in-law.

She watched for a moment or two Simons' growing dismay; saw him struggling inwardly with his riotous thoughts. Suddenly, she leaned forward and said quietly: 'If you wish for the truth for yourself, you must, in your turn, be honest with me.' She met his startled gaze and smiled. 'You have risked a great deal already, by coming to me. Do you think I'm such a fool that I don't know why you are asking me this question? Do you imagine that I am ignorant of the desire of many Yorkists to replace Henry Tudor with either one of my sons, or with the son of my brother-in-law, Clarence?'

There was another silence, broken only by the rustle of a mouse scampering through the rushes at their feet. Simon stared at the fleas hopping in the dirt, abstractedly crushing a louse under his shoe.

'You are the mother of the Queen,' he muttered and Elizabeth Woodville shrugged.

'You must have thought of that before you came to me. Don't worry! I shan't betray you. I shall not assist you, but

I shall not betray you, either.'

Simons looking into her face seemed satisfied and the story came tumbling out. A friend of his, an Oxford organ-builder called Thomas Simnel, had a son, Lambert, who was not only the same age as the young Duke of York, thirteen, but also looked extraordinarily like him. Lambert was to be taken to Ireland and crowned as King Richard the fourth. Then, after a successful invasion of England, the real Duke was to be substituted for the pretender.

'And my eldest son, Edward?' the Queen Dowager hot at Simons and saw again the nonplussed look on his face.

'We were sure . . . almost certain. . . . '

'That he was dead?' Elizabeth Woodville rose to her feet with a mirthless little smile. 'And so he is, Master Simons.' She noted his look of relief and laughed. 'They are both dead.'

To her surprise, this piece of information did not dismay the priest as she had expected. He merely nodded in a business-like way and said: 'Then Lambert must be the young Earl of Warwick.' He added carelessly: 'We were prepared for that eventuality. It may have escaped Your Grace's notice, knowing the two boys as well as you did, but the Duke of York bore a strong resemblance to his cousin, the Duke of Clarence's son, and they were both about the same age.'

'My son was, my nephew is, Plantagenet,' Elizabeth Woodville remarked bitterly, 'if that is what you mean. Whereas Edward. . . . ' She broke off, unable to continue.

Simons smiled. 'Precisely! King Edward the fifth took after Your Highness's family.'

He would have expatiated on this theme, but Elizabeth Woodville interrupted him.

'Just now,' she said harshly, 'you remarked that "*we* were prepared." I take it that you have support for this rebellion?'

The priest winced a little at the uncompromising word, but nodded briskly. 'The Dowager Duchess of Burgundy will help us, with both money and men. However, our main support lies in Ireland where, as you know, loyalty to the House of York is very strong. We have definite promises of help from the Earl of Kildare and the other Fitzgerald chieftain, the Earl of Desmond.'

The Queen Dowager caught her breath and Simons noticed a muscle of her throat work convulsively. With an effort, she achieved a wan smile.

'If the Earl of Desmond is to aid you,' she said, in a constricted tone, 'then you should be thankful that my sons are dead. He would never have supported any child of mine.'

'Your Grace knows him?'

'I knew . . . his father.'

She moved to the door, indicating that the interview was at an end. She would soon be fifty years of age, but it occurred to the priest that she was still a remarkably attractive woman. As he followed her from the room and joined the Earl of Lincoln and John of Gloucester, still waiting in the shadows, Richard Simons thought that time had dealt kindly with Elizabeth Woodville. Indeed, it had, if anything, had a mellowing effect upon her; as though her experience of life had softened the harsher nature of her youth.

The Queen was in labour. Any time now the baby would be born and, as her mind hovered just above that circle of pain through which she would fall in just a few moments, she realised that it no longer mattered to her that the child was Henry's.

In the week's following Richard's death, she had considered putting an end to her existence. It was only when she had forced herself to contemplate the act, itself, that she had known she could not do it. She had learned on that day that she loved life too much, and that the depth of her despair was not great enough to bring her to suicide. This knowledge had been a shock to her, but the struggle to come to terms with her emotions about her uncle had helped to mitigate Henry's almost insulting indifference.

That Henry did not like her because she was the daughter of her father and the scion of the House of York, he had made obvious from the start, emphasising it by his delay in marrying her and his continued refusal to have her crowned. Her feelings for him had not then existed; even her wedding night had aroused in her neither pleasure nor revulsion. It had been the knowledge that she was pregnant and the bearer of Henry's child that had finally shaken her out of her absorption in Richard and the past, and dragged her back in to the reality of the present. For nine months, she had felt a bitter resentment, but now, at the instant of birth, this was being replaced by a new and stronger emotion. As she heard the baby's first cry, it no longer concerned her that the child was Henry's and not Richard's.

Before she obeyed the midwives' behests and tried to sleep, Elizabeth insisted that her little son, Prince Arthur, be put into her arms.

17

FEBRUARY of the year 1487 was cold and damp. No ray of sunlight, however tenuous, penetrated the thick, grey barriers of cloud. The rivers ran full, overflowing their banks and then receding to leave borders of mud and yellowing slime; and the fields were turned to morasses by the never-ceasing rain.

At the palace of Sheen, Henry, impervious to the dismal weather, the chill and the draughts alike, devoted himself to what had now become the chief motivation of his life; the retention of that throne which fate had so unaccountably tossed into his lap. Even now, after eighteen months, he could not really believe that his luck would hold; terror-stricken that in another year, perhaps less, he would find himself once more a fugitive at the court of France. No fool, he had known from the start that it would merely be a matter of time before the Yorkist partisans, shattered and stunned by the totally unexpected defeat at Bosworth, would begin to stir. And, as he remarked bitterly to Jasper, there was no lack of potential kings in the remaining Plantagenet heirs.

Foremost, and far the most dangerous, was Clarence's son, the young Earl of Warwick. Second in importance were the Earl of Lincoln and his brothers, Edmund, William and Richard de la Pole. Then there were the girls; Warwick's elder sister, Margaret Plantagenet, whom Henry had made one of his wife's ladies-in-waiting, and Elizabeth's four sisters, Cicely, Anne, Katherine and Bridget. Last, but by no means least, were the ghosts of his two young brothers-in-law.

On the advice of Archbishop Morton, Henry had made, in the early days of his kingship, discreet enquiries as to the burial place of the boy's two bodies. He had received confirmation of their deaths from his mother-in-law, but found that neither she nor Elizabeth had any idea as to the location of the graves. Those who could have told him, the former Constable of the Tower, Sir Robert Brackenbury, and his servants, had died with Richard at Bosworth, along with one of the assassins, Sir Richard Ratcliffe. The other murderer, Sir William Catesby, he had had executed a week after the battle on the advice of the Stanleys – a piece of inept bungling that in no way endeared his step-father's family to him. To have persuaded him to sign the death-warrant of a man whom they should have realised to be of importance was unforgivable;

the more criminal because he, himself, should have known better. Four years ago, the late Duke of Buckingham had mentioned Catesby and Ratcliffe to Reginald Bray in connection with the possible murder of the Princes. Bray had passed on the information and Henry had, inexcusably, forgotten it.

One possibility had remained open to the King. At the time of Bosworth, Richard's close friend and personal servant, Sir James Tyrrell, had been Governor of Guisnes Castle and had, therefore, not been in England on that fateful August day. At first, Henry had stripped Tyrrell of all his offices, but, finding him co-operative and more than willing to serve his new sovereign, had restored them to him in exchange for Sir James' future good service and such information as he could impart concerning the Princes' fate. Unfortunately, this was no greater than that already in Henry's possession: the bodies had been buried temporarily under some stairs in the White Tower, but had subsequently been moved. King Richard had expressed so firm a resolve to have this done, that Tyrrell had no doubt that his intention had been translated into action.

'A great pity,' Morton had remarked. 'To have been able to display the bodies would have done us much good, in that it would have proved beyond doubt that the boys were dead and scotched all rumours to the contrary.'

Jasper's gruesome suggestion that two bodies of the same ages and in the same stage of decomposition, should be found and exhumed, was greeted with a shudder by the Archbishop and vetoed by Henry. Caution was of the very essence of his nature, and although Bosworth had been won in despite of it, to move carefully was still one of the cardinal rules of his life. In spite of everything, he could not rid himself of the vague fear that one, at least, of the boys might not, after all, be dead. Tyrrell swore to having seen the bodies, but Henry wanted to see the proof with his own eyes. And he did not know where, in all the great, grey mass of the Tower to start looking.

The beginning of 1487 brought the first news of the Simnel rising. A young boy, purported to be the Earl of Warwick, had been rapturously received in Ireland, and not even Henry's parading of the real Edward Plantagenet through the London streets perusaded the Irish that they were being duped. Their only reaction was to laugh at the Londoner's gullibility, saying that the boy exhibited was probably one of the late King Edward's bastards.

To exacerbate Henry's already over-stretched nerves, news

came from Flanders that Francis Lovell and the well-known adventurer, Martin Swart, were to sail for Ireland at the head of two thousand German mercenaries, provided by the Dowager Duchess of Burgundy in support of her supposed nephew. And as though this were not enough, the Earl of Lincoln fled the country to join them.

Henry was not altogether surprised. His spies had told him of the visit of Richard Simons to Winchester, and of those people to whom he had spoken. Henry had not, at the time, paid it much attention, merely adding the information to that store of trivia which might, one day, prove to be of importance. The news that Simons was one of the chief motivators in the impending rebellion, coupled with Lincoln's disaffection, now revealed those meetings at Winchester to have been of the utmost significance. Henry wasted no time. John of Gloucester was consigned to the Tower, never to be seen again, and the Queen Dowager deprived of all her estates. She was placed under close arrest and immured in the convent of Bermondsey. Before she went into what was virtually imprisonment, she saw her son-in-law for the last time.

Elizabeth Woodville looked at Henry Tudor with a faint, supercilious smile. 'Did you really think that I would join a conspiracy,' she asked, 'for the son of George of Clarence?'

Henry returned her look. He was not interested in the fact that she had suppressed information concerning possible treason. He knew, whatever she might say, that she had never been his friend; she resented her daughter's lack of power, but this did not trouble him. His dislike sprang from her oft-repeated conviction that he was King only because of his wife; and because she had sat here, at the heart of government, during his years of exile. He needed to inflict retribution for all the misery and uncertainty of those years, and he needed to visit it in full upon the members of the House of York. Elizabeth Woodville's greatest crime in his eyes was that she had spurned him for her daughter, and had been content to throw herself and her children on the mercy of King Richard. Moreover, she had written the letter which he was now pushing towards her with hands that shook – a thing which he, himself, observed with the utmost disgust.

'You wrote that,' he said, and his tone of voice left no room for denial.

The Queen Dowager picked up the paper curiously, then recognised it as a letter which she had written to her son, the Marquis of Dorset, while he had been with Henry in Brittany. She had forgotten its existence, but memory came flooding back and she knew, without looking, the particular part of it to which her son-in-law referred. She quoted: 'My dear son, why do you not come home? Richard will treat you well.' And to add insult to injury, Dorset had obeyed her behest. Only his recapture by two of Henry's men, as he had been about to embark at Brest, had prevented his return. Now, staring into Henry's eyes, Elizabeth Woodville laughed.

He called the guards and she knew a moment of terrible desperation. She glanced around her. A mere four years ago, she had been here at Sheen with Edward, still Queen of England. Two months later, Edward was dead and tragedies had crowded thick and fast into her life. Now, she was going into what might well prove life-long imprisonment, and the hot tears stung her eyelids. Then the royal blood of the House of Luxembourg, inherited from her mother, came to her rescue. She drew herself up and looked imperiously at Henry.

'Before I go,' she said, 'I should like you to know that I wish the conspirators good-luck! Particularly the Earl of Desmond.' There was a look on her face which the King was at a loss to interpret, as she added: 'I owe him that much, at least.'

Henry rode with his army through the June countryside, from Nottingham towards Newark; through glades of dappled shadow and stretches of open ground, where the light quivered as bright as a sheet of pressed metal; by villages and hamlets, whose houses threw thick wedges of blackness on to the sun-baked streets; and along narrow, rutted tracks, fringed with fox-glove and campion that turned ragged, dusty faces towards the marching host.

A little under a month ago, on the twenty-fourth of May, Lambert Simnel, the organ-builder's son, had been crowned King Edward the sixth at Christ Church in Dublin, with a diadem taken from a statue of the Virgin. On June the fourth, Lincoln and Lovel had landed with their German mercenaries and wild Irish clansmen at Furness in Lancashire. With them came "King Edward" and his "tutor", Father Richard Simons.

Henry had moved hurriedly from Kenilworth to Nottingham, where he had been joined by Jasper Tudor, Oxford and the Stanleys – his step-father, Lord Stanley, his step-brother, Lord Strange, and his step-uncle, Sir William. The King had viewed these latter with a jaundiced eye and thanked them with an elaborate show of politeness for coming so promptly to his aid; a piece of sarcasm not lost upon Lord Stanley, who realised with increasing bitterness that Henry would never forgive them their delay on Bosworth Field. And there were times, in the secret places of his mind, when the new Earl of Derby experienced incipient regrets for the outcome of that battle.

He knew one of those moments now, as Henry, slewing himself round in the saddle, remarked with grim jocularity to Lord Strange: 'Let us hope, my dear George, you don't fall into the hands of the enemy today. Your father still has other sons.'

Both Stanley and Strange flushed at this reminder of a painful episode in their past, when, before Bosworth, Richard had demanded the certainty of Stanley's support in exchange for his hostage son's life. Stanley had sent back the answer: 'I have other sons,' and trusted in Richard's mercy not to carry out his threat. But Stanley could not say to Henry: 'I trusted Richard Plantagenet,' any more than he could suppress the thought that, in similar circumstances, he would never had the same confidence in his step-son.

The rebel army, striking eastwards across the Pennines, had moved south by way of Doncaster and Rotherham, and were now, on this day of June the fifteenth, reported to be encamped at Fiskerton ford, a few miles south of Newark. Its failure to march into Yorkshire, Richard's country, and still, nearly two years after his death, a seething cauldron of discontent, Henry attributed to Lincoln's leadership. Henry Percy, sitting, as usual in moments of crisis, upon his estates, had lain in the rebels' path and it was conceivable that he would have fought if forced to it. As little as anyone else did he believe in the validity of "Edward the sixth". His loyalty, however, had not been put to the test, for, as Henry shrewdly surmised, Lincoln and Swart would not risk a battle and possible defeat before coming to grips with the King, himself. With the memory of Bosworth still green in their memories, their chief hope must be that Henry, like Richard, would fall in the forthcoming battle.

Henry, however, had no such intention and when, on the following morning, he stared across the old Roman road of the Fosse Way to the rebel ranks beyond, it was from his position as commander of the rear-guard. The van he had entrusted to Oxford, and the centre to Jasper and Rhys ap Thomas. A notable absentee from the battle was his brother-in-law, the Marquis of Dorset, whom he had clapped in the Tower. He did not trust Elizabeth Woodville's son.

At nine o'clock, Henry gave the signal for the attack. Lincoln had chosen his position with care, on a wooded hill affording cover for his troops, and from which he hoped to create havox among the climbing enemy. Unfortunately, he had reckoned without the impetuosity of his ill-disciplined Irishmen. There bare-legged savages from the hills and fens, wearing nothing but their kilts, their sole protection round, leather-covered shields, threw themselves, yelling and chanting, down the slope, heedless of Lovell's and Lincoln's furious adjurations that they return. For a moment, Oxford's troops wavered, terrified by the appearance of this horde of 'brute-beasts,' as they were later to refer to their oponents. But Oxford, rallying his men, soon proved to them that breast-plate and sword, battle-helm and axe were more than a match for the Irishmen's clubs and knotted ropes.

Even so, the battle lasted three whole hours, thanks mainly to the incredible courage of the Irish in the face of appalling odds, and the superb fighting ability of Swart's German mercenaries. But, in the end, superior armour and the sheer weight of numbers told their own tale. By mid-day, the field was Henry's. The Earl of Lincoln and Martin Swart lay amongst the piles of their own dead, and Henry, breathing more easily than he had done at any time since first hearing of the landing, could afford to be lenient. He consigned the grovelling Richard Simons to prison and sent Lambert Simnel to be trained in his kitchens as a scullion. Desmond and Kildare he pardoned.

But as Henry and his commanders looked back on that death-wracked hill, and saw the ravens swooping low over the wounded and the slain, not one of them could have foretold that he had just taken part in the last battle of that long and bloody struggle, to which his descendants would give the euphemistic title, 'Wars of the Roses.'

Francis Lovell, flying through the night and leaving behind him the carnage of Stoke, reached Minster Lovell in a brilliant dawn. Down under the banqueting hall he went, an animal burrowing its way into the safety of the earth, shutting the door of the secret vault thankfully behind him. But the mechanism that controlled the lock had never been mended and Robert Percy's prediction, made on that summer's morning two years previously, was fatally fulfilled, and Lovell found himself condemned to the lingering death of starvation, locked in a living tomb.

18

It was November the twenty-fifth, a day of damp and cold that struck through the clothes and skin to the very bones beneath, sending little red-hot pincers of pain darting along arms and legs, making shoulders and knees ache like a bad tooth. But today, the Londoners cared nothing for their twinges of their troubles: today was the coronation of King Edward's eldest daughter.

Henry had at last been persuaded to see the wisdom of this course.

'You cannot afford to lose the good-will of the people,' Morton had told him, and was endorsed in his opinion by Richard Fox, now Secretary of State.

'Your late father-in-law was very much beloved of the Londoners and they admire the Queen because she is his child.'

At any other time, this argument might have aroused all Henry's opposition, but he had his own reasons for agreement. Not only was he pleased at the birth and progress of Prince Arthur, now a year old, but he wished to distract his subjects attention from the setting up of a new court which was to be held in the Star Chamber at Westminster. This court, which was primarily to concern itself with offences affecting the Crown interests, was Henry's method of speeding up the law's ponderous procedure, and was empowered to take such short-cuts as were necessary to stifle opposition to the King.

John Morton, while rejoicing at Henry's acquiescence to his wife's coronation, sighed, nevertheless. Here was a man over whom the Archbishop would never have complete power; into whose mind he would never have total access. Behind the quiet face was a mind as devious as it was brilliant; that calculated every move, every word with only one aim in view: to keep Henry Tudor King of England. At this very moment, the Londoners were acclaiming Henry's decision not to comply with Pope Innocent's demand for support in a crusade against the Turks. But what the people did not know was the actual wording of their sovereign's reply.

'I need,' Henry had written, 'all monies raised by taxation for myself.'

Apart from Elizabeth's coronation, Morton had triumphed in another matter. He had advised the creation of a new Tudor symbol by the combining of a Yorkist with a Lancastrian badge. In this, Henry had not been so tractable, but his belief that it would prove difficult had been speedily disabused. One of the two main Yorkist badges was the White Rose, and amongst the insignia of Lancaster was the comparatively little-used one of the Red Rose. The two, as Morton pointed out, could easily be fused, but only the assurance that the Red Rose should be the larger, incorporating the smaller and, therefore, less significant White Rose, reconciled Henry to it.

It had pleased the people, however, and was everywhere prominently displayed as Elizabeth stepped ashore from the barge which had carried her from Greenwich to the Tower.

Henry, going forward to greet her and bowing punctiliously over her hand, noticed that she looked rather pale and was moved with unexpected compassion.

'Are you well?' he enquired in an undertone and she responded with a quick look of surprise.

'It was merely that I had visions of being burnt alive,' she answered, a gleam of laughter momentarily lighting her eyes. 'The bachelors' barge, as you can see, was determined to set the Thames – literally – on fire.'

A glance across her shoulder showed Henry a number of gaudily-dressed young knights flocking ashore from a barge whose prow resembled the Red Dragon of Cadwallader. From the dragon's mouth, a sheet of flame was belched forth every few minutes, fanning out over the water in tongues of orange and gold, and sending up a shower of little red sparks to the imminent danger of all the other shipping.

Henry snorted, while his mind turned on the possible provider of such outrageous ostentation: someone with more money than sense, that was obvious. Someone, too, who could afford to pay his King a little more in taxation than he was already doing. He would set Morton to solving the problem first thing in the morning.

Meanwhile, he was pleased to note that his Queen, at least, was not lacking in taste. Nothing could have been more elegant than her dress of white and gold lace, trimmed with ermine and ornamented with gilt tassels, her beautiful fair hair streaming down her back from beneath a circlet of precious stones; a lovely young woman whose obvious likeness to her father was inciting the Londoners to hysterical adulation. Henry's brief sympathy for her faded before this realisation, and he handed her perfunctorily into her litter of silk and cloth-of-gold.

The litter lurched its perilous way along the uneven cobbled streets between the screaming, stinking masses of people and was borne by some of the King's newly-created Yeomen of the Guard. Formed shortly after Bosworth, it had provoked the late Earl of Lincoln to one of his rare outbursts.

'Your husband,' he had told Elizabeth, scornfully, 'is the first English sovereign who has ever felt the need of a personal body-guard.'

And at the thought of John de la Pole, Elizabeth felt a return of that desolation which had beset her ever since the battle of Stoke. She remembered with a sudden clarity, that morning in Richard's apartments, all those years ago, when she had been playing with Lincoln, Mary and Cicely, and Richard's two children. She saw again her uncle Clarence bursting in, falling over the younger of the two Johns; she recalled the way in which Katherine had run to Richard when her father had left for the Tower; and she felt the security and happiness of that moment as though it were yesterday. And now, of all the people in that room on that Good Friday morning, only her sister, Cicely, and herself were left.

The shock of Lincoln's death and John of Gloucester's disappearance had fallen upon a mind already numbed by her mother's sudden imprisonment. Her affection for Elizabeth Woodville had never gone deep, but the Queen could not believe that her mother would have conspired against her own daughter and grandson. Elizabeth could not understand Henry's motives in doing what he had done, for he never allowed her to see into his thoughts or presented to her anything more than a polite, empty façade, hiding the real man beneath.

Cicely Neville, for whom Elizabeth longed more and more every day of her life, was now a recluse in good earnest; a broken-hearted woman, living out her remaining years in utter seclusion. Elizabeth knew that she would never see her grandmother again. Of her sisters, Cicely had been married to Lord Welles, one of Henry's kinsmen, and the other girls, for whom no doubt, safe Lancastrian alliances were being planned, had never been close to their eldest sister. Elizabeth was doubly grateful, therefore, for the companionship of her cousin, Margaret Plantagenet, a quiet, pious, but affectionate girl, whose grief at the continued imprisonment of her brother, the Earl of Warwick, never stunted her sympathy for the afflictions of others. But Elizabeth knew that Henry and his mother were already planning Margaret's marriage to Sir Richard Pole, a kinsman of Margaret Beaufort. And although this was an almost insulting match for the daughter of George of Clarence,

Elizabeth was glad of it, if only for her cousin's sake. For Sir Richard Pole was a kindly man who could be relied upon to protect his future wife from all those dangers which now beset anyone who bore the name of Plantagenet.

Near Westminster Abbey, Elizabeth alighted from her litter, but, as she was greeted by a bevy of 'angels' and virgins' singing her praises, she felt a stab of fear. Never before had she known the Londoners in so wild and uncontrollable a mood. She had seen them angry, like prowling animals; sullen like beasts at bay. She had seen them as happy as excited children; as dignified as though each man were himself a King. But this near-hysteria was both new and terrifying. It was as if the people saw in the coronation of Edward the fourth's daughter, their last link with an older, more carefree and more chivalrous era, when a man's duty to his overlord was greater than that to this new, more impersonal, but far more implacable master, the State. A new age of reason was already replacing the superstition of the old, but the people, loth to let the past go, were grabbing at this moment with eager, predatory hands in a last, desperate attempt to stay the passing of time.

One of the people's perquisites at coronations was the embroidered cloth on which the sovereign walked to Westminster Abbey, but today the Londoners could not wait until the Queen had entered the building. Elizabeth realised in horror that the last of her attendants were barely being allowed to pass along the carpet before it was being hacked and torn in pieces. People were everywhere pushing and shoving. Margaret Plantagenet fell violently against the Queen, and Elizabeth glimpsed the bracelet which her cousin always wore. It was a silver chain from which hung a miniature wine-butt, a constant reminder of Clarence's death; that death encompassed by Elizabeth's mother's family.

The Queen shivered and just at that moment, the men-at-arms, realising that the encroaching mob had become entirely out of hand, laid about them with their swords. One man fell dead almost at Elizabeth's feet, his blood spotting her beautiful gold and white gown. And as she passed into the gloomy depths of the Abbey, suppressing a strong desire to scream like a frightened child, she felt that her blood-spattered dress might well be an evil portent for the future.

Henry and his mother watched Elizabeth's coronation from behind a lattice screen, etiquette not permitting the King's presence in the Abbey proper. But while Margaret Beaufort's thoughts revolved around that other coronation of four-and-a-half years ago, when she had held Anne Neville's train and been of relatively small importance, her son's were occupied with matters of state.

At present, Henry had two main preoccupations. His biggest headache was his attitude towards France's month-old invasion of Brittany, during which time Vannes had fallen to the French. King Charles naturally expected Henry's assistance against his rebellious vassal. Had it not been French money and men that had helped Henry Tudor to his throne? On the other hand, the English seemed to think it natural that they would be called upon to support Brittany because, first and foremost, they hated the French, but also because they assumed that their King would wish to aid a people amongst whom he had lived for so long. Although why, Henry thought savagely to himself, everyone should assume him grateful for that enforced stay in Brittany, was past his comprehension. His natural inclinations were towards France, his grandmother's country.

His skilful policy of non-participation in the feud, was overset in the May following Elizabeth's coronation. On a wet summer's evening, when the rain hung in a curtain over house and street, when hills and sky merged together in a vast, dreary expanse of grey the colour of a stagnant pond, Henry listened in cold fury to the tale of Sir Edward Woodville's latest exploit. A thin whiplash of a wind arose, keening amongst the rooftops and ruffling the surface of the Thames into a myriad miniature tidal-waves. Along the banks, marsh-marigolds gleamed in patches of faded gold.

Henry turned away from the window, back into the spartan comfort of a small, chill room on the ground floor of Westminster Palace. Richard Fox stood shivering before the tiny fire, but this was not entirely due to the cold. When Henry was angry, there was something very frightening about this silent young man of thirty-one.

'Tell me again what happened,' the King instructed and the Secretary spread deprecating hands.

'It was at Southampton, Sire, last week. On the thirteenth, to be precise.' It was always well to be precise with Henry. 'Sir Edward Woodville and his two-hundred men boarded a ship that had just docked with a cargo of salt. They overpowered the crew and then forced them, at sword-point, to carry them to Brittany. Unfortunately – '

'Most unfortunately,' Henry interpolated bitterly.

' – the vessel was attacked by the French. Sir Edward and his men not only repelled the boarders, but captured the ship as well and took it with them to St Malo to augment Duke Francis' fleet.'

There was an irrepressible note of triumph in Fox's voice which, together with the mention of St Malo, made Henry's thin lips set so close that they almost disappeared. Could this smug fool of an Englishman not see that King Charles the eighth of France would construe this as a government-sponsored attack upon one of his vessels; a tacit declaration of English support for Brittany?

But worse was to come in the months ahead. On the second of July, at St Aubin, the Bretons were overwhelmed by the French, and Sir Edward Woodville and his men were killed almost to a man.

In September, while the English were still clamouring to avenge their compatriots' deaths and inveighing against Henry's extension of peace with France, Duke Francis died, leaving the duchy to his only child, his eleven-year-old daughter, Anne. Every Englishman's chivalrous instincts were now at fever-pitch and Henry realised with disgust that he would have to pretend, at least, to make some move against France. For this, ships and munitions were required – and for ships and munitions, money.

Which brought him to his other perennial problem; how to amass a large enough fortune to be financially independent of Parliament. And it was at this moment, that Henry Tudor made one of his rare mistakes; when his instinct for making money deserted him.

It was on a late winter's day of steel-grey shadows and sharp white light, that the King received in audience a tall, emaciated Italian who had been living in London for some months now, in a state of near-starvation, making a precarious living drawing globes, and all in hope of seeing the English King.

'Your name?' Henry enquired in French, as the man drew himself upright from his deep bow.

'Bartholomew Columbus,' the Italian replied, also in French. 'I hope it will please Your Grace to accept this map.'

'And your business?' Henry asked, taking the map and glacing at it briefly.

'I am here, Highness, to ask help for my brother, Christopher. He believes that men can reach Asia by way of the Atlantic ocean. He begs that Your Grace will provide him with money and men.'

Henry hesitated. Such an expedition might turn the thoughts of his restless, belligerent subjects from Brittany to 'Brazile,' that land which men still believed to lie somewhere west of

Ireland. But he doubted it. The English were obsessed at present by another war with France, and once their interests were set, it was hard to divert them from their purpose. He must play along with them; pretend that war was brewing, and for that he needed money. He had none to spare for hazardous, and probably abortive, expeditions to Asia by a western route.

So, he refused and the two men parted; Bartholomew to his bug-infested lodgings, where he wrote regretfully to his brother that Spain was now their best hope; Henry to his council-chamber to announce the levying of a new tax to meet the cost of rearmament.

19

ON a day of fitful April sunshine, Henry Percy rode reluctantly towards York, for his was the dubious honour of collecting the new subsidy from the men of the north.

Parliament had been persuaded to grant one hundred thousand pounds for the cost of a war against France. Apart from the normal taxation methods of tenths and fifteenths, the clergy were to pay a quarter of the required sum, and a levy of one and eightpence was to be made on every ten marks' worth of a man's property. But, correctly guessing that even these measures would not make up the full amount, Parliament required a further subsidy to be extracted from an already over-burdened population who, however much they might clamour to take up arms against France, did not wish to pay for the privilege of doing so.

Henry Percy knew that the men of Yorkshire and Westmorland were as embittered about the new tax as the rest of their fellow countrymen, but here, in the north, their bitterness had deeper roots; it sprang from seeds which had been sown nearly four years previously, on a hot August day hear Leicester. As he rode into Thirsk, Henry Percy felt a growing sense of uneasiness.

In later years, Sir Francis Bacon would write that: 'The memory of King Richard lay like lees in the hearts of the northern men: one had only to stir the dregs for it to rise up and pervade the whole.' And although Henry Percy would not have put it so poetically, it was a sentiment with which he would have entirely agreed. The men of the north had not, so far, been overt in their actions against the new government, but their passive resistance was expressed in dozens of little ways. Northumberland was aware, for instance, that it was becoming popular in Yorkshire for a man to name any white horse foaled in his stables White Surrey, the name of the horse which Richard had ridden to Bosworth.

As far as possible since that August day, Henry Percy had kept aloof, particularly from the citizens of York. He was conscious of their enmity each time one of them looked his way: there was no sense in courting disaster. And now, King Henry had insisted that he, of all people, should be responsible for collecting the subsidy. Northumberland had protested in vain and it was small wonder that he rode today with an armed escort.

A thin mizzle of rain obscured the horizon and black clouds scudded across a lowering sky. A wind blew in from the moors, bringing the bitter-sweet smell of the heather, and, from a long, long way off, a hint of the sharp, salty tang of the sea. It scattered the refuse along the cobbled street; bits of onion skin, tossed like pale, transparent wings; old turnip-rinds and apple-peel brushing the horses' hooves.

It was a mile or two outside Thirsk that Henry Percy saw them, a rabble of men blocking his path, and he instinctively huddled inside the protection of his cloak.

'What do you want?' he demanded, reining in before them.

'We've come to protest,' was the answer, 'against this latest tax.'

With some impatience, the Earl began to recite King Henry's many reason's for the subsidy. At which precise moment he started to recognise particular faces was uncertain. But it was when he caught sight of a set of strong, red features bobbing up momentarily on the edge of the crowd, that his uneasiness turned to fear. John Sponer, former Sergeant of the Mace at York, had been with Richard at Bosworth and bore towards Nothumberland an undying hatred for his failure to array the Yorkshiremen in time for the battle, and for his refusal to support Richard during the fight.

A movement to his left made Henry Percy turn sharply. Another face disappeared into anonymity, but the fleeting glimpse afforded him had suggested the harsh visage of Thomas Wrangwysh, sometime Mayor of York. And that, surely, was Alderman Tong . . . and Richard Vavasour . . . and Richard York. Northumberland felt the palms of his hands grow wet with sweat. What were men of that calibre doing with the scaff and raff of the countryside?

It was then that he began to see more familiar faces, this time amongst the scaff and raff, themselves; faces that stirred chords of memory, invoking a spate of little pictures in his mind's eye; pictures of scenes over seven years old, but clear enough, nevertheless. He saw rioting in the streets of York as the followers of Wrangwysh and Richard York fought each other over the results of the mayoral election; he saw some of these men before him, sentenced to prison for their part in the disturbances; and he saw those men released on orders from the Duke of Gloucester.

The Earl realised that he had stopped speaking and that his breath refused to come. This was no ordinary rabble of angry citizens protesting against taxation; these were men consumed by hatred and intent upon murder – his murder!

He gave a choking cry and turned to call up his escort, but it had gone. Men on whom he had relied, in whom he had trusted, were now no more than the thudding of distant hooves and the faint, far jingle of harness.

The men of York were all around him now, their eyes glowing oddly red, as though the lust for blood was reflected from their souls. He saw someone raise his arm with a flash of steel, and remembered, in that second of supreme terror, the inconsequential fact that the man's name was John Chambers. The arm bore relentlessly down, a trickle of something red and warm was oozing between the fingers.

There was a great cry from the rest of the mob, and, suddenly, they were all hacking and screaming together. A bird rose screeching above their heads, a dark shape against the leaden mass of the sky, and the churned-up earth around their feet soaked up the blood and the rain.

Then, just as suddenly, all was quiet again. The men dispersed, creeping silently away, merging into the grey landscape as though they had never been. Only their handiwork remained to testify to their presence there on that drizzling April day. For the mangled body of Henry Percy, fourth Earl of Northumberland, lay on the road outside Thirsk, as dead as the man whom he had betrayed four years earlier at Bosworth Field.

It was with mixed feelings that Henry Tudor heard of Henry Percy's death. His first reaction was one of quiet pleasure that the man who had played such a waiting game at Bosworth and nearly cost him his life, had been set upon and killed. But later, when it began to dawn upon the King that the motive for this murder had not been anger at the subsidy, but loyalty to Richard, his fury was aroused. He sent an army north to capture as many of the assassins as could be found, and it appealed to his sense of the ironic to place at its head a man who had fought, and fought valiantly, for Richard at Bosworth Field.

The Earl of Surrey, son of that first Howard Duke of Norfolk killed during the battle, had recently been released, along with the Marquis of Dorset, from the Tower. Thomas Howard, accepting the change of dynasty philosophically and with an eye to the restoration of his father's title, had readily agreed to be Henry Tudor's man as soon as he had been given the opportunity. And, on reaching York, he had no compunction in rounding up and hanging men, some of whom had been his companions-in-arms a few years before.

With that little matter satisfactorily settled, the King could now give his undivided attention to foreign affairs. On the twenty-seventh of March, 1489, a month prior to Percy's death, Henry's envoys had signed, at Medina del Campo, a treaty with Isabella and Ferdinand of Spain. One of the chief clauses was the proposed marriage of Prince Arthur and the young Infanta Catalina; another, inserted by the wily Ferdinand, was that Henry should begin hostilities against France as soon as his truce with that country expired. Consequently, in April, the English King reluctantly despatched an expeditionary force to Brittany, which occupied Guingamp, hurriedly evacuated by the French.

But Henry, whose dislike of war was fast becoming an obsession, preferred to put his trust in more peaceful methods and, in August, he renewed England's old treaty with Portugal. Amongst his ambassadors sent to Lisbon was Sir Richard Edgecombe, a blunt Devonian who had done his King good service in many quarters of Europe. But although staunchly Henry Tudor's man, Edgecombe was not above consorting with known Yorkists if it suited him.

'You may stay in their flea-bitten Poruguese inns,' he told the rest of his fellow envoys. 'I shall lodge with Brampton and his good lady.'

Edward Brampton, who had once escorted Henry Tudor to St Malo, had been knighted in 1484 by King Richard the third; the first man of Jewish birth to be so honoured. Since Bosworth, he had at first lived in Flanders, but was now residing in his native Portugal. Like Edgecombe, he could value a man for himself in spite of his political beliefs, and welcomed Sir Richard with open arms.

Dinner was a splended affair, with all the best Portuguese dishes and finest wines, but Edgecombe, refusing a custard made of whipped cream and sherry, said, laughing: 'Too damn rich for me, Ned. All these foreign foods! They upset the stomach.'

'Pooh!' exclaimed Brampton. 'Don't tell me that you haven't got used to them by now, after all the jauntering about you've done. Scotland, Brittany, France, Ireland! By the way, I hear you did good work there, persuading the Earl of Kildare to sign an oath of allegience to Henry Tudor.'

A bitter note had crept into Brampton's voice and his guest shifted uncomfortably. Lady Brampton, sensing the tension, interjected quickly: 'Let's have some music,' and she beckoned to a young man who had quietly entered the room a few moments before. As the boy moved into the pool of candlelight illuminating the table, Sir Richard, glancing casually in his direction, stiffened and uttered a startled oath.

'God's Body!' he breathed. Then, turning towards his host, he muttered in an undertone: 'What an extraordinary likeness! I take it that he's one of the late King Edward's – er – by-blows?'

Brampton grinned. 'It is an uncanny resemblance,' he agreed, 'and you can well be pardoned for what you're thinking. But the plain fact is that, so far as I know, the lad has no drop of Plantagenet blood in him. His name is Peter Warbeck and he and his parents once lodged with us in London. They come from Tournai, and when we were in Flanders we met them again. The upshot was that my wife, who had been fond of Peter when he was small, persuaded John and Clara to let her bring the boy to Portugal for a while.'

'The young Warbeck, a tall, fair, seventeen-year-old, began to sing and Edgecombe stared at him, mesmerised. When the boy had finished, bowed and withdrawn, Sir Richard turned once again to Brampton.

'It's impossible,' he averred, 'that anyone could look as he does and not be a Plantagenet.'

'We-ell,' said Sir Edward slowly, casting a quick look of apprehension at his wife, who had set her lips in a thin, repressive line. He hesitated, then laughed. 'My good lady doesn't like my saying this, but I have sometimes wondered if, perhaps, the boy was . . . shall we say adopted? I recall that the late Duke Charles of Burgundy once remarked – admittedly in one of his more vicious moments – that he had married the greatest whore in Europe.'

Edgecombe's eyes narrowed for a second, then dilated in

sudden understanding. 'You mean . . . the Dowager Duchess Margaret. . . .'

'I don't mean anything,' Sir Edward responded emphatically. 'I'm just saying that what with the boy being Flemish . . . and the likeness . . . and . . .' His voice tailed off as Lady Brampton rose majestically and begged, in arctic tones, that the gentlemen would excuse her.

'Well,' remarked Edgecombe, as he resumed his seat, his hostess having departed in a cloud of displeasure, 'it's a good job that they can't see the boy in Ireland.'

Brampton directed a look of enquiry at him, as he recharged Edgecombe's glass.

'Oh yes,' Sir Richard went on, sipping the wine and feeling a glow as warm as its colour spread through his veins. 'There's still a lot of unrest over there. The Irish still hanker after the House of York; even Kildare. I don't believe that his oath to Henry is worth the droppings from my nose. Yes, indeed! They would love young Warbeck there.'

He stretched his legs and arched his back luxuriously. He had been right; this was better than any Portuguese inn. He noticed, idly, that his host was looking thoughtful. Ned Brampton was getting broody in his middle-age.

On the twenty-ninth of November, 1489, the Queen gave birth to her second child, the Princess Margaret, a strong, healthy baby who, at a few weeks old, was the possessor of an outstanding pair of lungs which she did not hesitate to use.

Outside, the December winds whined through the streets and wailed around the roof-tops; died, then, gathering momentum, arose once more in a swift squall of sleet. Lying in her haven of warmth, her daughter in her arms, Elizabeth felt content. She knew that many people thought her lot an unhappy one because Henry excluded her from both his counsels and his affections. But she, who had seen the desire for power ravage both her mother's and father's families and tear them apart, had never wished for political influence. As for affection, her husband's very nature prevented him from treating her with anything but punctilious, if chilly, courtesy, and this was all she needed. Henry Tudor had nothing more acceptable to offer her than that which he already gave. The love that she had wanted had not been hers to take, but the fulfilment of her passionate nature had come with her children.

Elizabeth had discovered that she was a natural mother, and as long as Henry wanted heirs she would give them to him. Arthur was the light of her life and not even the fact that he bore an ever-increasing resemblance to his father could detract from his beauty in her eyes. And now she had a daughter. She accepted with apparent meekness the King's decree that the child should be called after his mother, and contented herself with descrying daily in the little Margaret new and growing likenesses to Elizabeth Woodville. She held inside herself a secret bubble of laughter that this should be so.

More than ever now, that inner life was Elizabeth's refuge and her strength. Within the charmed circle of her mind, she was safe: she could say and do things which would never be tolerated in Henry Tudor's Queen. Only the very discerning recognised that behind the façade of fashionable decorum and wifely acquiescence to her husband's will, there dwelt the wild and affectionate creature who was the true Elizabeth Plantagenet.

She bent now to kiss the top of her daughter's small head and, as she did so, remembered with a shudder that today the Abbot of Abingdon was being executed at Tyburn for his part in yet another plot to place the Earl of Warwick on the throne. An unexpected anger welled up inside Elisabeth; anger that men such as the Abbot should continually plot against her husband and so jeopardize the lives and inheritance of her precious children.

And, looking back on that moment in later years, to that cold December day of 1489 that had brought the first flurry of snow, the Queen would realise that it had been one of the great turning points of her life. It had marked the moment when she had stopped thinking like Elizabeth Plantagenet, daughter of King Edward the fourth, and had started to think like Elizabeth Tudor, mother of the future King Arthur.

20

THE Princess Margaret was just over twelve months old when, during the Christmas festivities of the following year, 1490, her father dined in state with the Archbishop of Canterbury.

John Morton, planning the banquet with the officers of his household, had been in something of a cleft stick. Fast becoming Henry's most indispensable administrator, he had inaugurated a new approach to the old problem of relieving over-mighty vassals of their money. Sir William Stanley had recently had a taste of it.

'He had the effrontery,' the outraged knight had snorted to his brother, 'to inform me that as my hospitality, both to the King and to others, had been so great in past months, it must be assumed that I was even wealthier than he had supposed. I am, therefore, to be more heavily taxed in the future.'

Lord Stanley – people still seemed to call him that, rather than the more imposing Derby – had laughed sourly.

'Then our friend is having his cake and eating it, too,' he had answered. 'He told me the other day, that as I was not a lavish host, I must be salting my money away for my own purposes. I, also, am to be more heavily taxed. It seems, my dear brother, that we are caught on a two-pronged fork. Morton's fork!'

Sir William had let rip with a volley of oaths, but Lord Stanley had merely stood, glowering. His wife, Henry's mother, had recently taken a sacred vow of chastity and, in consequence, eschewed her husband's bed and, as far as possible, his company. All her time was now absorbed by her son. Undoubtedly, the victory at Bosworth was turning to dust and ashes in Stanley's mouth.

He waited, with a certain grim satisfaction, to see how the Archbishop would manage his own Christmas feast, for Morton dare not now be too prodigal nor yet too niggardly when entertaining his King. But after much cogitation and innumerable changes of plan – Morton's Sergeant of Confectionary told the Sergeant Usher of the Household that he would very likely end by cutting his throat – John Morton managed to strike just the happy medium.

'Which he always has done and always will do,' Sir William grunted in his brother's ear as they sat at the high table, watching the Archbishop's mummers begin one of their elaborate disguisings. 'What's our revered Secretary of State looking so pleased about?'

Lord Stanley, glancing briefly at Richard Fox replied curtly: 'I hear that Stillington is dead. No doubt our foxy friend is hoping for the bishopric of Bath and Wells.'

'Which he'll get, never fear,' Lord Strange put in from his father's other side.

Before Stanley could reply, a diversion was created. A young boy, some twelve years of age, who had been standing behind the Archbishop's chair, suddenly leapt in amongst the players and, with apparently little effort, created and mimed a part for himself as he went along. The actors were in no way disconcerted, a fact which suggested to Henry that they were used to this particular form of interruption.

'Does he often do this?' the King enquired of his host and Morton said that he did, shouting out: 'Bravo, Tom!'

And when the boy, flushed and triumphant returned to his place, the Archbishop laid an affectionate hand on his sleeve.

'It is my opinion, Sire,' Morton said, turning to Henry, 'that this boy, if we live to see it, will prove to be a marvellous man.'

Henry looked thoughtfully at Master Thomas More. The Archbishop was probably right; he was an astute judge of men and the King respected his assessments. But in the sweet young face that stared respectfully back at him, Henry detected just such a hint of obstinacy, that same slavery to conscience, that Morton had so deplored in the late King Richard the third.

The thought of Richard Plantagenet, as always, brought Henry up short. That old familiar feeling of hatred and envy still have the power to catch him by the throat. It was the more infuriating now that it was so senseless. Richard was dead; had lain in his obscure grave in the Greyfriars' Church at Leicester for over five years and Henry Tudor wore his crown. And yet, his memory, even now, could arouse this unreasoning sensation of jealousy.

Henry rose abruptly from the table. The dancing was beginning and he had no liking for it. Very occasionally he danced with Elizabeth, but that was all and she was not present tonight. She was pregnant yet again – a prolific woman like her mother – and had pleaded fatigue. And if Henry and John Morton suspected that it was her dislike of the Archbishop which dictated her absence, neither would openly acknowledge the fact.

'You have something to show me,' Henry reminded his Chancellor and allowed Morton to usher him into a small, private chamber where a log-fire threw flickering light over floor and ceiling, and glinted on the silver in a corner cupboard.

Henry's eyes flickered, too, towards that cupboard and its contents, and Morton, perceiving it, hurriedly produced a letter which he held out to his sovereign with a compelling hand.

'John Hayes sent me this, from Winchester. He used to be in the Duke of Clarence's employ, as Your Highness knows. He received it last month from an old friend of his, John Taylor of Exeter. Taylor was one of King Edward's customs officials, an ardent Yorkist and now in voluntary exile in France.'

Henry took the paper and began to read, his practised eye skimming the page and picking out almost by instinct the salient words and phrases.

' . . . the words we spoke in St Peter's church at Exeter . . . the King of France, by the advice and consent of his Council . . . help for your late master's son.'

Henry's lips compressed. His support of Brittany had won for him the French King's enmity. Charles – or rather, the Lady of Beaujeu – regarded him as an ingrate who now refused to take in friendship the hand that had helped him to a throne. Had he been a fool, allowing Ferdinand to blackmail him into supporting the Duchess Anne? Was the future and problematical marriage of Arthur and the Infanta Catalina worth the price he had paid? Perhaps; perhaps!

He read on. ' . . . his friends and servants . . . may be assured of safety in France . . . The King will give men, silver and ships . . . and they may come into England. . . . '

Why not? thought Henry. What Charles and his sister had done once, they could do again. They had helped to replace Richard Plantagenet by Henry Tudor; why not Henry Tudor by Edward, Earl of Warwick?

'Enlist those of like mind. Thomas Gale of Dartmouth will stand your friend. . . . The time of help is coming . . . written at Rouen, this fifteenth day of September. . . . '

Henry laid the paper down. The glow from the fire, playing over his face, revealed nothing to the watchful Archbishop. The features were expressionless; a mask. But the eyes of the two men met and a glance of mutual understanding passed between them. One day, it said, perhaps not yet, but one day, the son of George, Duke of Clarence, must be put to death.

The bitter weather that made life in England almost unbearable during that winter of 1490-91, affected the whole of Europe, but Edward Brampton was not the man to be deterred by a little thing such as the cold. On a frost-bitten January morning, against all the advice and importunings of his wife, he went for his usual walk to his favourite wine-shop and ensconced himself cosily at a corner table.

'Duarte Brandao!'

It was so long since he had been called by his Portuguese name, even here in Portugal, that Brampton did not immediately realise that he was being addressed. It was only when the name was repeated with a certain gentle insistence, that he looked up.

'Duarte Brandao!'

'Pregent Meno!'

The two men embraced, a flood of Portuguese pouring from their lips. When their first surprise and rapture was spent, they sat, beaming contentedly at one another.

'Well, well! Pregent Meno!'

'Well, well! Duarte Brandao! But I mustn't call you that, must I? I should give you your English title.' Meno made an attempt to twist the words off his tongue and failed, laughing. 'No! No! I can't do it. An evil barbarous language!'

'Never mind that,' said Sir Edward. 'What are you doing in Lisbon? In fact, what are you doing with yourself, generally?'

'Oh, I buy and sell,' Pregent answered with a grin. 'Successfully, of course! As to my being in Lisbon, I travel to many places. I see many countries – France, England, Spain, Burgundy, Flanders, Ireland – '

'Ireland?' Brampton's voice cut sharply across that of his friend. 'You mean you visit Ireland?'

'Often! I. . . . '

But Brampton had lost the thread of Pregent Meno's discourse. He was busy with thoughts of his own. Suddenly, he said: 'Pregent, do you stand in need of a servant? A fine, upstanding boy who will do you excellent service?'

Pregent Meno, arrested in mid-sentence by this peculiar and totally unexpected demand, stared open-mouthed. 'Another servant? You mean . . . one of yours? I can always do with a good man, Duarte, but why – ?'

'I want this boy – this man; he's nearly eighteen – to go to Ireland. I have neither the time nor money to go myself, or I would have taken him.'

'Is he Irish?'

'No, a Fleming.'

'Then, why?'

'Oh,' Brampton said, swilling his wine around in his half-empty mazer and watching the swirling patterns of crimson and black, 'the boy has a desire to see the country.'

But, later, when he had been taken home by his friend and had been introduced to Peter Warbeck, Pregent Meno expressed doubts on that score.

'It doesn't seem to me, Duarte, that the lad has any particular desire to visit Ireland. Now, what are you playing at? Be honest with me and then, who knows? I might be induced to employ the young man. I like him.'

Edward Brampton hesitated; then, encouraging his friend to draw nearer the fire and help himself to more wine, lowered his voice to a confidential whisper.

'Listen carefully, Pregent. Here is all that I would want you to do. . . .'

Winter gave way to spring; to March winds and the fragile budding of early primroses; to wood-anemones, the wind-flowers, tossing in clouds of white and palest purple beneath the bare, still blackened branches of the trees; to clumps of sweet violets, their tiny, veined faces peeping from between heart-shaped leaves, and sending their delicate, haunting perfume rising like incense in the dark, vaulted shadows of the woods.

In Yorkshire, it was still bitterly cold, but in the Magistrates' Court it was hot and sticky with the press of many bodies. The Mayor glared impartially at the two men before him.

'John Burton, you have accused John Payntor of seditious talk. You say that he called the late Earl of Northumberland a traitor because he betrayed King Richard at Bosworth. John Payntor, what do you have to say for yourself?'

John Payntor's face turned a dull red and he stuck out his underlip belligerently. He shot a baleful glance at his accuser, a school-master at St Leonard's Hospital, out of the corner of his eye.

'I deny it, Your Worship. John Burton said the King Richard was a crouchback and a hypocrite and had been buried fittingly – in a ditch, like a dog.'

A low growl broke from the onlookers and the Mayor flung up a restraining hand. If he were not careful, he would have his court turned into a treasonable gathering against the reigning sovereign.

Payntor's voice went inexorably on. 'And I said Burton was a liar – ' He caught one of the magistrate's fulminating eyes upon him and something of that worthy's anxiety communicated itself to him. His tone dropped to a more moderate note as he added: 'I replied that King Richard was not buried in a ditch, but that King Henry had interred his body fittingly as became a man of gentle birth.'

All the magistrates breathed again. 'That accords with the deposition which I have here from the Prior of Bolton Abbey.' the Mayor agreed, rifling through the papers in front of him. 'This conversation took place, I understand, in the presence of three witnesses at the house of William Plumer. Stand forward, William Plumer.'

The gentleman so named detached himself from the ruck of

onlookers, and came forward. Also called was Richard Flint, a chaplain, one of the men present at the time of the alleged treasonable conversation. The look which he directed at John Burton boded no good for the school-master.

Plumer gave his evidence quietly, confirming Payntor's story, but the little chaplain was of a more pugnacious spirit.

'It was more than flesh-and-blood could stand, Your Worship, he shouted, 'with that man there – ' he indicated Burton with a vicious stab on his grimy forefinger – 'calling King Richard a caitiff and a crouchback and . . . and . . . and other execrable lies.' His voice had risen almost to the pitch of hysteria, and when Burton retorted: 'It's true! He was!' there seemed likely to be a most unseemly brawl. The spectators were muttering dangerously and one or two threatening movements were made in Burton's direction, so that the magistrates rose to their feet as one man, in an uprush of scarlet silk.

'Silence!' roared the Mayor, and as soon as he could make himself heard, he added in scandalised accents: 'I will not have my courtroom turned into a bear-pit!'

Two other men then gave their evidence, following which there was an unscheduled exchange of personalities between Burton and one of the witnesses. Finally, after a brief consultation with his fellow magistrates, the Mayor delivered his verdict.

'I find John Payntor innocent of the charges brought against him and I bind you both over to keep the peace on pain of a fine of one hundred marks. Don't let me hear from either of you again.'

There was a ragged cheer from the crowd which turned to a hiss as John Burton pushed his way into the chilly street. Much he had got out of it, the citizens gleefully remarked to one another, trying to bring a charge of sedition against a loyal man like John Payntor. They did not say loyal to whom: they had no need to do so.

But in the minds of the more thinking element, there was cause for perturbation. It was the first time that they had ever heard the late King Richard so slandered. The words 'caitiff' and 'crouchback' had an ugly ring to them. And mud, once thrown, had an unpleasant habit of sticking.

21

SHORTLY before the birth of her third child, on a bright spring day when the earth glimmered like a cupful of dancing, iridescent light, Elizabeth visited an old friend at the Sign of the Red Pale in Westminster Yard. She did not know then that it was to be the last time, but it did occur to her that William Caxton was looking older and more tired than she had ever seen him before.

Accompanied by her cousin, Margaret Plantagenet, and her aunt, Catherine Woodville, she had been into the city to see the new buildings being erected under the auspices of Thomas Wood, the goldsmith. Situated on the south side of Cheapside, they comprised ten houses and fourteen shops, each four storeys high, to be known as Goldsmith's Row. Elizabeth had been enchanted by the symmetry of the buildings, while her ladies had exclaimed rapturously over the decorations – the Goldsmith's Arms and a frieze of lead, gilt-covered figures depicting woodmen riding on fabulous beasts.

It had been on impulse that Elizabeth had stopped her litter at the printing works and gone inside to see William Caxton. It was dark after the sunshine outside and the Queen's vision was shot through with greens and oranges, giving everything she looked at a blurred halo of light. The clatter of the presses was deafening, and Caxton, hurrying to meet his distinguished visitors, was quick to usher them into his private room and close the intervening door.

'Your Grace, I am honoured.' Caxton bowed and kissed Elizabeth's hand. He still spoke with the faintest trace of an accent, the legacy of his long years abroad, as Head of the English Merchants in Bruges. Then he showed the Queen and her ladies some of the books which he had printed over the years; *Le Recueil des Histoires de Troy,* Chaucer's *Canterbury Tales,* Malory's *Morte d'Arthur* and the *Dictates and Sayings of the Philosophers* by Elizabeth's uncle, Anthony Woodville. And Caxton also showed to Margaret Plantagenet *The Game and Play of Chess,* with its dedication to her father.

Elizabeth was never sure afterwards how it happened, but suddenly she and her cousin were listening, enthralled, to Caxton's stories of two little boys, George and Richard Plantagenet, the brothers of England's new King, Edward the fourth.

'They were wild times, with Queen Margaret's troops hammering at London's gates, and the Duchess Cicely – Your Grace's grandmother – sending her two youngest sons to Burgundy for safety. And then we heard that Your Grace's father had been elected to the crown instead of the mad King Henry. What excitement!' the gnarled hands, stained with ink, were flung up in a gesture of approbation; the blue eyes gleamed through the sagging flesh. 'Duke Philip – he'd been very cold, very circumspect till then – had your father – ' he smiled at Margaret – 'and your uncle Richard brought to Bruges to do them honour. But little boys of that age – the lord George was eleven and his brother only eight – need more to amuse them than honours. So the Duke took them to his palace at Hesdin.

'The marvels of that place! Your highnesses would never believe! And neither did Your Grace's uncles until they saw them with their own eyes. There was a room where every kind of storm could be simulated.' Caxton's hands flew up and down like nesting birds, searching for a gesture worthy to express the marvels of that fairy-tale palace. 'Snow, thunder, lightning, tempest! To stand in the middle of that room, was to stand in the eye of the storm.

'And then there were the ponds.' The old eyes began to twinkle. 'Over every lake was a little bridge which could be collapsed at the twitch of a cord. How lord George and lord Richard laughed when some of the Duke's attendants were told to demonstrate this wonder for them. I may say that the poor unfortunates who fell into the lakes didn't find it so amusing. And neither did Your Grace's uncles when they were shown Duke Philip's books. Some of the books, you see, were filled with a fine, white dust that blew into the reader's eyes when he turned to certain pages.

'But the library proper, what splendour, my dears, that was!' (The old fool was waxing not only poetical, but familiar, thought Catherine Woodville acidly, bored to tears.) 'The illuminations of those manuscripts defy description! Every margin, every initial letter was a riot of birds and flowers and exquisite little figures. Beautiful! Beautiful!'

Caxton lapsed into the forgetfulness of age, lost in a past that was so much more vivid than the present: the present, he had found, had turned a little sour.

His partner, Collard Mansion, entered in a flurry of grey robes. One of the boys had told him what was happening. Did William not realise that it was dangerous nowadays to talk about the late King Richard? And in front of the Queen, of all people! The man was mad!

But Elizabeth, far from being put out, seemed to be engrossed in Caxton's stories. As she rose to go, she took the old man's hand, clinging to it as though he were some last link with the past; a link she feared might soon be broken and which she could not bear to see snap.

The Duchess of Bedford, watching her niece, wondered if she had, after all, been correct when the monstrous suspicion had first crossed her mind that Elizabeth had loved her father's own brother.

And Elizabeth and Margaret Plantagenet went out into the sunlight, each busy with her own secret thoughts concerning those two little boys who had laughed and been enthralled by Hesdin a long, long time ago.

'We will come back again soon,' the Queen said gently to her cousin and Margaret's eyes brightened.

But before they could do so, William Caxton was dead.

Elizabeth's third child, another boy, was born at Greenwich on the twenty-eighth of June and christened Henry, after his father.

It was obvious from the start that this baby was neither Tudor, Beaufort nor Woodville: he was pure Plantagenet and, from the first, bore a startling likeness to his maternal grandfather. It made him at once his mother's favourite child and the least beloved of his father. But he was another boy to consolidate the Tudor dynasty and, as such, was precious enough in the eyes of both parents.

And his birth proved to be opportune, for, by the time he was four months old, Henry's spies in Ireland were sending back extremely disquieting reports in connection with a certain Peter Warbeck, who had recently arrived in that country in the train of a merchant, one, Pregent Meno. Warbeck's incredible resemblance to the Plantagenets had immediately attracted attention and, by early November, the first stirrings of rebellion were afoot. The only trouble was, the Irish chieftains could not quite make up their minds whom the young man was really meant to be. Early rumours made him once again the Earl of Warwick.

Henry laughed. 'Kildare and Desmond will be fools if they play that card for a second time,' he remarked to Morton. 'For one thing, they know – or they should do by now – that I have the real Edward Plantagenet safely in the Tower. More important for them, however, is that they acclaimed Lambert Simnel too loudly and with too many protestations of faith to be able to support Master Warbeck in the role. If they do, they'll lose face.'

'Not the present Earl of Desmond,' demurred the Archbishop. 'That was his brother, the late Earl.'

But Henry dismissed this as a mere quibble. All the Fitzgeralds, he remarked austerely, had been involved; they were all tarred with the same brush.

'There is an old saw, my dear Archbishop, which you may know. It goes: "The vice of the French is lechery; that of the English, treachery." The second line might, in my estimation, equally well apply to the Irish.'

The next report to reach the King's ears, was that the young man in Ireland was now reputed to be John of Gloucester, Richard's illegitimate son. Henry was not unduly disturbed. For one thing, a bastard made a poor figurehead; for another, he had the comfort of knowing that John of Gloucester was dead.

But before the early snows of December had time to do more than powder the roof-tops with the faintest feathering of white, affairs in Ireland had taken a much more serious turn. Peter Warbeck had been acclaimed as the younger of King Edward the fourth's two sons, Richard, Duke of York, and had been vouched for by a number of ardent Yorkists, among them John Taylor of Exeter, now busying himself in Dublin.

It was Henry's secret fear come true; the fear that one day, one or both of his two brothers-in-law would be found to be still alive. He knew it for an unreasonable, more, a ridiculous fear, and yet he could not rid himself of it. It dogged his waking thoughts like his jealousy of Richard, that humiliating emotion that should have been exorcised by Bosworth Field, but continued, incomprehensibly, to haunt him.

John Morton, noting Henry's anxiety, sent at once to Guisnes, and Sir James Tyrrell replied yet again with assurances that the boys had indeed been murdered. Had he not seen the bodies with his own eyes? The Queen, too, was called upon to reassure her husband and even Elizabeth Woodville was prevailed upon to write from her convent-prison that her sons were certainly dead.

But Henry could not be satisfied. The women had never seen the bodies and Tyrrell had been Richard Plantagenet's man. Suppose that he had been lying all these years, lulling Henry Tudor into a sense of false security; biding his time.

'For what?' asked Margaret Beaufort, the only person to whom Henry would reveal even a glimpse of the terrors that beset him. 'Tyrell has proved himself your man over and over again. He was wounded at Dixmude in the action there, and everything he has he owes to you. Small benefit to him, then, to exchange Henry Tudor for the son of Edward the fourth. Henry,' and she laid an urgent hand on her son's arm, 'you know that this Warbeck is an impostor.'

Henry did know it, but his practical nature cried out for some proof. If only he could find the boys' corpses! Where had they been buried?

Fortunately, he had other cares to distract his attention. It seemed extremely probable that Anne of Brittany would marry Charles the eighth of France. A number of suitors had been proposed to her (among them Catherine Woodville's son, the Duke of Buckingham) and she had even gone through a form of proxy marriage with the Hapsburg Maximilian. This, however, had been annulled and the fourteen-year-old girl was at present besieged in Rennes with her garrison of Bretons, Flemings and English.

The latter were behaving after their usual fasion when abroad, badly; getting drunk, raping the women and generally indicating that their contempt of foreigners was no ill-founded rumour, but a very real and deep-rooted emotion. It was hardly surprising, therefore, that as preparations were made at the English court for yet another Christmas, word should reach Henry Tudor that Anne, thowing in her hand, had married Charles of France at Langeais in Tourraine, on the sixth of December.

Henry's, until now, assumed animosity towards France was aroused in good earnest. The enlargement of French possessions by the annexation of Brittany – a territory in perilous proximity to England – had turned France into an immediate enemy. However much he might dislike the idea, and however much it might go against his secret inclinations, Henry perceived that the war would now have to be prosecuted to the full.

Spring came late in the year 1492, after an eventful winter which had seen an abortive Breton plot to resist French domination, and the fall of that last Moorish stronghold, Granada, to the armies of Isabella and Ferdinand. But it could not come late enough for Elizabeth Woodville in her convent, for her physicians had warned her that before the spring was out, she would be dead.

The stomach pains which she had first experienced some years previously, had increased so much of late that she could no longer rise from her bed and the doctors had only confirmed what she had already suspected.

On the tenth of April she made her will, a document pathetic in its brevity.

'As I have nothing to leave to my dearest daughter, the Queen's Grace, nor to any of my children, as I would have wished, I bequeath to her and to her issue, with as good a heart and mind as is possible, my blessing, as I do to all my aforesaid children.'

Elizabeth Woodville had smiled a little as she had signed it. She had insisted on that qualifying clause 'with as good a heart and mind as is possible' against the advice of her lawyer. It was the sting in the tail of her forgiveness and she hoped that it would not pass unnoticed by either Henry or Elizabeth.

She closed her eyes, clenching her teeth against the white-hot onslaught of pain. Perhaps she did not mind death as much as she might once had done. Her generation was dropping off, one after another – her brother-in-law, Suffolk, as well as Caxton, had died last year – and a new, forward-thrusting generation was taking its place. At fifty-five, she found modern youth very hard to understand. All this restlessness, this desire to be up and doing, searching for new worlds to conquer, had been quite unheard of in her young days. Europe had been the world then, and quite big enough, too. No one had dreamed of trying to find a new route to India by sailing down the African coast, as Bartholomew Diaz had done only a year after Bosworth Field: as well would men have contemplated a journey to the moon.

The pain receded and she stirred, opening her eyes again. She was alone and terribly afraid. There was so much in her life that she wished she could undo; so many tragedies that might have been avoided. These last few weeks, she had had the same dream, recurring again and again. Always she was wandering down a long corridor to a tiny room at the end, and always, when she opened the door, she saw the bodies of two children lying inside. Sometimes they were the bodies of her own two sons, but at others, they were those of the Earl of Desmond's children.

And on a cold, rainy night in late April, when the wind moaned through the draughty passages and mingled with the voices of the nuns at prayer, Elizabeth Woodville dreamed it for the last time. As she opened the door into that little room, she gave a great cry, sat up abruptly in her bed, then fell forwards into the comforting arms of the Mother Superior, who had been called earlier to her side. The Mother Superior, laying the dying woman back among her pillows, caught the one word, 'Thomas!' But whether Elizabeth was calling her son, the Marquis of Dorset, or speaking to someone in the past, no one would ever know. Elizabeth Woodville, one-time Queen of England, was dead.

22

Henry sat in his tent before the walls of Boulogne, listening to the spasmodic barking of his siege-guns.

It was October, six months since the unregretted death of his mother-in-law, and he was here, in France, at the head of his armies. Sluys had capitulated a few weeks earlier and the English were determined that Boulogne should go the same way before they were forced to retire on Calais for the winter. They were excited, pleased to be fighting once more in France. and anyone who was rash enough to surmise that the present King would emulate his predecessor, Edward the fourth, and make a profitable peace with the enemy, was set upon and beaten.

Henry said nothing, but Jasper, noting the familiar set of the lips and half-veiled eyes, opined to Sir William Stanley that his nephew was up to something. Sir William thought it extremely likely. His opinion of his brother's step-son was reaching its lowest ebb, and the fact that Henry's two pet lawyers, Edmund Dudley and Sir Richard Empson, had inflicted on him yet another tax, in no way ameliorated this feeling. He considered Henry secret, devious and, above all, a coward. One had, Sir William reflected, only to look at that narrow, sallow face to realise that the King was in the grip of fear.

Jasper Tudor had also noticed Henry's apprehension. He knew, none better, his nephew's dislike of physical violence, but, unlike Sir William, he knew also Henry's tremendous force of will which could make him overcome any terror. There was something more in the King's attitude than immediately met the eye; some inner perturbation which manifested itself in the sharpened tone, the tautened body and the nervous plucking at the chin. Without really expecting any reply, Jasper asked of his nephew if anything were troubling him.

Henry said nothing for a while, then, to the Duke's astonishment, answered: 'Jasper, I'm haunted by the little Duke of York.'

Jasper stared. He was uncertain whether or not to take this literally, and his nephew, had confided in him that he was unprepared for what he considered to be a flippant reply.

'Just because Charles has invited this Warbeck to the French court?' he enquired incredulously, adding, with a bracing laugh: 'You don't set any store by that do you? It's just a move to annoy you; to make you more amenable to ending the war. Peterkin Warbeck!' The laugh rang out again, full and round; the hearty guffaw of an unimaginative man. 'I hear that he's prancing round the French court like a popinjay. Giving himself airs and making himself thoroughly ridiculous. Duke of York, indeed!'

Henry looked at his uncle from under his heavy lids. He should have known better than to try to make Jasper understand. His uncle had not a sensitive bone in his body – but perhaps that was as well: the grandson of the mad King Charles the sixth of France could not afford too great an imagination.

It was the knowledge of this taint of madness in his own blood that always made Henry keep a tight rein on his temper and curb his more extravagant flights of fancy. And it was the reason for his anxiety over this obsession that he now had concerning his youngest brother-in-law. He could not rid himself of the notion that the boy was still alive and that this Warbeck might well be him.

Henry, however, was too astute to be impressed by the French King's professions of satisfaction with the imposter. He did not need Jasper to tell him that this was a carrot dangled before his nose; an added inducement to persuade him into a treaty of peace. He smiled to himself. Had Charles but known it, he had wasted his time and money by fostering Peter Warbeck's pretensions. Henry had long ago made up his mind to another Picquigny. And the loss, yesterday, of one of his best captains, Sir John Savage, ambushed outside the walls of Boulogne, together with all his men, had merely hardened Henry's resolve.

It was with all honour and courtesy, therefore, that, towards the middle of the month, Henry welcomed into his camp a deputation of Frenchmen, headed by Phillipe de Crève-Coeur, whose title, the Seigneur d'Esquierdes, had earned for him amongst the English the name of 'Lord Cordes'.

'Oh Lord! It's Cordes!' some wag would shout, every time

the valiant and chivalrous Seigneur appeared in the enemy lines, and the name had become so associated with him, that Henry found himself inadvertently using it over the council table.

'Lord Cordes' laughed, drawing his furred cloak about him, for it was chilly in the tent. He knew enough about the English to realise that the bestowal of a nickname usually betokened affection and he wondered if Henry Tudor had one. Somehow he doubted it.

'My master,' he said, 'offers to bear the entire cost of your defence of Brittany, to be paid in annual instalments of fifty thousand francs.'

Henry's eyes flashed wide open and it was, thought Sir William Stanley contemptuously, as though all the wealth of France was momentarily reflected in those pale, almost opaque, blue orbs. Then the lids closed and Henry inclined his head noncommittally. Phillipe de Crève-Coeur continued: 'The growth of commerce between our two countries is naturally to be encouraged. There will, of course, be a separate trade agreement.'

'And?' prompted Henry, after a pause, and 'Cordes' laughed.

'And, Sire, King Charles gives his pledged word not to assist any pretenders or aspirers to your throne.'

'The young man at present . . . er . . . gracing your master's court?'

'Will, of course, be sent packing.'

But packing where? It was but a short step from France into the Netherlands and the welcoming arms of the Dowager Duchess Margaret. However, that was a problem for another day. Henry's present one was to persuade his counsellors and captains to accept the idea of peace.

Rather to his surprise, he found them less recalcitrant than he had expected. It was the soldiers, not the generals, who wished to prosecute this war. The commanders were only too well aware of the difficulties; the failure of Maximilian to support them; the suspicion that Ferdinand and Isabella were about to make their own peace with France; the feeding and quartering of troops during the winter months. Certainly they would agree to end hostilities – and be home in time for Christmas, into the bargain!

So it was, that on the third of November, 1492, at Etaples, England concluded her second lucrative peace treaty with France within the span of twenty years.

The English were restive. Not only had they been baulked of

making war in France, but the uneasy suspicion had been implanted in their minds that never again would a King of England make a serious attempt to regain the lost empire of Henry the fifth. Inactivity fretted the English soul, not merely the commoners but the lords, also, and the elevation of John Morton to the rank of cardinal did nothing to appease such disgruntled spirits as Sir William Stanley.

Pope Innocent the eighth had died at last and Rodgrigo Borgia now reigned in Rome as Alexander the sixth. He it was who had bestowed the hat. This father of six children had expressed the pious hope that Morton would do something to unify the English church, for it was well known abroad that while the English never omitted any outward ceremony, they had as many and as diverse opinions about religion as there were flowers in the fields.

The Pope, himself, was preoccupied with the threatened invasion of the French, for, having subdued Brittany, Charles had turned predatory eyes towards the divided land of Italy, a colony of warring city-states. Alexander's appeal for material aid went unheeded by Henry Tudor, who was conserving his resources to meet whatever emergency might arise from the situation in Flanders. Peter Warbeck had been received there as Margaret's long-lost nephew, and Maximilian, angry at Henry's treaty with France, had been inveigled by his step-mother-in-law into lending the pretender his support. Moreover, Henry's spies in Scotland reported that King James the fourth was extremely prone to the view that Peter Warbeck was indeed the Duke of York and, as such, rightful King of England. It was a situation which might explode at any moment, like a faulty gun-barrel and Henry, therefore, had no intention of sending men and munitions to the Pope.

He was, however, prepared to assist in other ways and see to it that Alexander's behest to John Morton was carried through to its logical conclusion – the setting up of stakes and the burning of heretics at Smithfield. It was, as Sir Robert Clifford remarked in grim jest to Sir William Stanley, one more faggot on the fire of Henry's unpopularity and he, for one, was getting out and joining Peter Warbeck in Flanders.

Sir William experienced a feeling of surprise. Until now, he had always assumed Clifford to be very much Henry Tudor's man, and, just for a fleeting second, a note of warning sounded inside his head: it was ignored. Sir William Stanley was not so subtle a man as his brother and had never heeded his intuition. It did not even occur to him as strange that Sir Robert should risk confiding such a treasonable piece of information to the step-uncle of the King.

'Faugh!' he exclaimed, laughing. 'You're never going to tell me that you believe in Peterkin Warbeck.'

Sir Robert, reclining at ease in his companion's house, cast a quick look around him. Rumour had not lied when it had made Sir William out to be one of the richest men in England. He recognised many pieces of furniture and plate belonging to the late King Richard; and a particularly fine sapphire and ruby brooch, which now adorned Sir William's tunic, had once been worn in the dead man's hat.

'Oh, I don't know,' he answered. 'It's never been proved that the boys are dead. Just a spate of rumours every so often – and no bodies were ever produced, neither by Richard nor Henry. And this young man bears a quite remarkable resemblance to the Plantagenets, or so I've been told.'

Sir William put a doucette into his mouth and chewed on it thoughtfully. 'Mmm. I must admit that it has sometimes crossed my mind to wonder why, if Richard killed his nephews, he didn't put their corpses on show. If he feared rebellion on their behalf, to have them murdered and then tell no one . . . well . . . it seems such a contradiction in terms.' Sir William sucked his teeth and offered his guest more wine.

'Precisely,' agreed Sir Robert, accepting the mazer and sipping in his rather finicky way. 'But, the validity of Warbeck's claim apart, do you want to stay in the same country as Morton and Empson and Dudley?' He threw yet another appraising glance at his surroundings. 'You may be doing very nicely now, but in another five years. . . . Who knows? You may be taxed out of existence.'

'Five years!' ejaculated Sir William wrathfully. 'I'm damn near ruined now.'

Sir Robert permitted himself a tiny, incredulous smile, but his host failed to see it. Sir William was off again, riding the hobby-horse of his latest grievance.

'I'll tell you something else,' he said. 'This insane decision of Henry's to expel all the Flemings from England because of Maximilian's support of Warbeck, will do nothing but harm. The wool trade will lose hundreds of pounds because we can't do without them. The only people who will profit will be the Hanse merchants and the English won't like that, let me tell you.' He sucked in his cheeks, then puffed them out again with one of his deep chuckles. 'Oh no! There will be trouble over that, mark my words.'

'Come to Flanders with me, then,' Sir Robert pressed. 'I'm

sailing tomorrow. The Captain could manage another passenger.'

But Sir William thought of his houses and his lands and, in spite of the crippling taxation, his not unpleasant life and declined. He saw a shade of disappointment in Clifford's face and patted his arm consolingly.

'I'll say this to you,' he said. 'If Warbeck should prove to be the son of Edward the fourth, I won't lift a finger against him.'

And with that, Sir Robert Clifford had to be content. He sailed the next day, on June the twenty-third – a month to the day after Maximilian's own treaty with the French at Senlis – leaving England, as Sir William had predicted, simmering with dissatisfaction and unrest.

It boiled over on a cold, drizzling day in mid-October, with an attack by the London apprentices on the Steelyard, the home of the Hanseatic merchants. Sir William rode with his brother to see what was happening, and was rewarded by the sight of a furious, roaring mob of young people, vainly trying to break through the massive iron gates.

'They'll never do it,' Lord Stanley remarked regretfully, ducking a sling-shot and retiring rapidly to a safer point of vantage. 'Those gates can withstand an army, let alone a rabble of apprentices.'

His brother was more sanguine. 'I don't know. They might do it – just!' He dismounted, gentling his frightened horse.

'They say,' remarked a pleasant, slightly foreign voice behind him, 'that a carpenter and several blacksmiths have been smuggled inside and that they are reinforcing the gates.'

The brothers, turning, saw a smiling, obviously Italian gentleman standing within a few feet of them and he introduced himself as Giovanni Cabot. 'But in Bristol, where I live, I am known as John.'

'Bristol, eh?' said Lord Stanley, shouting to make himself heard above the din. 'What are you doing there?'

John Cabot jumped aside to avoid a flying splinter of wood and replied with unimpaired calm: 'I know all about the spice trade, and as the Bristol merchants want to take the English trade away from Southampton – ' he paused to pull Sir William clear of a fresh wave of apprentices, screaming filth and abuse at the 'Easterlings' – 'they find me very useful.'

'They do, eh? And what do you find them?' Sir William waved on the newcomers with an encouraging gesture of his hand.

'Oh,' said Cabot with a laugh, 'I find them useful, too. I have a theory that by journeying westwards across the Atlantic, one can reach the east coast of Asia. But to prove it, I need sailors and, more important, money. Bristol is a very rich city and her men have already made several voyages to find the Island of Brazil.'

By this time, the air was acrid with drifting smoke, the apprentices having set fire to a pile of brushwood outside the Steelyard's main gate.

'What the devil do they hope to gain by that?' snapped Sir William. 'The fools will never burn it down. The place is a fortress.'

'Anyway, here comes the Mayor with the Watch,' was his brother's lugubrious answer. 'That will soon put an end to it.'

He was right. A short, sharp battle ensued, ending with the majority of the apprentices in ignominious flight and the ring-leaders marched off under guard.

Lord Stanley and Sir William leisurely remounted their horses, but of their talkative Italian friend from Bristol there was now no sign. He had disappeared among the crowds of sightseers who were dispersing slowly, grumbling to one another about the wild, misguided ways of modern youth.

'The eastern coast of Asia by sailing westwards across the Atlantic!' Lord Stanley snorted to his brother. 'The man's mad! All foreigners are mad! He'll never do it.'

23

THE name of Peter Warbeck was no longer one to be spoken of with disdain; no longer an idle jest to be mentioned in the same breath as the latest bawdy joke.

In the November of 1493, he was present in Vienna at the funeral of the Emperor Frederick the third, Maximilian's father, and was afforded every honour and courtesy due to a reigning Prince. His extensive retinue of servants, provided and paid for by the Dowager Duchess Margaret, all flaunted the White Rose of York on their surcoats and his banner displayed the full arms of England. Afterwards, he returned with Maximilian to Flanders, to be greeted once more with extravagant affection by his 'aunt' and with more reserve by Duke Philip, Maximilian's son; heir not only to his mother's patrimony of Burgundy, but also to his father's vast Hapsburg domains. This extraordinarily handsome young man took few pains to conceal his scepticism of the English 'Duke of York'.

Between Margaret Plantagenet and Peter Warbeck there existed a peculiar relationship; a tacit understanding that neither would ever admit the imposture, not even when alone. By prefacing many of her sentences with the words: 'Do you remember?' the Dowager Duchess was able to convey certain facts to her protegé which it was essential he should know, without her ever seeming to instruct him.

As they walked together in the winter-garden of Peter's Antwerp home, a magnificent building put at his disposal by Maximilian, she said to him: 'Do you remember your wedding-day? I wasn't there, but I heard all about it of course.

She went on talking quietly, telling him of Anne Mowbray, of the processions, who had accompanied whom, all in the most normal way as though she were simply recalling to mind events of which he, also, had the clearest recollections. But underneath, her thoughts raced off down little by-ways of memory; jagged fragments of thought stabbing her conscious mind.

She saw Richard and George sprawling on the nursery floor at Fotheringay; heard again the frightened shouts of the Londoners as Margaret Anjou hammered at the gates of the city; glimpsed the lust in Edward's eyes when they rested on Eleanor Butler; and chattered once more with her niece, Elizabeth, as she twisted, dissatisfied, before a mirror of polished steel.

Margaret's feelings had changed towards Elizabeth whom she regarded unfairly, as a traitress to her family and House. The Duchess judicial instincts might tell her that her niece had had little option in becoming Henry the seventh's wife, but her more irrational impulses prompted her to enquire bitterly of her friends if Elizabeth need have produced so many and such healthy heirs for the usurping Tudor line. Margaret was forty-seven years of age; not a young woman any more, and it was her greatest ambition to see the House of York restored to the English throne before she died. For this, she would go to any lengths; she would even lend her support to an impostor, for a rebellion was nothing without a focal point. Once Peter Warbeck's invasion was successful, then would be the time to release her favourite brother's son from the Tower and place on the Earl of Warwick's head that crown which Clarence had so long and so vainly coveted.

A footfall sounded on the cinder path behind them, and

Margaret and Peter both turned their heads, almost guiltily. But it was only Sir Robert Clifford, hurrying to tell them of the latest outrage perpetrated by some of Antwerp's English visitors.

'They have torn down Your Highness' coat-of-arms from the front of the building,' Sir Robert informed Peter Warbeck, raising horrified hands, 'and they are shouting abuse in the street.'

'Is that what we can hear?' The Dowager Duchess shrugged indifferently. 'They'll sing another song when my nephew is restored to his throne. Sit down, Sir Robert. I have something I wish to discuss.'

She indicated a rustic bench, now rimed with frost, and Clifford reluctantly seated himself. The cold struck up through his backbone, making him shiver and he set his teeth firmly together to stop them chattering. But he inclined a dignified ear.

'What is the position now in Ireland?' demanded Margaret. 'Sooner or later, the Duke of York must return there to prepare for his invasion. The eastern littoral of England will be too well guarded, and so the attack will have to come from the west.'

Sir Robert pursed his lips. 'There is no time like the present,' he advised. 'The Irish chieftains have always been loyal – '

'Not the Butlers,' the Duchess interpolated, and Clifford conceded the justice of her remark with a spread of his beautiful hands.

'True, but Desmond and Kildare – in fact, the entire Fitzgerald Clan – will do all in their very considerable power. As I said just now, there is no time like the present and the Duke of York cannot be expected to kick his heels here in idleness while he should be claiming his rightful inheritance.'

Margaret was inclined to agree, but, a week or so later, had cause to change her mind in a hurry. Her spies at the English court reported the presence there of the Earl of Kildare, seeking Henry's pardon and his reinstatement as Lord Deputy of Ireland. The Duchess also had cause, for the first time, to doubt the validity of Sir Robert Clifford's advice.

Elizabeth, seated at Henry's right hand at the high table, was aware of a certain tension in the atmosphere. This did not emanate from the Earl of Kildare, in the place of honour, nor from the lesser Irish chieftains further down the board. They were all as rowdy and carefree as the bulk of the guests who graced the main body of the hall; rather, it was the uneasiness on the face of Cardinal Morton, mirrored in those of Reginald Bray and the Bishop of Bath and Wells. Indeed, Richard Fox had eaten very little, his nervous glance jumping towards every servant who entered, as though he expected any moment to be confronted by a gorgon.

Elizabeth looked at her husband. Henry's face rarely gave any indication as to his feelings, but tonight she caught a glimpse of suppressed amusement; a quiver of the thin lips betokening anticipation. After eight years of marrige, Elizabeth knew this look; a gloating expression which meant that someone was about to be embarrassed.

This pleasure which Henry derived from other people's humiliation was partly an inherited tendency; but it stemmed, also, from his broken and lonely childhood, when he had been nothing but a penniless adventurer, to be used or discarded at will by the Princes of Europe.

Elizabeth caught the flash of an imploring glance between Henry and Morton and guessed that the King and his councillors were not at one in this matter: whatever her husband was up to, it did not have their full approval. But the banquet was drawing to its end and nothing had so far happened. Relief gleamed in the eyes of Bray and the Cardinal. It seemed as though Henry had changed his mind and decided to behave himself.

Richard Fox felt the relaxing of tension. He motioned for another portion of rosewater junket to be put on his plate, and found his voice for the first time that evening. Raising it, he deplored the Vatican's refusal to grant the King's request for the canonisation of Henry the sixth. 'That most blessed martyr, foully done to death by Richard Plantagenet.'

Elizabeth felt the sudden surge of anger and pain which always affected her when she heard her uncle reviled. But she knew better than to refute the slanders.

Not so the Earl of Kildare, who laughed outright. 'I've never heard that before,' he said, slewing round to look the Bishop in the eye. 'Indeed, I've always understood that it was King Richard who had King Henry's body removed from Chertsey to Windsor as a more fitting burial place. Hardly the action of a murderer towards his victim.'

Fox was taken aback by this unexpected onslaught. One grew accustomed to vilifying the late King without fear of contradiction. 'Richard was in the Tower on the night of the murder,' he said defensively.

Kildare shrugged. 'Oh, of that I have no doubt. Nor do I doubt that he concurred with his brother's decision to remove the old man. But that is a different matter. The tenor of your words, my lord, implied Henry's murder at Richard's own hands and at his personal instigation.'

'I . . . I . . . You mistake.' Fox had become flustered and his inability to withstand Kildare's remarks merely added fuel to the flame of Henry's wrath. This Irish chieftain, this 'wild man of the woods,' had not only dared to contradict the Secretary of State at a public banquet and make him look foolish, but had done it on the one subject most calculated to enrage the King. And to think that he, Henry, had planned to embarrass Kildare at this feast and had been within an ace of bowing to his minister's entreaties not to do so. Turning in his chair, he beckoned imperiously to a young man who had been standing in the shadows.

'More wine, my lord?' he said to Kildare. The wine-bearer came forward and knelt. 'You know my server, I think.'

Kildare and Lambert Simnel regarded each other. The other chieftains, each aware by now that something unusual was toward, were staring silently in their direction.

Henry continued: 'Now he shall kneel to you as you once knelt to him – when you did him homage as King of England.'

Jasper Tudor gave a bellow of laughter and Oxford began to snigger. Someone else tittered and there were grins on many faces, even on those of the Irish. But not on Kildare's. He had been offered a slight which he would not forget in a hurry.

As one of his countrymen shouted: 'Come to me, boy! I'll drink the wine if it's good, whoever offers it to me,' Kildare turned away, his heavy features suffused with colour. And he took no further part in the evening's entertainments.

Morton sighed and exchanged a speaking look with Sir Reginald Bray. They had small hope now of keeping the Fitzgeralds' fingers from dabbling in the pie of Peter Warbeck's making.

The year that followed was an uneasy one. In the spring, Maximilian and Philip put an embargo on English cloth; in the autumn, the French armies swept over the Alps and down into Italy; and throughout Ireland trouble was rife for the entire twelve months.

The Fitzgeralds and the Butlers fought openly in the streets of Dublin, a sure sign that Kildare had determined to back the 'Duke of York,' and his kinsman, the Earl of Desmond, was hot in his support.

It was this fact which Elizabeth offered to her husband as

the strongest proof of Warbeck's identity.

'The Earl of Desmond,' she assured Henry, 'knows this youth for an impostor – or, at least, strongly suspects that he is one. The Earl would never support the son of my mother. What this Warbeck provides him with is the opportunity to insult, and maybe harm, Elizabeth Woodville's daughter and grandchildren.'

Henry, although giving no sign beyond a small, cold smile, was impressed by her reasoning and was grateful for the alleviation of his fears. He knew, as did everyone, the old story concerning Desmond's father and Elizabeth Woodville, and knew, also, that the enmity had lingered on in the hearts of all the murdered Earl's children.

It was Reginald Bray's suggestion that the King should create his youngest son, Henry, now just over three years old, Duke of York, thus robbing Peter Warbeck of his pretensions to even the lesser of the two titles which he claimed.

So it was, that on the first of November, 1494, this sturdy, golden-haired child was carried into Westminster Hall in the arms of the Earl of Shrewsbury. Elizabeth and Henry, wearing their crowns, paced before him, themselves preceded by the Archbishops and Bishops of the realm. Everywhere there was colour and light; the dull warmth of crimson and the brilliance of scarlet; the glitter of gold and the pale iridescence of silver; the glow of blues and purples and the arrogant flash of bright orange. The torches and cressets hissed on the walls and the candlelight set the many gems twinkling and sparkling with a thousand facets of light. To the little Henry it was as though a rainbow had been broken into a myriad pieces and scattered about the hall for his delight.

Seated at the table with his mother and father, he stared happily about him, only breaking into a scream when he failed to get all his own way. Elizabeth, watching him, was reminded with a dreadful clarity of her brother, the former Duke of York, on his wedding day; the day when her father had announced the trial, for high treason, of his brother, George, Duke of Clarence.

Elizabeth jerked her mind back from the painful past, only to find herself looking straight into the eyes of Clarence's daughter, now Lady Margaret Pole. Her cousin had been married a year or so previously to Sir Richard Pole, the son of Margaret Beaufort's half-sister, and Elizabeth was thankful to note that she seemed very happy in her marriage. It was some small compensation for her father's murder and her brother's continued imprisonment.

After the banquet, which to Elizabeth dragged on interminably, there were the usual entertainments, with the Princess Margaret, a self-possessed five-year-old, awarding prizes for the wrestling. Elizabeth knew that Henry was planning to offer this, his eldest and, so far, his only daughter, to King James the fourth of Scotland as his future wife. The fact that James was already twenty-one years old did not bother Henry; the disparity in age was of small importance in dynastic marriages. To Elizabeth, however, it seemed of considerable moment, but she knew better than to protest. No words of hers would weigh with Henry, nor would he expect her to proffer her opinion. The only people who could in any way influence him, were his mother, the Cardinal, Bray and Fox. Elizabeth's chief hope lay in James' own obvious animosity towards England and the improbability that a young and highly intelligent man would look kindly upon a marriage with a child sixteen years his junior.

The music had started and Elizabeth glanced sideways at Henry, but it was apparent that the King was not dancing tonight. The Queen recalled her father, a King who would be remembered as the man who had cried: 'I will dance with the prettiest lady in the room,' holding out his hands to his little daughter. Henry would never be remembered like that. His face was set and secretive, a smile hovering on his thin lips. Idly, Elizabeth wondered if it had anything to do with Sir Robert Clifford's return from Flanders.

24

THE Tower of London was bitterly cold in this January of 1495. Even the royal apartments, filled to capacity since Henry's decision to hold temporary court here, oozed damp beneath the lavish hangings. The river rushed grey and dark outside, all the filth and rubbish of a great city floating on its surface; a grey-green scum slapping the sides of ships whose profusion made the Thames one of the busiest water-ways in the world. And it lapped past those dim, underground dungeons, fuller now of prisoners than they had been for many decades. For with the burgeoning of a new learning and culture centred upon that dreaded task-master, the State, had come, in natural corollary, a lessening of regard for the right of an individual conscience.

Elizabeth, staring out of her window at the murky ribbon of water, remembered how often her father and her uncles had forgiven men who had fought openly against them, because the right of personal choice was an integral part of the old Christian way of life. But in this modern world, with its fast-rising breed of new men who called themselves humanists, humanity was sadly lacking. It was unwise these days to even plot against one's King, much less to take up arms; as Sir Robert Ratcliffe and Sir Simon Mountford had discovered to their cost a month ago.

The return of Sir Robert Clifford from Flanders had been the signal for extensive arrests. Ostensibly rejecting Peter Warbeck as an impostor and throwing himself on Henry Tudor's mercy, Sir Robert had unburdened his conscience in exchange for five hundred pounds. There were many people, however, including the Queen, who were of the opinion that Clifford had always been one of Henry's agents; and, judging by the scope of his information, one of the best. As well as Mountford and Ratcliffe, Lord Daubigny had also been beheaded, while lesser men had suffered at Tyburn. Several priests and Dominican friars had been arraigned on conspiracy charges and only their cloth had saved them from death. William Worsely, the Dean of St Paul's had also been implicated, but too little could actually be proved against him: nevertheless, suspicion now clouded his life. Oh, undoubtedly, Clifford was one of Henry's best agents. And not only that, but, as was soon to be proved, an *agent provocateur*, also.

It was Margaret Pole who brought the incredible news to her cousin that Sir William Stanley had been arrested.

'Sir William Stanley!' The Queen was at first incredulous. Sir William was the brother-in-law of Henry's mother and the man who had placed Richard's battered coronet on Henry's head at Bosworth Field.

'On what charge?' she demanded of Margaret. Surely a Stanley would never jeopardise almost limitless wealth and high position to snatch at the insubstantial shadow of Peter Warbeck. The Queen signed to her cousin to sit down.

Margaret did so and they sat side-by-side, the daughters of two brothers who had once been known as the handsomest princes in Europe; long ago in those green years before doubt and deceit, treachery and betrayal had warped and discoloured the interwoven threads of their lives.

'It cannot be possible,' Elizabeth said, but Margaret was emphatic.

'My husband was present when it happened. He came straight to tell me.'

'But what is the charge?' The short winter day was drawing to its close and Elizabeth shivered. She hated this place. If she listened hard enough, she could still hear the screaming and cannonading of that summer's afternoon when the Bastard of Fauconberg had led his attack. And somewhere, in an unknown grave within these grim walls, her little brothers were buried.

Margaret was speaking. 'Sir Robert Clifford maintains that Stanley once told him that if Peter Warbeck were indeed the son of your father, he would never lift a finger against him.'

Elizabeth got up, striking her hands together. 'But the charge is so nugatory. Sir William denies it, of course?'

'No; that's just it. He admits the charge, but says that no reply is necessary to such a triviality.'

The Queen had no affection for Sir William Stanley. On the contrary, she had always hated him as the betrayer of the man whom she had loved. But time and circumstances had blunted the edge of both love and hate and she could not but admire his contemptuous defiance in the face of danger.

'Henry won't harm him,' she told Margaret confidently. 'He will imprison Sir William for a short while, just to teach him a lesson, then let him go.'

But Elizabeth was wrong, for she had forgotten two most important factors in the case. Sir William was, thanks to his plundering of King Richard's estates, the richest commoner in England; and although he was the man who had placed the crown on Henry Tudor's head, he was also one of those who, by his caution, had almost permitted Henry's death at the hands of that same Richard Plantagenet.

And so, on the fifth of February, on a bitterly cold day of hard frosts and east winds, Sir William Stanley went to his death on Tower green. Henry, moved by an unexpected pricking of his conscience, paid for the funeral expenses.

Whoever might rejoice and whoever might quail at Sir William Stanley's downfall, there was one person for whom the news of his execution did nothing but lighten her dying days.

Cicely Neville was seventy-six years of age and felt, as spring approached, that she had very little longer to live. She was glad that Berkhampstead where she had spent so much of her life, was to see its close.

'I shall be dead before the summer is out,' she told her

weeping women and cursed them for a pack of soft-hearted fools. 'Do you think that I want to survive until I'm a hundred and see that man's son King of England?'

'Your great-grandson,' they reminded her and were rated soundly for their pains.

'Arthur!' she exclaimed. 'A stupid, silly, simpering sort of a name.' The alliterative sentence was spat at them with venom. 'And a stupid, silly, simpering sort of a boy to go with it, I shouldn't wonder. None of mine or my granddaughter's making, I'll be bound.' She had forgotten for the moment that Elizabeth was the child of Elizabeth Woodville and that son whom she had renounced after his brother's death. She remembered her only as the beloved granddaughter who had stood beside her on that long-gone day, when the bodies of husband and son had been re-interred in the Collegiate Chapel at Fotheringay.

Well, a small portion, at least, of the Plantagenet and Neville blood would be inherited by the descendants of Henry Tudor and his mother; but at the thought of Margaret Beaufort, the Duchess was moved to another paroxysm of rage.

'Pious, mealy-mouthed, treacherous, little vixen,' was her slanderous summing-up of her cousin's character for the edification of her ladies, all of whom begged her, vainly, to rest. It did no good, they pointed out, to dwell on the unpleasant memories of the past. Cicely laughed. She might be dying, but the venting of her spleen brought her a curious refreshment of spirit.

'Margaret Beaufort! She was always an unpleasant creature, even as a child. Always running to tell tales behind the other children's backs. And so clever and sharp-witted that it was a wonder her tongue didn't cut her own throat. Faugh! God save me from the woman who is as learned as a man – because she's never half so clever as a woman who is not.'

Having delivered herself of this piece of philosophy which was totally at variance with much that she had preached all her life, Cicely lapsed into silence. Her ladies, thinking her asleep at last, were about to tip-toe from the room, when the voice from the bed was raised again.

'And praise God that justice has been meted out to Sir William Stanley.' She smiled. 'I never thought that I should live to see the day when the victorious curs were at each other's throats. Let us hope that Henry Tudor has enough sense to rid himself of his step-father, as well. The Earl of Derby, indeed! And why, pray? Just so that his precious wife could style herself Countess. Lord Stanley was good enough before.

It was good enough when he married a Neville, my niece. Warwick's sister!' The Duchess raised herself on one elbow and fixed her women with a basilisk stare. 'And he betrayed my nephew, Warwick, even as he betrayed my son.'

She fell back and her ladies crept silently away. She must, she told herself, be careful: she was becoming garrulous in her old-age. But as one got older, there seemed so much more to say and fewer people who were interested enough to listen.

Cicely watched the pale evening sunlight filter through the windows, bringing the faint scent of scythed grass. In two days' time, it would be June, the beginning of summer. A confusion of pictures clouded her mind; vague, shadowy figures drifted through her thoughts, never taking definite shape. Once, one emerged clearly from behind the veil of anonymity; a tall, handsome man, an archer called . . . Blackburn! Yes, that was it. There had been some scandal attached to Blackburn, but she was too tired to remember what it was.

During the night, she was restless, tossing from side to side, trying to break through that barrier to the people who beckoned from beyond. Who where they? She must know!

Then, suddenly, the mist lifted. She knew them all quite plainly, standing around her bed; her husband, her sons and daughters – and her mother, strong-minded, practical Joan Beaufort, admonishing her as she had so often done in the past.

'Time to get up,' Cicely heard her mother say, quite distinctly. 'A beautiful May morning and time to get up.'

And she got up, the funny part being that she could see herself, still lying on the bed. Even as she stretched out her hands to her mother, her ladies fell on their knees, sobbing.

For Cicely Neville, Duchess of York and mother of two kings, was dead.

Five weeks later, Peter Warbeck set sail from Antwerp with fourteen ships and some fifteen hundred men, all supplied by Margaret or Maximilian. Warbeck and his immediate entourage wore black, in mourning for his 'grandmother,' the Duchess Cicely, whose body was now buried alongside that of her husband in the Collegiate Chapel at Fotheringay.

The Dowager Duchess Margaret had been against this attempt on the south-eastern sea-board of England, but she had been overruled by Warbeck's other advisers. Was not Kent, they argued, the cradle of most English rebellions? Were not the Kentishmen, descendants of the Jutes, among the most restive and belligerent members of a nation noted for its constant dissatisfaction with the *status quo?* Margaret had, perforce, to give in, but she would commit neither men nor money to the enterprise until she had Warbeck's solemn assurance that he, himself, would not set foot upon English soil until he had tested the climate of public opinion; and, should it prove hostile, that he would sail on to Ireland.

According to his promise, therefore, on a cold, blustery July morning, Peter stayed aboard his flagship whilst officers and men from two of his other ships landed on the beach at Deal. They were met by the Sheriff of Kent, Sir John Peachey, and an apparently apathetic band of the town's inhabitants.

'Who are you and what do you want?' demanded the Sheriff, although he had a remarkably good idea of the answers to both his questions.

'We are the Duke of York's men,' replied Captain Corbett, 'and we come to claim England in his name. He is your rightful King.'

'Splendid! Splendid!' was the gratifying response. 'We are all your men. We will live and die with you. Call your comrades ashore and in the meantime I'll rouse the people of Deal to your master's standard.'

While some of the men, under the command of Captain White, rowed back to the waiting ships, the remainder were regaled with beer and cheese, brought to them by the seemingly friendly housewives.

When Sir John's message was received on board the flagship, Warbeck was with difficulty restrained from going ashore himself. But older and wiser men remembered that had Henry Tudor once gone ashore at Poole, he would not today be King of England.

And, in the event, their caution was justified. No sooner had the men from one of the other ships joined their comrades on land, than they were set upon and utterly routed by the Sheriff and an armed body of men. A hundred and twenty were killed, while many more were taken prisoner, to be dragged to London and wholesale execution.

Peter Warbeck, saddened but by no means dispirited, sailed on with the rest of his fleet to Ireland and a royal reception by Maurice, Earl of Desmond.

Henry heard the news of Warbeck's defeat whilst being entertained at one of his mother's great houses in Lancashire. He displayed no elation, merely rewarding the messenger with a little more than he might otherwise have given him. But inwardly, he was jubilant. His spies were everywhere and he was perfectly well aware that the Milanese ambassador had recently written to his master: 'The people are afraid of the King: he is not loved because he is an avaricious man. . . . If some lord of the royal blood of England were to rise up and oppose him, Henry would fare ill. . . . The people would not support the King.'

The Italian had been proved wrong. The majority of the English wanted no more civil war; they were tired of the struggle for the crown.

'When Parliament meets in October,' Henry told his step-father, 'I shall make it a part of English law that no on fighting for his King can be made a traitor by any usurper.'

He and Lord Stanley were standing on the roof of the house so that the King might admire the breathtaking panorama before him, but he had no eyes for the distant hills touched by the dying finger of the sun, nor for the magnificent sweep of the valley, patched with its clusters of trees.

Lord Stanley laughed, but it was not a pleasant sound. 'In fact,' he said, 'an exact reversal of the law which you made after Bosworth.'

'Of course!' Henry glanced contemptuously at his step-father, 'I shall make it a part of English law that no one

He stepped nearer the parapet as he spoke, feigning an interest in the view before him. He was vaguely conscious of a figure crouched in the shadows, his step-father's jester, who had been following them about. Suddenly, the man sprang forward, gripped Lord Stanley's arm and said urgently: 'Tom, remember Will.'

Henry, whose reflexes in moments of danger had always been extremely fast, withdrew from the edge almost before the meaning of the words had penetrated his brain. He looked briefly into his step-father's eyes and saw there such hatred that even he, accustomed as he was to dislike, felt shaken. Thomas Stanley would never forgive him for the death of his brother.

But neither, thought Henry cynically, after a moment's calm reflection, was Stanley ever likely to do anything about it.

25

As the year 1495 drew to its close, Jasper Tudor died at the age of sixty-five. Shortly afterwards, James the fourth of Scotland gave his answer to the proposed alliance between himself and the Princess Margaret by inviting Peter Warbeck to his court. Not content with treating the young man like a prince and bestowing upon him one hundred pounds a month, James gave Peter his own cousin, the Lady Catherine Gordon, as his wife.

This act startled not only the English court, but most western European ones as well. There were few princes who really believed in the claims of this Flemish adventurer, and many, like Ferdinand and Isabella, who openly scorned his pretensions. And Henry, grateful to the Spanish sovereigns for their support, refused all help to those Jews fleeing from the horrors of the Inquisition and seeking refuge in England.

In early March of the following year, the King again visited Bristol, and among the people whom he met was a certain Italian called John Cabot.

'You are a Venetian, I understand,' said Henry.

'A Genoese by birth, Your Grace, but a naturalised Venetian.' Cabot bowed low. 'May I have the honour to present my three sons: Ludovico, Sebastiano and Sancio.'

Henry, who, in the years of his exile, had become very sensitive to the inflections in a voice, was quick to perceive that Cabot was not over-fond of his second son, and was soon to discover the reason. Sebastiano, or, as he preferred to be known, Sebastian, was a self-opinionated, self-possessed twelve-year-old, far brighter than either of his brothers and already promulgating theories in direct opposition to his father's. Nor was he shy of contradicting Cabot in public and in the presence of the King.

'You may say what you like,' he told his parent contumaciously, 'but I am convinced that this land which we shall find in the Atlantic is not a part of Asia, but a separate continent.'

John Cabot, looking very much as though he would like to slap his son's precocious little head, silenced him with a glare and returned to his task of persuading the English King that his projected voyage of discovery would be of immense value to England.

Henry agreed. He had, in the past years, regretted his peremptory refusal to Bartholomew Columbus, and so, on March the fifth, he rectified his previous error by granting letters patent to John Cabot.

'Henry, by Grace of God, King of England and France and Lord of Ireland, to all whom these presents shall come, greeting.

'Be it known that we have given to our well-beloved John

Cabot, citizen of Venice, and to Ludovico, Sebastian and Sancio, sons of the said John, and to the heirs of every one of them and their deputies, authority to sail to all countries and seas of the West and North, under our ensign, with five ships . . . to seek out and to find isles, countries and provinces of the heathen wheresoever they be . . . which until now have been unknown to Christians.'

There was a good deal more in much the same strain, and a condition that Henry should have a fifth part of any goods or money with which they returned.

Cabot was so excited that even the news of another royal birth, that of the Princess Mary, seemed to him like an anticlimax. But the Bristolians were delighted and sped their King on his way with vociferous cheering. The scent of money and of discovery was in their nostrils, and they had no time to waste before building and fitting out those ships which Cabot so urgently needed.

A month prior to his visit to Bristol, Henry had completed an agreement with Duke Philip of Burgundy and his father, Maximilian. It was primarily a commercial treaty to restore the free flow of trade between England and Flanders, but it also contained a clause which stipulated that neither country should offer shelter to the rebels of the other.

In July of the same year, 1496, the King joined the Holy League, an alliance between the Vatican, Milan, Venice, Spain and the Hapsburg dominions, directed against France. But as Henry made it perfectly clear that he had no intention of actually taking up arms against his French neighbours, unless goaded to it, Charles the eighth also remained his friend.

In consequence, almost every European door was now closed against Peter Warbeck and his Scottish allies. James the fourth's bid to marry the Infanta Juana of Spain was rapidly and effectively repulsed by the simple expedient of making her the wife of that beautiful young man, Duke Philip.

Thoroughly enraged, James professed more faith than ever in his now somewhat embarrassing guest, and in the autumn of 1496 mounted a full-scale invasion of England on the pretender's behalf.

'More money,' Henry snarled to John Morton.

He was all but forty years of age and looked older. The Cardinal surmised that it was not so much the cares of kingship which sat heavily upon Henry, but the fear of losing them. Those years of exile haunted Henry Tudor's every thought and influenced his every action. He was missing his uncle, too, more than he cared to admit, even to himself. Jasper had been a link with his youth and however bitter the past, it was, nevertheless, an integral part of his life. And, at forty, Henry was becoming aware of the need to say: 'Do you remember?' Now, there was no one who could answer his questions.

Morton was conscious of Henry's unhappiness, but could not divine its cause. He could, however, predict its consequence. In misery, men turned to a variety of palliatives – women, food, drink. But Henry Tudor consoled himself by amassing yet more money: it was the only way he knew to make himself feel safe.

The cost of this new war against the Scots, coming as it did upon Henry's costly reinforcement of the Navy – the *Harry Grace a Dieu,* alone was valued at fourteen thousand pounds – could only have one end. The King confirmed this.

'When Parliament meets in the New Year,' he told Morton, 'I shall demand increased taxation.'

The new levies and subsidies were deeply resented throughout the country, but nowhere more so than in the south-western counties. To the people living there, Scotland and the north of England were so remote that it was like asking them to pay for a war in a foreign country. Bitterness and unrest were rife everywhere, but, for once, the men of Bristol were too busy with their own affairs to spare more than a passing grumble for the increase in taxation. Their thoughts were riveted upon the possible riches that John Cabot might bring back, and the boost to their trade.

On a bright, clear morning in early May, Cabot stood on the deck of his ship, *The Matthew,* and regarded the cheering crowds on the quay. He looked at the sea of faces; those swarthy Bristol faces with their curious blend of artfulness and ignorance, apathy and acute self-interest. They were a strange people, thought the Venetian, with the ox-like strength of their Saxon forebears and the fox-like cunning of their Welsh neighbours across the Bristol Channel. But he loved them, as much for their arrogance and greed as for their generosity and vision; as much for that most peculiar of English vices, pride in their own shortcomings, as for that most peculiar of English virtues, embarrassment at their own good deeds.

His friend, the Sheriff, Richard Ameryk, embraced him before going ashore.

'If you find a new country, Giovanni,' he said, laughing, 'I solemnly charge you to name it after me.'

Cabot smiled and raised his voice a little above the celebratory clamour of the bells.

'I have often wondered . . . it's not an English name, surely?' He was tentative. One had to be so careful with these English.

But Ameryk, unoffended, shook his head. 'It's Welsh,' he said. 'My father was called ap Meryk, but with the English passion for shortening words. . . . ' He left the rest of the sentence to speak for itself and they both laughed again.

There was a final embrace, then the Sheriff clambered ashore. The people screamed and cheered, and the ships glided slowly down river and into the Bristol Channel.

The citizens dispersed to their homes and, during the next few days, suffered from the anti-climax following any great event. In consequence, they had time to give fresh thoughts to their financial affairs. Even now, however, they were so excited at the prospect of Cabot's return, that they could summon up no really deep resentment against the government. But merchants and beggars and itinerant friars, coming from other parts of the region, had a different tale to tell. Somerset and Devon were in a ferment, but nowhere were the disturbances so alarming as in the wilds of Celtic Cornwall.

The Cornish were normally a tolerant race, especially towards the foibles and follies of human nature. This sprang from an unexpressed, almost unconscious conviction that anyone who was not Cornish was to be pitied and might as well be mad or eccentric as anything else. But like all people possessed of a strong measure of forbearance, they could eventually be pushed too far and, when roused, were a force to be reckoned with. Inarticulate themselves, they needed someone who could put their thoughts and feelings into words and, on this occasion, the hour had produced two men who were able to speak Cornish and English fluently: Thomas Flammock, a lawyer, and Michael Joseph, a farmer, both of Bodmin.

On Bodmin Moor, Joseph addressed the huge mass of people gathered together from all over Cornwall, in their native Cornish.

'Men of Kernou,' he shouted, 'are we going to allow ourselves to be ground to powder because of a small commotion made by the Scots, which, so I hear, has already been settled?'

His words, carried on the summer breeze and passed by word of mouth to the outermost perimeter of the vast, human assembly, were greeted with an earth-shattering yell of: 'No!'

'It is not the King who is to blame,' Flammock informed

them, 'but his counsellors. Is the King not one of us? Is he not descended from Arthur, whose mother, Igerne, came forth from Gorlois' hall, here in this fair land of Kernou, to be the wife of Uther, the Pendragon of Britain? We will go to London! We will put our case before the King. He who is our kinsman will surely not refuse us his ear.'

If there were those who considered this assessment of the situation to be met with in London as over-optimistic, no voice was raised in protest and the amorphous mass of labourers, farmers and miners set out on the two-hundred-mile journey to the capital.

To the Cornishmen, the majority of whom had never been beyond the confines of their own villages, this was an incredible adventure. They stared in amazement at the vast wilderness of South Devon and gazed in awe upon the Flowering Thorn of Glastonbury, that ancient cradle of Christianity which their forefathers had known as Ynys Gutrin. At Wells, they were honoured by the presence of the rash and aggrieved James Touchet, the young Lord Audley, who placed himself confidently at their head and proceeded to harangue them in the market-place; only to find that his audience was dwindling away.

'Where have the fools gone?' he demanded angrily of Flammock.

But the fools – or as many of them as the outraged monks would allow – had crowded into the Cathedral to look at the most marvellous piece of machinery they had ever seen; a clock whose face showed the sun and the stars and the phases of the moon, and whose little knights fought each other on horseback every time the hour was struck.

A more wonderful sight, however, was the walls and church towers of London which they viewed from Blackheath in the middle of June. But their spirits were low. Not only had the men of Kent refused to join them, sending rude messages to these outlandish west-countrymen as they had encamped about Farnham, but their King, the descendant of Arthur, seemed curiously indifferent to the voices of his kinsmen. London was in a state of siege and Henry Tudor was sending an army against them, led by Rhys ap Thomas and Lord Daubeney.

On a summer's evening as dismal as their prospects, in their tent beneath the dripping trees, the three leaders held agitated council.

'We must withdraw,' said Flammock. His face was an unpleasant putty-colour and runnels of sweat furrowed the dirt on his forehead. 'We cannot fight them. All our men have are crowbills and scythes.'

'And courage,' declared Audley in a ringing voice.

'One brave man,' observed Michael Joseph sententiously, 'is worth ten cowards.'

'Which is to say,' snapped Flammock, 'that the King's army is made up of cowards. I don't believe it. We came to speak peacefully to the King. If we can't do that, it were better to go home.'

'No!' said Joseph and Audley as one man.

'You'll regret it,' warned the lawyer, and he was right.

Towards evening on Saturday, the seventeenth of June, the royal army, now augmented by the Earls of Oxford and Essex and a very reluctant Edmund de la Pole, Earl of Suffolk – his father's dukedom had been denied him as a result of his brother, Lincoln's treachery – crept out of London and surrounded the unsuspecting Cornishmen. The first attack almost demoralised them, but, with incredible bravery, they rallied and fought back with such ferocity that Daubeney was captured and hundreds of his men felled by their enemies' primitive weapons.

But the advantage thus obtained could not last: the superiority of armour and fighting skill was bound to tell. Before it became necessary for Henry, commanding the reserve, to move his forces into action, it was over. The Cornish were routed and the massacre lasted far into the night. More than fifteen hundred of them died, and their three leaders were taken; Audley to suffer execution on Tower Hill, Flammock and Joseph to die traitor's deaths at Tyburn.

The quarters of their mutilated bodies were sent to be nailed over the gates of Cornwall's principal towns, a gruesome and horrible warning, which, it was hoped, the inhabitants would be quick to heed.

26

In August, the court was at Woodstock, entertaining the Spanish envoys who had come for the proxy betrothal of Prince Arthur and the Infanta Catalina. Also at court, and attracting far more attention than the Spaniards, was the silk-clad figure of John Cabot. A fellow Venetian wrote home proudly that:

'The English run after him like mad men. He is called the Great Admiral and is paid every honour.'

Elizabeth, seated beside her husband, listened with interest to the things which the explorer had to say, but felt, when he had finished, that Cabot's achievements hardly warranted the extravagant acclaim with which he had been greeted. He had indeed discovered land, but the sight of snares and needles for making nets some little way inshore, coupled with that of felled trees, had sent him and his men scurrying for the safety of the *Matthew*.

'You saw no sign of the inhabitants, then?' enquired Henry.

'Alas, Your Highness, no! With only one ship and crew, we dared not risk an encounter. These people are doubtless very ferocious; probably the subjects of the Grand Khan.'

'And these other two islands which you say that you saw on your way home, you did not land?'

Cabot spread his arms, his wide silk sleeves rippling in the light. 'Perhaps on the next voyage, who knows? Our supplies were limited. We could not spare the time.'

The King seemed satisfied and ordered a grant of ten pounds to be paid to 'him that has found the new isle.'

Cabot had not, after all, called his discovery by the name of his friend. Ameryk, preferring the simpler and more direct Newfoundland. He hoped that Henry would grant him permission for yet another voyage, but was shrewd enough to see that this was not the moment for broaching the subject: the King was plainly preoccupied.

King James was ravaging over the Border again, bringing with him his great siege-gun, 'Mons Meg,' and although the Earl of Surrey was more than likely to put him to rout, it was the implications of these present raids that seriously worried Henry and his advisers. For Peter Warbeck had, earlier in the summer, returned to Ireland.

'These forays are mere distractions,' Morton said, as he paced Woodstock's gardens by Henry's side. As he spoke, he could not help but remember how, in similar circumstances, King Edward used to lay his arm across his counsellor's shoulders, the easy familiarity making the most solemn occasion convivial. But Henry disliked physical contacts; he kept his body, like his mind, to himself.

The sunlight lay hot and still about them and overhead a bird called shrilly to its mate. Their shadows bobbed in front, to the side, behind; now long and emaciated, now grotesque and squat, as they turned first one way, then another, along the winding paths.

'Distractions for Warbeck,' the King concurred, then added: 'He must strike soon. Six years this charade has gone on and still I cannot get to grips with him.'

There was a hint of panic in Henry's voice which the Cardinal was quick to detect. He smiled to himself. It was reassuring to know that this self-contained young man – forty years of age was still young to a man of seventy-seven – could feel uncertainty and fear.

'You will come to grips soon enough now,' he soothed. 'Warbeck and his supporters know as well as anyone that his time is running out. The governments of Europe are tired of him. If he is what he claims to be, why does he not make a push to seize his kingdom? He cannot go on any longer drifting from one European court to another, living off his pretensions. Even the Irish are becoming desperate, thanks to Your Grace's foresight.'

Henry glanced swiftly at the Cardinal-Archbishop, but Morton's face betrayed only respect. All the same, Henry knew that Morton considered himself equally responsible for the state of affairs in Ireland. It had been on his advice that Henry had sent Sir Edward Poynings to that troublesome island and Poynings' new laws had brought the Pale more firmly under English domination than it had been for centuries. And this was an added incentive to the Geraldine chieftains to see their protégé upon the English throne, and that as soon as possible. Yes; certainly Warbeck must strike in the very near future.

'But where?' murmured Morton, diplomatically giving his sovereign the opportunity to supply the correct answer.

Henry snorted, and 'Cornwall!' was his trenchant reply.

Cornwall was still in a state of unrest, particularly around Bodmin, for the cause of the late, ill-fated rebellion, the subsidy, had not been removed.

Peter Warbeck landed at Whitsands Bay, near Land's End, on September the seventh and, leaving his wife on St Michael's Mount, proceeded northwards with his Irish troops, gathering the Cornish to his standard as he went. At Bodmin, he proclaimed himself King Richard the fourth and issued a declaration concerning his 'uncle,' Richard the third.

'Although desirous of ruling our land, in all other actions he was noble and loved his country and the welfare of his people.'

By September the seventeenth, Peter was at Exeter, but the gates were barred against him. The Earl of Devon was firmly entrenched behind its walls, together with most of the local nobility – a fact which was as disturbing to Warbeck as his lack of armaments and men. Not one person of note had joined him, and his spies in London told the same story: Buckingham, Daubeney, Sir Willoughby de Broke had all hastened to lay their services at Henry Tudor's disposal, for no one really believed in the identity of this pretender.

Whilst in Flanders, Peter and the Duchess Margaret had tried to enlist the support of Sir James Tyrrell, but the Governor of Guisnes Castle had simply laughed.

'I know that you're an impostor,' he had told Warbeck scathingly. 'I saw the real Duke of York after he was dead. Oh, I know what you'll tell me: that you were not truly dead; that somehow you miraculously recovered, and King Richard hid you for fear of further attempts on your life. Well, I don't believe it and neither will anyone else. Other people may not be as certain as I am that you're a fake, but let there be the smallest doubt and no Englishman of importance will support you. To risk his life, a man has to believe in what he is prepared to die for.'

And so, as Peter found himself isolated with his wild Irish and Cornish men, his belief in his destiny, never very strong, faded. Yet even so, he would not go down without a fight. He could have escaped then, before the royal army arrived from London, but there was that in his nature which forbade his abandoning his followers to their fate. This young Fleming had an innate dignity and responsibility which, together with his looks, had made him a natural choice for the part he had been called upon to perform. And now, in this moment of crisis, he also displayed courage and a talent for improvisation. Having no artillery, he ordered the felling of trees. While some of his men created a diversion by scaling the walls, others used the hastily made battering-rams against the eastern gate. Scythes and axes were also used in an effort to break down the massive timbers. When these attempts failed, Warbeck ordered piles of branches and dried grass to be heaped against the gate and lit.

The wood was at last burned through, but defeated its object by making it as impossible for the invaders to burst through the ring of flames as it was for the defenders to get out. Reluctantly Peter abandoned the siege and withdrew his decimated army in the direction of Taunton, but the news that the King was already at Wells finally convinced him that his cause was lost. Without properly equipped troops he could do nothing; the invasion had been doomed before ever it had begun.

Tearfully disbanding his army, he rode for Southampton and there, unable to find a ship to carry him to France, made for the sanctuary at Beaulieu.

Peter Warbeck rode captive through the streets of London, while the Londoners screamed abuse.

'Son of a Jew,' somebody yelled, and his tired, confused mind tried to grapple with this strange insult. Why did they call him that? Neither of his parents was Jewish. Then he remembered Sir Edward Brampton in whose house he had once lived. Peter had almost forgotten that Brampton had been of Jewish birth.

The crowds pushed closer, jostling him and his frightened horse, a sorry nag that reared its head in terror. His guards laughed, calling him King Perkin in derision. Ever since his attempt to escape from Beaulieu, his life had become a nightmare. He had been caught and dragged to Taunton to the King. There, he had made a full and frank confession about his birth, parentage and state, and had been brought back to the capital in Henry's triumphant wake. What would happen to him now, he wondered; what had the English King in store?

Truth to tell, Henry was in a dilemma. No sooner had he clapped eyes on Peter Warbeck than the fears which had haunted him these past six years had faded into insubstantial shadows. Why the sight of this boy should so convince him that he was not the Duke of York, son of Edward the fourth, Henry did not know. The young man had looks, manners, breeding, but the two latter were indefinably false; a carefully acquired veneer which, if once cracked, would peel away to reveal the hardy peasant underneath. And Henry, despising his terrors, thirsted for revenge: he wanted Peter Warbeck's life in exchange for the loss of his self-esteem. Unfortunately, the boy was a foreigner and, as such, could not be accounted a traitor. The most that Henry could do was to keep him in custody, separated from the wife he adored.

Catherine Gordon was brought to Sheen and made one of Elizabeth's ladies-in-waiting. The Queen was sorry for her, for she was plainly in great distress, but Elizabeth remarked sapiently to her sister, Cicely: 'Whatever Catherine may say now, she will marry again. She is the marrying kind.'

Lady Welles eyed her sister sharply. 'You talk as though Warbeck were dead.'

The Queen smiled and shifted uncomfortably in her chair. She was six months' pregnant and feeling hot in spite of the

December cold. Soon it would be Christmas and her sisters had joined her for the seasonal festivities. Cicely was twenty-nine now, two years younger than Elizabeth. It was hard to believe that this quiet, rather repressed woman had once been the headstrong, extrovert girl whom Elizabeth remembered so well. Cicely's childless marriage to a man many years her senior had been the catalyst.

Anne, now twenty-two, the wife of Lord Thomas Howard, Surrey's son, looked up. She, too, was so far childless, but seemed happier than Cicely.

'Elizabeth is right,' she said. 'Catherine Gordon is not the celibate type. She grieves intensely and loves the same way. She would not make a satisfactory widow if – and I only say if – Warbeck were to die at any time.'

The Princess Katherine, who, at eighteen, bade fair to rival her grandmother Neville's celebrated beauty, and was the wife of William Courtenay, the son of the Earl of Devon, got clumsily to her feet, for she was also pregnant. Her tender heart had been deeply touched by the plight of Catherine Gordon, and the fact that her father-in-law had, in no small measure, been responsible for Warbeck's overthrow, made her feel guilty. She did not like to dwell upon the possibility of Peter's death.

'I have had a letter from Bridget,' she said, changing the subject. 'She will take her final vows very soon now.'

'A nun!' exclaimed Cicely, going over to warm her hands at the fire. 'Well, Bridget always was a pious little soul. But the Queen of England's sister a nun! What does Henry say about it?'

Elizabeth hesitated, then said, almost furtively: 'He approves. It will, after all, save him much of the cost of her dowry. The nuns at Dartford are unlikely to drive so hard a bargain as a husband.'

There was silence, broken only by the crackle of the fire. Then Cicely gave an incredulous little laugh. Never before had she heard her eldest sister venture even an oblique criticism of the man whom she had been forced to take as her husband. What had happened to Elizabeth? Was it that she was getting older and felt more secure? Or was she poking gentle fun at a person for whom she felt a measure of affection? Lady Welles could not make up her mind.

Sitting beside her sister, she began to talk, but, as always, any attempt to probe her relationship with Henry had the effect of making Elizabeth withdraw inside herself. It was a subtle and complicated emotion, this feeling for her husband, held by the tenuous threads of a mutual affection for their children, and based on a fear that the great love of her life had been evil; an incestuous passion that must be expurgated by channelling it in a less dangerous direction. But what had begun as a purely artificial emotion, as brittle and as fragile as a glass butterfly, now had, on occasions, the flashing and brilliant hue of the genuine article. Elizabeth did not love Henry and never would do so, but twelve years of marriage and its attendant intimacies had engendered a warmth rather than a cooling; a drawing together rather than an estrangement.

But here, at Sheen, she had felt that delicate, carefully tended affection wavering in the balance. A sudden and startlingly vivid recollection of her uncle, connected with the old palace, had destroyed her peace of mind and made her acutely aware of Henry's many imperfections, not least the way he tacitly condoned every foul-mouthed slander that could be heaped upon the name of Richard Plantagenet. It was only when she reminded herself of Henry's lonely and unhappy childhood and the long years of captivity in Brittany that Elizabeth experienced a return of something like her former state of mind. All the same, she would be glad to leave Sheen for Westminster and felt, as she rode away from it on a grey, late December day, that she would be happy never to see it again: it held too many best-forgotten memories.

She had her wish. On the morning of the twenty-second of December, her ladies woke her with the news that the Palace of Sheen had been razed to the ground by fire during the night.

27

THE destruction of Sheen was welcomed by Henry as well as Elizabeth but for an entirely different reason. It was not that the King had particularly disliked the palace, but it gave him the opportunity to indulge one of his favourite pastimes; the planning and refurbishing of his many properties. And in this, he was joined by that other indefatigable builder, John Morton.

Since Henry's accession, he had re-surfaced Greenwich Palace, enlarged Westminster, improved Eltham, practically re-built Baynard's Castle and erected a poor-house on the site of Gaunt's old palace of the Savoy. For his eldest son he was building Tickenhall in Worcestershire; was re-planning Westminster Abbey; and six years earlier, had put up two large breweries at Portsmouth, thus earning for himself the undying gratitude of the inhabitants and of all the thirsty sailors who passed in and out of the town.

Morton had kept pace with his master. He had repaired and extended his palace at Canterbury and also his residences at Maidstone, Charing and Aldington Park. He had started Hatfield House, repaired Rochester bridge and put a superb roof on the nave of the church in his native Bere Regis. In Norfolk, he had brought the fens under cultivation and now joined enthusiastically with Henry in planning the great house which should replace Sheen. Both men were agreed on a change of name and it was the Cardinal who sauvely suggested Richmond; the earldom held by Henry's father and, later, by Henry himself. The King was pleased and, with his father still in mind, christened the son born to him and Elizabeth in March, Edmund.

This baby was less than a month old when news reached England of the death of Charles the eighth of France and the succession of Louis the twelfth, a young man who, with his country's interests in view, obtained a hurried divorce from his wife and married the widowed Anne of Brittany.

Henry's own matrimonial schemes for his children were beginning to show signs of fruition. In February, Ferdinand and Isabella had ratified the marriage treaty between Arthur and Catalina, while James of Scotland had at last been persuaded to look upon the proposed alliance with the Princess Margaret in a favourable light.

In May, Cabot set out on his second voyage, having first entranced his royal patron with the prospect of limitless wealth from the territories of the Grand Khan, and, as high summer drew on, Henry had every reason to feel complacent. Life was finally settling into a recognisable pattern and with the acceptance of his leadership both at home and abroad, came a sense of security hitherto lacking. But it was Henry Tudor's fate never to be left in peace for long: two events happened in quick succession, both equally disturbing.

The first was Peter Warbeck's escape from the Tower, an item of news brought to Henry as he sat in his bath, by the unfortunate Richard Fox. The fragrant spices made the Bishop sneeze and through his watering eyes he saw the cold, set face of the King.

'When and how did this happen?'

'Last night, Your Grace, at midnight. It is thought that he bribed his gaolers.'

'I have no wish to know what is thought,' Henry said witheringly. 'I want to know exactly what took place. Find out!'

He looked at Fox's sullen features and recalled the younger man of Brittany. Good living, the King reflected, had impaired a character whose usefulness to his Sovereign had lain in a needle-sharp mind. This man with his slightly swelling paunch was but half the man whom the impoverished exile had known.

As Henry heaved himself angrily out of the scented water, it did not occur to him that his own failing health could cloud his judgements, nor did he think of himself as an ailing man. But the truth was that the strain imposed upon his slender body by the long, incessant fight to keep his crown, had vitiated a constitution which had never been robust. His disinclination for hunting and tennis were as much a sign of his physical deterioration as his thinning hair and rotting teeth.

Fox did not return. It was the wily Morton who brought the pleasanter tidings that Warbeck had been recaptured, hiding in a Carthusian monastery near the burnt-out palace of Sheen. Henry regarded his Chancellor with an unspoken question in his myopic blue eyes, but the Cardinal Archbishop regretfully shook his head.

'We cannot put him to death for that,' he said. 'It was merely a bid for freedom by a man who, as a foreigner, is still nothing more than a political prisoner. No treason was involved.'

Henry rubbed his back where it was aching and looked speculatively into the fire. In spite of the June weather it was cold and a fierce, dry wind had blown all day, bringing down the rose petals in a shower of red and white.

'But if treason were involved. . . . ' His voice trailed away and Morton smiled.

'Ah, now that would be different. A bid, for example, to put not himself but . . . shall we say Clarence's son on the throne?'

Henry raised his eyes from the contemplation of the fire. 'Two birds with one stone, in fact.'

The Cardinal nodded. 'As you say. . . . '

The brief phrases died. There was a moment's silence while the wind moaned about Westminster Palace and whipped the trees into a frenzy. The clamour of the city was faint today, a thin quiver of sound in the distance.

'Let Warbeck have a taste of the stocks before he is returned to the Tower,' Henry advised. 'Make him repeat the confession he made to me at Taunton.'

'And when he returns to the Tower?' prompted Morton.

'I think . . . yes, a change of rooms. Let him have some companionship. Move him closer to the Earl of Warwick.'

Morton smiled with complete understanding and went on his way to attend to these matters.

Before summer had faded into autumn, however, trouble had flared in another quarter. Edmund de la Pole, Earl of Suffolk, as wild as his brothers, Richard and William, were quiet, killed a man in a tavern brawl in Cheapside and was arrested by the Officers of the Watch.

Henry raged inwardly. Not only was Suffolk first cousin to his wife, but, after Clarence's son, the next male heir in the Yorkist line of succession. With plans fermenting in his head for the Earl of Warwick's execution, Henry felt that he dare not use this heaven-sent opportunity to rid himself of Edmund de la Pole. Two such judicial murders so close together would look too obvious and it was absolutely essential that Edward Plantagenet should die. It would dispose of the Yorkists' main hope and placate Ferdinand and Isabella who, through their ambassador, De Puebla, were expressing doubts of the Tudor dynasty's stability as long as that unfortunate young man remained alive.

So Edmund de la Pole was tried and convicted by the King's Bench instead of the Star Chamber, and Henry granted him a pardon. Suffolk, however, far from being grateful, considered himself disgracefully ill-used and resented the fact that he had been taken into custody at all.

'It was an accident and everyone knew it,' he said, airing his grievances around London and refusing to retire quietly to his estates. 'I am the cousin of the Queen and, as such, should never have been arrested in the first place.'

A year of such petty annoyances was crowned for Henry by the disappearance of Cabot's ship somewhere in the vast uncharted deeps of the Atlantic. And, with John Cabot, went the dream of the Grand Khan's treasure.

The New Year began no more auspiciously than the old. Another 'feigned boy' arose in the person of Ralph Wilford, a cordwainer's son from Bishopsgate, claiming to be the Earl of Warwick and trained by an Augustinian friar, Father Patrick.

The people, however, were growing used to Henry's rule: they might grumble about taxation, but after fourteen years of peace no one wanted a return of the civil wars. The plot failed for lack of support, and by the end of February Wilford had been hanged and Father Patrick imprisoned for life.

Nevertheless, the incident – for it was little more – confirmed Henry in his determination to rid himself of the Earl of Warwick. Moreover, De Puebla was emphatic..

'If the proxy marriage of Prince Arthur and the Infanta is to take place in May,' he told Morton, 'my sovereigns must have the assurance of the Earl of Warwick's death.'

The Cardinal Archbishop smiled. 'It is . . . being arranged.'

The Spaniard looked long and thoughtfully at the ageing, clever face before him and then nodded. He was satisfied that Morton would do what was necessary and wrote accordingly to Ferdinand and Isabella.

And so, on Whit Sunday, the nineteenth of May, at Bewdley in Worcestershire, De Puebla stood as proxy for the Infanta Catalina and exchanged vows with Prince Arthur, now thirteen years old. Privately he thought that the boy did not seem at all strong and wished that he had the constitution of his younger brother, Henry, a bouncing eight-year-old. The latter, too, was far more popular than Arthur, a fact which the Spaniard was quick to attribute to young Henry's uncanny resemblance to his maternal grandfather, Edward the fourth. He had the same blond hair, the same big frame. 'And the same roving eye for the women,' as De Puebla remarked drily to one of his friends.

'And his father intends him for the Church,' was the sardonic reply, which made the ambassador chuckle.

Yes; perhaps it was as well that Henry was not the one to marry the Infanta. The morals of a true grandson of Edward the fourth would never suit a daughter of Isabella the Catholic.

Elizabeth, watching her second son enchant the visitors at his brother's proxy wedding, still felt troubled about Henry. Young as he was, she was already aware of a streak of cruelty in him which had not manifested itself in her father until his later years. This, allied to a certain rigidity of thought, inherited from Margaret Beaufort, and a conscious rectitude which was entirely his own, made the Duke of York a very dangerous young boy to cross; the more dangerous in that these faults were buried deep beneath the outer layers of charm. Few people as yet had the insight to penetrate that outer crust – certainly not Desiderius Erasmus when a month later, he visited the royal children at Eltham in the company of his friend, Thomas More.

Elizabeth was seated with her children in the great hall when the two men entered, and she rose immediately to greet them. More was a good deal younger than his companion whom the Queen judged to be in his early thirties; a thin, frail man with an extremely hesitant manner and a tendency to blush fierily whenever he thought himself insulted, which was often.

'And how do you like our country?' Elizabeth enquired upon More's informing her that this was his friend's first visit to England.

Erasmus bowed. 'So much so that I have written to my friend, Fausto Andrelini, in Paris, telling him that if he but knew the blessings of this land, he would put wings on his feet and fly here. Also,' he lowered his voice confidentially, 'I love the English woman's habit of kissing everyone she meets.' As soon as he had said this he became flustered and stared fiercely at his feet, while the colour surged into his pallid face.

'You are not the first stranger to remark favourably upon that particular custom,' the Queen said easily. 'And now you must meet my children.'

The baby, Edmund, was too small to attract any attention and lay placidly in the arms of his nurse. But Henry, dragging the four-year-old Mary by the hand, his elder sister, Margaret, following, came forward at once and pushed a scrubby paper into Erasmus' hand.

'A poem,' he announced. 'For you! I wrote it. You may keep it if you like.' He smiled, his most enchanting smile. 'I shall expect something which you have written in return though.'

Erasmus, overwhelmed, bowed and backed away, cursing More under his breath for not having warned him what to expect.

'I wasn't to know,' hissed the younger man. 'Say that you will send him something in a few days' time.'

'You'll have to lend me the money for pen and ink,' was the muttered reply and More raised resigned eyebrows. He was becoming accustomed to Erasmus' cadging ways.

Elizabeth, an amused spectator of this little scene, was diverted by a touch on her arm. Turning, she found her aunt, Catherine Woodville, at her elbow.

'Have you heard the latest gossip?' enquired the Dowager Duchess and, when the Queen shook her head, went on: 'Your cousin, Edmund de la Pole, has run away again, this time to Guisnes. He's staying there as the guest of Sir James Tyrrell.'

Elizabeth looked grave. Henry would never forgive Tyrrell for this.

The Queen was correct in her assumption. Not all Tyrrell's assurances of his good faith, nor even the fact that Edmund de la Pole eventually returned to England, could repair the damage done to Henry's trust in King Richard's former Master of the Henchmen. Henry's trust was extended towards people only so long as they earned it. One slip, one deviation from the straight and narrow path of his service, was neither forgotten nor forgiven. The Governor of Guisnes Castle had not learned sufficiently well the lesson of Sir William Stanley.

But Tyrrell could wait. Henry's most pressing problem was the disposal of Warwick and Warbeck.

'Claymound knows what he must do?' the King asked tersely of Morton.

'He is one of our best agents.' Morton sat down in compliance with a sign from Henry. He was feeling his age today; his body refused to behave itself, sending sharp little messages to his brain that all was not well. 'Claymound has persuaded Warwick that he will soon be executed in any case, and might as well attempt an escape now. Not a difficult task, he tells me. The boy is . . . young for his age.'

'Simple?' enquired Henry and he knew a totally unexpected qualm of conscience.

'Fourteen years of imprisonment have not . . . improved him, shall I say?' Morton shifted. That pain in his left knee was an old friend, but this dull ache in his hip was something entirely new.

'And Warbeck?'

'He will clutch at any straw to escape. I have instructed that he and Warwick be allowed to spend some part of each day together: that will establish collusion. Warbeck, although he doesn't know it, is now involved in a plot to put Clarence's son on the throne.'

'Evidence?'

'Claymound has told Warwick that if he gives him a wooden image that once belonged to the late Duke of Clarence, it will ensure him sanctuary at Westminster after the escape. In actual fact it will prove Warwick's complicity in the plot.'

Henry said nothing. Through the window he watched the autumn leaves drift slowly to the ground, harbingers of winter and of death. Winter would mean that he, Henry Tudor, had sat for more than fourteen years on the English throne; death, Warwick's death, would mean that he might sit yet another fourteen years in even greater safety.

Suddenly the King got up, pacing about the room, and Morton stared at him in amazement. It was the first time that he had ever seen Henry display that outward agitation of body which betokened inner perturbation of the mind.

Henry himself was utterly confused by his emotions. His uncle Jasper had once told him, in a moment of exasperation, that he was a 'cold fish' and Henry had accepted it as a fair estimate of his character. He had often thought that he was devoid of conscience in so far as he could do those things necessary to hold his own without any great qualm or soul-searching. His own opinion of himself was all that mattered to him, and so it had always been for as long as he could remember.

Perhaps that was the trouble now. He had provoked Sir William Stanley to his death and regarded him as fair game. But there was something about this present plot – the duping of an innocent boy, retarded by his own ill-treatment, and a young man who had largely been a pawn in other and more ambitious hands – that stuck in his throat. Nevertheless, it had to be, for the sake of the Tudor dynasty. If that frail plant were to survive, it had to be grafted on to older and more established stock. And so, if Spain made provisos they must be honoured.

It was late October when the escape from the Tower was contrived and mid-November when Warwick and Warbeck went to their deaths; Warbeck at Tyburn and Warwick, still bewildered, to the block and the axe on Tower Hill.

It was the end of the year. And the end of a century.

28

It was just over a hundred years since Henry of Bolingbroke had deposed and murdered his cousin, King Richard the second, and so plunged England into decades of schism and civil war. There had been uneasy peace under Henry Tudor for fourteen years, but, as men pointed out to one another in the ale-houses and the taverns, this was only two years longer than the period between Edward the fourth's return from Burgundy in 1471 and his death in 1483. Even now there were many people who regarded the Tudors as a temporary phenomenon and who still speculated on Henry's successor when he should die: Prince Arthur's peaceful succession was by no means regarded as certain.

Henry, always conscious of the need to underline his position, decided that the old forms of regal address, Your Grace and Your Highness, were no longer suitable, and that the more awesome Your Majesty should be substituted instead. This should be sufficient to remind anyone, when approaching Henry Tudor, that he was indeed speaking to his sovereign-lord.

The instability of the Tudor dynasty, however, was soon to be demonstrated by two serious misfortunes, the first of which occurred in June whilst Henry and Elizabeth were in Calais, entertaining Philip of Burgundy.

It was a glittering occasion, a reconciliation between the two rulers now that Peter Warbeck was dead. Not that Philip had ever been a really serious supporter of that unfortunate young man, but his father and the Dowager Duchess Margaret had dabbled incessantly in English political affairs to Henry's discomfiture, and Philip was now determined to end this situation. A complete resumption of trade between the two countries was the outcome of the talks, and the company could then devote themselves whole-heartedly to the lavish entertainments provided by the English.

'How is my aunt? Elizabeth enquired of Duke Philip as he led her out to dance.

The Duke laughed. 'Always active. A true Plantagenet.' It was a guarded reply. Philip was conscious of Henry Tudor within ear-shot and he had no wish to offend again this man whom he regarded as one of Europe's cleverest statesmen. He changed the subject.

'Who is the young man who looks at us with such disapproval?' he enquired and Elizabeth followed the direction of his gaze.

'That is my mother-in-law's new chaplain, John Fisher. A very clever man, or so I've been told.'

'He does not look to be of the most convivial,' Philip observed and Elizabeth was bound to agree.

'I know what you mean,' she answered. 'There is something about him, perhaps his solemnity, that makes me feel that he will always be the bearer of bad tidings.'

Afterwards, it seemed as though she had had a premonition, for it was Fisher, acting on instructions from Margaret Beaufort, who broke the news to her of the young Prince Edmund's death. The sweating sickness was rife in England and the two-year-old child had succumbed after the briefest of illnesses.

If Elizabeth's grief went deep, Henry's went deeper, for his sorrow was tinged with fear. As, two weeks later, he watched his youngest son's body laid to rest near the shrine of Edward the Confessor, he could not rid himself of the conviction that this was God's punishment on him for the death of the Earl of Warwick. He confided his fears to John Morton.

'Nonsense!' exclaimed Morton bracingly. Now in his eightieth year, he was permitted liberties of speech which Henry allowed to no one else. 'Warwick was executed on a charge of high treason: attempted escape with a view to making himself King of England in Your Majesty's place.'

'I have heard it called . . . something else,' Henry reponded dourly.

Morton was frankly incredulous. 'Not,' he expostulated, 'in Your Majesty's presence, surely?'

'I know what's muttered behind my back,' the King said coldly; but realised only too well that it was really what he, himself, had thought in the secret recesses of his mind.

'This execution,' the Cardinal Archbishop replied, slightly stressing the last word, 'was a necessary . . . evil, if you must, but of vital importance to your sons. And Your Majesty still has two of those and will beget more. Their welfare must be your primary concern.'

Henry was moved, most unexpectedly, to clasp Morton's arm. It was good to have this counsellor and friend who always knew so well what his sovereign required him to say.

But the comfort of Morton's presence was soon to be denied to Henry, for the new century wanted none of him. On September the fifteenth, 1500, at Knowle in Kent, the Cardinal Archbishop died.

'I do not like that young man,' snorted Margaret Beaufort and although Elizabeth smiled an enquiry, she knew quite well that her mother-in-law was referring to the new Archbishop of Canterbury's chaplain.

'Son of a butcher,' the Countess continued in a low, furious voice. 'I never thought to see the day when such a man would be received at court. And you only have to look at him to see that he is inordinately ambitious.'

Elizabeth thought her mother-in-law's strictures unjust. Thomas Wolsey's rather bovine features conveyed no such impression to her, but Margaret Beaufort was a shrewd judge of character and she could possibly, be right.

The two ladies were walking in procession at Ludlow to yet another proxy marriage of Arthur and the Infanta Catalina; a fact which provoked more acidulated comments from the Countess.

'How much longer can this farce continue?' she demanded. 'I am coming to the conclusion that Ferdinand and Isabella have no intention of honouring this contract.'

But for once, Margaret Beaufort was wrong. In May of the following year Infanta at last set out from Granada.

A month later, Edmund de la Pole again fled abroad, to Maximilian, and this time was accompanied by his younger brother. Richard de la Pole had been aware for quite some time that his likeness to his uncle, Richard the third, was being remarked upon by those people who remembered the late King as he had been in life and not as the hunch-backed travesty it was now the custom to recall. He had decided that discretion was the better part of valour and that it was as well to leave England before the fatal similarity landed him in the Tower.

The two brothers had a rough crossing and the same wild summer storms which they encountered in the Channel, blew the Infanta's fleet back into the harbour of Laredo, where she had to wait until mid-September before setting out once more. Even then, the freak weather was not played out and the Spaniards were forced to land not at Gravesend, where Sir John Paston waited to greet his future Queen, but at Plymouth.

The Plymothians were delighted. They had suffered so much at the hands of the French that they looked upon this union with Spain as a blow aimed at their mortal enemies. As the Infanta came ashore, she saw burnt-out houses still thrusting upwards like blackened fingers of doom against the pale October sky, silent reminders of the latest French raid on the town. Nevertheless, she thought the broad stretch of turf and the little island away to her left very beautiful; some consolation to a desperately home-sick girl.

The manners of the English, however, she found execrable, everyone pushing and shoving behind her as she entered the church to give thanks for her safe arrival; the guttural voices clamouring incessantly in this rough language of which she knew barely a word. Her attendants, too, were scandalised by the familiarity with which these people called out to the Princess, addressing all sorts of personal remarks to her and staring the poor girl out of countenance. Theirs was not the respectful devotion, the quiet reverance accorded to Catalina in Spain, but a noisy, exuberant ovation; none the less sincere for that, as the Spaniards were quick to appreciate.

'The Infanta,' one wrote home, 'has been received everywhere as though she were the Saviour of the World.'

The Plymothians would no doubt have been startled had they been privileged to read these words, for there was very little difference in their attitude towards anyone on whom they chose to bestow their approval. 'There's dear of 'n' could apply equally well to the Almighty, a Princess of Spain or a beggar-child strapped to its mother's back. But the Spaniards were not to know this and, in consequence, the welcome given to the Infanta was seen as exclusively Spain's.

They rode on through the damp discomforts of an English autumn greatly heartened. They were not impervious to the dreary colours of the landscape or to the chill that struck through to the very marrow of the bones, but they felt now that these hardships were worth the endurance.

The King awaited Catalina's coming with Arthur and the Queen at Farnborough. Watching Henry, Elizabeth wondered how much he really wanted this alliance with Spain. His political sense told him it was wise, but his French blood, which ran strongly in him at times, surely must deplore it. He was no more communicative than he had ever been and, since the execution of Warwick, Elizabeth knew them to be drifting apart even more irrevocably than before. The scar on her soul was deep; her life crowded with ghosts that haunted her dreams and taunted her waking moments, reproaching her for those periods of intimacy with Henry when two terribly lonely people yearned towards each other in an agony of isolation. At such times the dead would push between them; a long, sad-eyed procession – John of Gloucester, Edward of Warwick, Elizabeth Woodville, Cicely Neville and, above all, Richard Plantagenet, King of England. Elizabeth had thought her passion for her uncle dead, but lately it had flared and burned in those unguarded moments when her thoughts had wandered into the forbidden realm of the might-have-been.

The Infanta's envoy, De Ayala, interrupted her cogitations and she realised guiltily that she had not been paying attention to the proceedings.

'It is not the custom in Spain, Your Majesty,' he was saying in a disapproving tone of voice, 'for the bridegroom and his family to see the bride before the wedding-day. My mistress will therefore remain at Dogmersfield tonight and then proceed separately to London tomorrow.'

Henry stared at the thin Spanish face before him, at the

high-bred look of disdain for barbaric English ways, and felt annoyed.

'The girl is in England now,' he answered coldly. 'Our customs are not yours.' He turned to Arthur, bidding him get ready to ride: they would go to Dogmersfield that night. 'And we shall see the Princess Catherine even though she has gone to bed,' he informed the outraged De Ayala.

'My God, these Spaniards think they own the earth,' he said later to Fox as they rode through the deepening dusk to the Bishop of Bath and Wells' palace, once Fox's property, but no longer so since his elevation first to the See of Durham and then to that of Winchester. Henry was bitter. Ferdinand and Isabella must be made to realise that this was an alliance between equal powers; England was not thanking Spain on her knees for the honour of marrying her chief son to one of its lesser daughters. Henry Tudor stood on a par with Isabella of Castile and Ferdinand of Aragon and everyone must be made to see this, and at once.

Catalina certainly did so when, amid the horrified cries of her ladies and the tearful protestations of her duenna, she consented to receive her prospective husband and father-in-law.

'We are in England now,' she told Donna Elvira. 'We must bow to the wishes of her King.'

'It is wrong,' moaned the duenna.

The young Princess considered this, then reluctantly shook her head, smiling. 'Nothing is wrong,' she answered positively, 'that does not contravene God's laws.'

It was this extremely Spanish regard for the laws of God as expounded by the Catholic Church, that first struck Elizabeth when she met her future daughter-in-law; and she was glad that she had chosen as her personal wedding gift a phial of the Virgin's milk and one of Her girdles.

The Queen and the Infanta looked at each other and Elizabeth saw a square-set young girl of sixteen whose chief pretension to beauty was an abundance of auburn hair – a legacy, smiled Catalina, through her interpreter, from her mother's ancestor, John of Gaunt. This fact made a fragile bond between them, for the Queen was Gaunt's great-great-granddaughter. On the Infanta's part, she saw a woman of some thirty-five summers, once very lovely but now a little faded and past her prime. There was something in the eyes, thought Catalina, infinitely sad; a tired look as though Elizabeth found the burden of life too heavy.

On the ninth of November the Infanta rode in state through the London streets to meet officially her husband and his family who were awaiting her at Baynard's Castle. Those closest to the Queen thought that she seemed ill, but for Elizabeth it was always a strain to be in her grandmother's old home: everywhere she looked, there was some reminder of Cicely Neville. Only that morning, she had found herself in that same room where, thirty years ago, she had played on the hearth with her sisters and Richard's two children.

She shook herself free from these thoughts and awaited Catalina's arrival. Beside her stood Arthur, a delicate fifteen-year-old, nervously biting his lip and playing with the jewelled buckle of his belt. Of all Elizabeth's children, he was the least known to her, for he had had his own household at Ludlow since early childhood. Sometimes, when he coughed and the thin shoulders shook under the velvets and silks, she could not help remembering those of her family who had died from that wasting disease; her aunts, Anne and Isabel Neville; Anne's son, Edward, The Prince of Wales; her own sister, Mary. She felt frightened: she and Henry could not afford to lose another son. If only Arthur had been as healthy as his younger brother!

That robust young man was enjoying himself hugely, escorting his sister-in-law-to-be through the packed London streets and receiving, as always, the adulation of the crowds.

'God bless "little Edward",' someone shouted and Henry knew that this was a reference to his likeness to Edward the fourth. He was pleased: he was aware how popular his grandfather had been, and standing up in the stirrups, he waved his gold-handled whip.

But the Infanta, too, excited a good deal of admiration, in her wide-brimmed Spanish hat over its tight fitting cap beneath. 'St Catherine' and 'St Ursula', who welcomed her with the usual long-winded speeches, were frankly envious of it; and in Gracechurch street, 'Policy' 'Noblesse' and 'Virtue' nearly fell out of their mock castle of red and white roses, trying to get a better view of Catalina's face.

Her Spanish ladies also attracted attention and in Cornhill 'Job' and 'Boetius' had to kick the operator of the clockwork signs of the zodiac before he could be persuaded to stop staring at the Señoritas and start the mechanism rotating on its ponderous way. At the Standard, in Cheapside, the procession of 'illustrious prophets' was equally hard pressed to attend to the matter in hand; while the City Recorder several times lost the thread of his discourse when the Infanta smiled at him.

But at last it was all over and Catalina gained the comparative calm of Baynard's Castle. Two day's later, on November the fourteenth, she and Arthur were married with as much pomp and ceremony as Henry could contrive. A careful man by nature, he also knew when money should be spent.

During the dancing which followed the great banquet, Arthur and his bride won much applause. But it was young Henry, throwing off his robe and capering about in his doublet, dancing first with his aunt Katherine and then with his sister, Margaret, who drew most of the attention. He was the sun to Arthur's moon. Elizabeth wondered uneasily if it would always be so.

28

WHILE the Prince and Princess of Wales held court at Ludlow, the Londoners settled back into the calm of everyday existence. Christmas came and went in the usual round of festivities, and the New Year saw the arrival in England of a thirty-two-year-old Italian named Polydore Vergil, collecting 'Peter's Pence' for Alexander the sixth. But whether Polydore would ever return to Italy was doubtful. Like Dominic Mancini before him, he found the English a fascinating study; a mass of contradictions; a people constantly in rebellion against, yet complying with, authority. Beneath the prejudices and blind bigotries which were so much a part of the English character, Polydore descried an enormous tolerance; a tolerance which would, he suspected, paradoxically stifle all opposition to the corporate will by absorbing rebellion and making it respectable. For nothing was deadlier to the revolutionary than to find himself an accepted member of that society which he sought to overthrow, or to receive sympathy and understanding when all he craved was contumely and a martyr's crown.

Between the Italian and the King there was immediate sympathy. Henry recognised in Polydore the sympathetic listener whom he had lacked since Morton's death; a mind in tune with his own. He accordingly made Vergil an Archdeacon of Wells.

'A poor honour for so learned a man,' Henry apologised. 'Unfortunately, my subjects abhor honours being given to foreigners.'

Polydore knew it. There were many thoughts and emotions rife in the world today which he thoroughly disliked, but none more so than the growing sense of nationalism. And nowhere was it more apparent than here, in this little, off-shore island of Europe; here, where for a hundred years or so strangers had been recording the Englishman's great love of himself and his contempt for all things foreign; here, where for decades they had paid nothing more than lip-service to the concept of Christendom.

The canker was spreading, also, to other countries. That wily monarch, Louis the eleventh, had made it fashionable to be a Frenchman first, a Christian second. In Spain, the final expulsion of the Moors, while it had struck a great blow for Christendom, had engendered the feeling that to be of Aragon or Castile was to be of the world's *elite*. And in the internecine feuds of his own country, Polydore saw that this new awareness of geographical identity could lead to wars as bitter as any between Christian and Infidel.

So Polydore was glad that Henry Tudor was enlightened enough not only to welcome foreigners at his court, but to attempt, also, to absorb them into the pattern of English life.

'You would have found my late master, the Duke of Urbino, much to your taste,' he told Henry as they walked together in the Greenwich gardens enjoying the warmth of an April day. 'An extremely liberal and educated man.'

Henry glanced quickly at the Italian to see if any slur on his own character were intended. Satisfied that it was not, he smiled, showing his rotting teeth.

'I have read your book, *De Inventibus Rerum,* and enjoyed it. To know the origins of things, language, religion and so forth, can only be of value.'

'Ah! So my kinsman, Cardinal Adriano Castelli, thinks. It was he who suggested that I should write it.'

The King looked around him. It was a beautiful day; thin pools of shadow lay under the trees, but everywhere else the spring sunlight was as clear and sharp as the citrus fruits of Spain. And at the thought of Spain, Henry's contentment grew. He had a great power linked to England in marriage and a treaty of perpetual peace had recently been concluded with Scotland: James was no longer adamant in his refusal to marry the Princess Margaret. At home, the coffers were full, thanks to Empson and Dudley who, however much they might be detested by the people had done very good work for Henry Tudor.

Henry noticed a patch of silverweed growing by the wall

and his thoughts winged back over the years. He had come a long way from Maude Herbert and that evening at Pembroke Castle when he had gone into exile with his uncle Jasper. But the King was always wary and never more so than when life seemed to be doing him homage: it had played him false so many times before. And Henry was right to be afraid.

Into the placid sunlight, cutting through Polydore Vergil's honeyed words, flapping greyly like some harbinger of doom, came Richard Fox, his face yellow with anticipated fear. For messengers had arrived from Ludlow; messengers on sweating horses, with terror-stricken eyes; messengers who wore about their arms the long black scarves of mourning.

The news of Prince Arthur's death less than five months after the marriage it had taken years to bring about, stunned the English court. But Elizabeth was more than stunned: she was heart-broken. It seemed as though all her life people near to her had been snatched away before they could reach old age. In the presence of the court, she hid her tears as best she could, merely saying: 'We are young and God is where He has always been.' But in the privacy of her own room, she gave way to her overmastering grief. Arthur was her eldest child, her first-born, for whom had first stirred that maternal devotion which, over the lonely years, had compensated her for so much else that was lacking. She desperately needed comfort but did not know where to turn.

Her sister, Katherine, was with her, but Katherine was busy with miseries of her own. Ever since the birth of her son, she had been afraid for both his safety and her husband's. To be allied to the Plantagenets and to produce heirs was not wise, as the Courtenay family was finding out. No: decidedly Katherine was of no comfort to Elizabeth.

Unexpectedly, it was Henry who came to his wife; the first time in all their married life that he had sought her out and offered her consolation. But when he sat beside her, holding her hand like a frightened child seeking reassurance from its mother, Elizabeth understood. Henry was not offering, but asking for comfort. The fear that he had made this marriage with Spain in the Earl of Warwick's blood, and that God had again shown his anger by snatching away yet another of Henry's sons, threatened to overwhelm him.

Henry's despair, however, was not of long duration. As he gripped Elizabeth's hand, he felt again the reassurance of survival surge through him as it had so often done in the past. He would placate God, pick up the pieces and go on.

But the King had been shaken more severely than ever before in his life, and a frightened Henry was even more dangerous than usual. When the two de la Poles had fled abroad the previous year, he had thrown their brother, William, in the Tower. Now he added all those from whom he sensed the slightest danger, either real or imaginary. His wife's half-brother, the Marquis of Dorset, was taken into custody – St Malo was neither forgiven nor forgotten – along with his sister-in-law's husband, William Courtenay. Henry remembered also that Sir James Tyrrell had sheltered Edmund de la Pole during his flight to Guisnes and, accordingly, sent Bishop Fox across the Channel to bring Sir James home under the assurance of a safe-conduct.

Tyrrell was wary. He had always been conscious of the invidiousness of his position as a former friend and servant of King Richard, but after seventeen years of devoted service, surely he had earned Henry Tudor's trust and could repay his King the compliment in kind. He knew that Henry had looked askance at the hospitality which he had extended towards Edmund de la Pole and had often cursed himself for being such a fool. The fact was that he had known Edmund as a child and had once been enamoured, albeit from afar, of the boy's mother, a sister of Edward the fourth.

When Tyrrell had first heard of the arrests made so suddenly in England, he had correctly judged them to be the work of a frightened and seriously rattled man, liable to pounce in any direction. Sir James had, therefore, together with his son, withdrawn into the fortress of Guisnes, where his instinct for danger was soon proved correct, and he found himself besieged.

'We can last out here for months,' he told his son, 'and, at the worst, there is always France.'

Tyrrell had consented, however, to receive Bishop Fox. The prelate was, as ever, extremely plausible.

'His Majesty guarantees you a safe-conduct. There have been certain ugly rumours abroad in England and the King wishes to give you an opportunity to clear your name.'

'And if I cannot – to His Majesty's satisfaction, that is?' The Bishop shrugged and spread the big, capable hands which betrayed his yeoman origins. 'Very unlikely! The King holds you in the greatest esteem. Come with me now and the matter can be settled within the month.'

Tyrrell glanced from the window to the siege-ships lying in the harbour. He did not fancy a life of exile and he could not withstand Henry for ever. Far better, as Fox had pointed out, to allay the King's suspicions once and for all.

'A safe-conduct is guaranteed?'

The Bishop smiled and inclined his head.

The next day, as the ship stood out in the Channel, just outisde Calais harbour, Sir James, held between two burly sailors, faced Sir Thomas Lovell, Chancellor of the Exchequer.

'You have a choice,' the chancellor told him. 'Either send a token to your son, commanding him to join you on board, or – '

'Never!' exclaimed Tyrrell furiously.

'Or be thrown overboard into the sea as you are.' And Lovell indicated the captive's bound hands.

Tyrrell's bluster died. He could feel the breath of the seamen hot upon his cheeks and had little doubt that the threat would be put into execution. So much for Henry Tudor's promise of a safe-conduct! Sir James spat, but hesitated all the same. Would he be luring his son to his death? He could not believe it. It was more than probably that the King had some shady mission he wanted Tyrrell to undertake and wished to hold the younger Tyrrell as hostage. Also, like many another before him, Sir James felt that where there was life there was also hope. Let him but once prove Henry's suspicions unfounded and he and Tom would be back again in Guisnes before April was out.

He agreed, therefore, to send the token and, with his son safely aboard, the crossing of the Channel was soon accomplished. But Sir James Tyrrell was to have no opportunity to speak to the King. On May the second, he was arraigned and tried at Guildhall on a charge of high treason and, four days later, still utterly incredulous, went to the block. His son, Thomas, though condemned, was later reprieved.

Henry was satisfied. The encompassing of Tyrrell's death had not been his original intention when he had sent Fox to Guisnes with his offer of a safe-conduct. Arthur's death, however, had driven the King into a corner. No one knew better than he that, with only one son standing between him and the end of the Tudor dynasty, Yorkist hopes would be stirring; had been stirring before Arthur was cold in his grave. And because these hopes could no longer centre upon the Earl of Warwick, whom everyone now knew to be dead, they would almost inevitably revolve around the two sons of Edward the fourth, whom no one could prove to be dead. It was the old story: could he but produce the bodies, or at least some evidence of the boys' murder, he might stifle the resurgent hopes of the White Rose adherents. But he had never known were to look for the remains and everyone connected with the crime was dead – everyone, that was, except Sir James Tyrrell.

Tyrrell had been the innocent bystander; the man who, in London by chance to collect the robes for the Prince of Wales' investiture, had been called in by Sir Robert Brackenbury to view the hideous work of Catesby's and Ratcliffe's hands. It was highly unlikely, therefore, that he could be induced to own himself the murderer. Such a confession might obviously have been wrung from him by torture, but who would seriously believe the words of a man broken by the rack and the thumb screw?

It had been at this moment in his train of thought that Henry had perceived the value of Tyrrell's execution. A dying man would naturally wish to unburden his conscience of its most heinous crime – and after Sir James' death, who would be able to refute any confession attributed to him? His son, who might or might not be a party to the truth, could be held in custody until such time as the story had gained credence. The King had permitted himself a smile; he could almost hear the ghost of John Morton applauding him. He would yet make all safe for his son.

And who better to disseminate the story than Polydore Vergil, a man who had no suspicion of the truth and who could, therefore, more easily believe what was told to him? The Italian was fascinated. The disappearance of the two boys had been exhaustively discussed throughout Europe when Vergil was in his teens and the probability of their murder widely canvassed. He was delighted to know that the mystery had at last been cleared up.

'This Sir James, he confessed before his execution?' he enquired of Henry. He was guest-of-honour at the Whitsun banquet when Henry and Elizabeth wore their crowns.

Henry's eyes slid sideways, encountering those of his wife for a brief moment. She was the only other person who knew the truth and he could not be completely sure of her reactions.

He need not have worried, however. Elizabeth knew that the 'confession' was false and that it would result in yet another calumny being heaped upon her uncle, Tyrrell having apparently declared that the murders were carried out at the instigation of King Richard. But she knew also that there was nothing she could do about it. If she got to her feet now and shouted out the truth, who would believe her? More important, who would want to believe her? There would be many, when the story was finally blazoned abroad, who would wonder secretly why Tyrrell's confession, if true, had not been read aloud from the scaffold; why copies of it had not been on sale as was customary; why it had not been nailed to the doors of the churches and other public places. But if they drew their own conclusions, would they speak? It was most improbable: the recent executions and imprisonments had served as cogent warnings. So the Queen said nothing, tacitly acquiescing in her husband's lie and smiling mechanically at Vergil's pious exclamations that the truth would out, no matter how well concealed.

'Particularly here, in England,' the Italian declaimed, fluttering expressive hands that glowed with an effulgence of emerald rings. 'Here, where man's pursuit of the truth has always been an example to the rest of an admiring Europe.'

30

In private, Polydore Vergil's flattering estimate of the English character was not nearly so generous.

'The English,' he wrote, 'are valiant fighters but do not over-exert themselves when it comes to working.' And he agreed with a compatriot of his who, two years earlier, had expressed the opinion that: 'England has very fertile soil, but only sufficient agriculture is carried on to ensure the people a living. If they would only work all the land able to be cultivated, they could sell large amounts of grain to neighbouring countries.' Laziness, Polydore decided, was the curse of the English nation; although the women, he reflected were harder working than the men and 'of an extreme beauty with skin so white that it resembles snow. The men are tall and fair with grey-coloured eyes.'

Another thing which the Italian, in common with many other foreigners, deplored was that the English were very irreligious; full of outward observance, but with each man having his own concept of God and maintaining that his ideas were right. But Vergil also had to admit that everyone was very quick with Biblical quotations; never more so than at present when the verse from Leviticus: 'You shall not look upon the nakedness of your brother's wife, for it is your brother's nakedness,' was being bandied from lip to lip.

The reason for all the pother was the proposal by Isabella of Castile that the widowed Infanta should be betrothed to Prince Henry, now Prince of Wales in Arthur's stead. If the marriage between Catalina – or Catherine, as she was now generally known – and Arthur had been consummated, it was out of the question: Leviticus was definite on that point. But *had* the marriage been consummated? Catherine declared not, but she was a good daughter of Spain and De Ayala had made it clear to her that her parents wished the alliance with England to continue. And then, there were Arthur's remarks; the first, 'Marriage is a thirsty pastime', made the morning after the wedding-night; and the second, made a short time later, 'This night I have been in Spain'.

It was the subject everywhere under discussion that summer and autumn of 1502, throughout the English court and beyond. Should Prince Henry be allowed to marry his brother's widow? Was Catherine a virgin-widow or had she truly been Arthur's wife?

The conjectures, both interested and obscene, the theological arguments, both for and against, went endlessly on until Elizabeth felt that she would scream. She was pregnant for the seventh time, had recently lost two sons and was thirty-six years of age. Constantly sick and tired, her sole concern with the projected marriage was whether the Infanta would make a suitable wife for her beloved son. She was of the opinion that Catherine would not.

'Oh, she is a charming girl,' the Queen told her sister, Cicely, 'and would have made an admirable wife for Arthur. He was so quiet and gentle.'

'Insipid,' was Cicely's astringent comment, but only to herself. Elizabeth looked ill and tired and Lady Welles had no wish to upset her.

'But she's not for Henry,' Elizabeth continued, warming her almost transparent hands at the fire crackling on the hearth. The November day was chilly and she shivered. 'Catherine is so Spanish; her sense of what is right and wrong very clearly defined in her own mind.'

'And Henry's is not?' Cicely enquired.

Elizabeth smiled. 'Henry's sense of right and wrong is . . . pliable,' she admitted reluctantly. 'It is very strong, but entirely his own creation.'

'So I have noticed,' Henry's aunt replied drily. 'I don't think that I have ever met a child who made up his own rules of life so young.'

'I think perhaps that our father did,' the Queen answered with a sigh. 'And our uncle Clarence.'

'Talking of our uncles,' Cicely said thoughtfully, 'do you believe this story of Tyrrell's confession?'

Elizabeth coloured faintly. 'Why not?'

'Why not, indeed?' Cicely's eyes narrowed. 'You know, I always thought you in our mother's confidence, so . . . if you say it's true, then it must be. I must admit, however, that I find our uncle's motives obscure. Why were our brothers murdered?'

Elizabeth shrugged, moving her chair a little nearer to the blaze. Strange that she should be so cold! Throughout all her other pregnancies she had been warm, even on the chilliest day. In reply to Cicely's question, she replied: 'To make Richard more secure, one must suppose.'

'Because Edward and little Richard were a focus for disaffection?' Lady Welles quirked her strongly marked eyebrows. 'Mmm. And yet he kept the murders a secret, so that no one has ever been certain whether the boys are dead or not. Now that is not the action of a rational man, do you think?'

Elizabeth rose quickly, her velvet gown whispering amongst the rushes as she paced agitatedly to and fro. 'Believe me,' she assured her sister, 'our brothers are dead and Richard knew it to be so.'

Cicely, seeing that Elizabeth obviously did not wish to pursue the subject, forbore to press her questions. She could not suppose that it mattered now, and guessed that her sister had not liked their uncle. This totally erroneous impression was gained from Elizabeth's constant disinclination to discuss Richard, and Cicely's complete ignorance as to the state of her sister's affections all those years ago when the marriage between uncle and niece had first been mooted. Nor, unlike her aunt, Catherine Woodville, had she ever had the slightest suspicion.

She went away after a while to inform her husband that Elizabeth looked ill and had no business to be bearing another child at her age. But Lord Welles was unsympathetic. Being related to Henry Tudor, he saw the necessity to ensure the succession to go from three sons to only one in less than two years was unnerving for the securest of monarchs.

'And your nephew is most certainly not that,' Cicely remarked and felt suddenly frightened. Elizabeth had become, over the years, more a part of his life than he had realised. It was only now, when he contemplated the possibility of losing her, that he knew how essential was her presence to his peace of mind. He had not wanted to marry her; had resented her entitlement to the throne and had been determined that no one should think him a king in right of his wife. He had, therefore, kept her in comparative subjection, the more so when he had become aware of her popularity with the people, who loved her because she was the daughter of her father. Added to this, there had been the barrier of his own nature; his inability to feel deeply about anyone except his mother.

'The English King is not uxorious,' the Spanish ambassador had once written, and it was true. The lonely years of humiliation and exile had done irreparable damage to Henry Tudor's emotions; had dried for ever his capacity to love. Even the emotion which he felt for Margaret Beaufort was a compound of respect and reverence; the former for her erudition; the latter simply because she was his mother.

'When Henry loves me, he loves himself,' the Countess had once remarked astutely to a friend, but without rancour.

Now, however, when Henry looked at Elizabeth's pale face and heavy eyes; when she pleaded sickness and was tired, he wanted to hold on to her, to prevent her going away. He had a premonition of her death, no matter how hard he tried to suppress it or how often the astrologers and fortune-tellers forecast her long life and good health. So he turned for consolation to his great love, building, and paid constant visits to Westminster Abbey to oversee the erection of his beautiful new chapel. With him would go Reginald Bray, an ageing man now and very ill. And when Henry looked at him, he shivered: the finger of death seemed to be pointing at so many of the people whom he most valued.

With the coming of winter, the burning interest in the question of the Infanta's virginity paled somewhat before the latest topic for discussion; the summer marriage of the Princess Margaret and King James the fourth of Scotland. But while the Queen supervised the preparation of her daughter's trousseau and made plans for her own ceremonial procession at the wedding, she could not rid herself of the fancy that she would never live to see it accomplished.

Never before had she had so much trouble with a pregnancy. Her body felt tired and too heavy to obey her commands; she awoke in the mornings with such a feeling of lassitude that she never wanted to get up again. It was unlike her and she was worried.

But she had other problems also. Her two surviving daughters were strong, healthy children like their brother, Henry; but whereas Mary, a vital, pretty creature of six, had the straightforward lustiness of her Plantagenet grandfather, Margaret, at thirteen, was reminiscent of her aunt Margaret of Burgundy. There was a sly urgency in her rapidly ripening womanhood that boded ill for the future. Her predatory eyes would flit from one man to another, never meeting their gaze in open invitation, but, by the voluptuous swing of her hips or the insinuating pout of her over-red lips, suggest to their bolting senses all manner of delights in store. Elizabeth could not imagine a husband nearly twenty years Margaret's senior holding the girl's volatile fancy for long. And that would spell trouble. Whatever their natural inclinations, queens could not play fast and loose when a royal succession was at stake. She tried to instil some of her own moral precepts into the girl, but it was plainly useless. Margaret was not so much immoral as amoral, impervious to everything except the dictates of her own young body. Not even that strict disciplinarian, Margaret Beauford, had been able to influence her namesake or to imbue her with any more pious aspiration than to sleep with the first man who offered himself. Fortunately, no one had so far done so: fear of Henry had precluded that contingency.

As Christmas approached, Elizabeth went to visit Bridget in her convent at Dartford. The serene face beneath the nun's coif was all Woodville and reminded the Queen of their uncle Rivers. Bridget was the distilled essence of all those ineffable yearnings of the soul which, in Anthony Woodville, had been vitiated by the need for material comforts and the sybaritic urgings of the body. As they walked together in the cloisters, the wintry evening glimmering blue and grey about them, the angular shapes of the buildings softened by the gathering dusk, Elizabeth spoke to this youngest sister of hers of her love for their father's brother, and of her fear for her immortal soul.

Bridget turned and faced her sister, holding both Elizabeth's hands in a light, strong clasp. Only the chiming of a distant bell broke the silence and a young novice, hurrying in answer to the summons, flitted for a second across their line of vision, then merged, ghost-like, into the cavernous shadows of the ancient stones. The bell clashed into silence and there was nothing in the whole world but the whisper of their breath hanging in a frozen cloud on the icy air, and the beating of their hearts.

Then Bridget said: 'You love him still.' It was not a question: it seemed she knew the answer. She went on: 'I should not say this to you, for I fear that it is not the answer of the Church. But there is so little love in this world that what there is, is most precious; an emotion to be garnered and harvested against those moments of loneliness and desolation which beset us all.'

'Ah!' cried Elizabeth, 'you can speak so because yours is the love of God. It is pure, untouchable; the flame of the spirit. But mine is not.'

'It could have been. Had our uncle been willing, the Holy father might have granted you a dispensation. And you have been a good wife to Henry.'

'My body has been his; my mind never. He did not seek it, nor did I offer it. We have been happy, nevertheless, after our fashion.'

Bridget released her sister's hands and they resumed their walk, their light footfalls echoing oddly in the quiet. At the end of the cloister, Bridget turned once more to look at Elizabeth, her face gleaming palely under the close-set wimple.

'I say this to you. I do not believe that any love is wrong. It is the greatest jewel in our earthly crown. Give it back to God as his most precious gift to you.'

Two days later, Elizabeth took her leave of Bridget and, because she felt within herself that this was the last good-bye, she gazed long upon the beloved features before climbing into her litter. She sent up a fervent prayer that this youngest of her ill-starred family should always know happiness and her prayer was destined to be granted. Bridget would die shortly before her nephew gave his orders for the dissolution of the monasteries.

January saw the proxy marriage of Margaret and James, and the attendant ceremonial left Elizabeth exhausted. She found herself, too, a prey to odd fancies and momentary delusions. As she descended one night into the banqueting hall at the Tower, the trumpets blowing their fanfares and the light from the cressets flowing over the silks and velvets of the bowing courtiers like the transient ripples on the surface of the sea, she thought that she saw Richard. She almost cried out, so strong was her conviction: then the illusion shattered. As the young man moved out from the shadows of the wall into the pool of light shed by the torch above his head, Elizabeth saw that he was fair-haired and rosy-skinned, the very antithesis of her imaginings.

But her ladies noticed that many times afterwards, the

Queen would start at the sound of a footfall or stand, watching, by a window as though she were waiting for someone.

At the beginning of February, she made her preparations for the move to Richmond where, Henry had decided, the new baby should be born. Elizabeth was eager to go. Richmond held no memories for her as did the other palaces of the Plantagenets. Richmond was as new as Henry Tudor, himself, and she would feel better there. Her departure was set for February the twelfth, the day following her thirty-seventh birthday, which would be celebrated in the usual way.

Elizabeth awoke early on the morning of her birthday and lay for a moment, looking at the pale filter of dawn through her window. Suddenly, she realised what it was that had awakened her; a sharp, insistent pain, warning her that labour had begun prematurely.

By midday, the Tower was in uproar. The child, a girl, had been born dead and the doctors shook their heads and pursed their lips over the condition of the Queen. Finally, one of them told Henry that it would be unwise to hope too much. Another, blunter but no less kind, advised the King not to hope at all: Elizabeth was sinking fast and it was doubtful if she would outlive the night.

Henry, his mind scrambling with confused thoughts, stood by his wife's bed and stared down at the once beautiful face, now emaciated by approaching death. Elizabeth had been his companion for just over fifteen years and her passing would leave a void which no one else could fill. She had been obedient, acquiescent and fulfilled all her marriage vows with the one exception, her promise to love. Well, he had not wanted that, nor did it strike him that he might have deprived her of the most necessary emotion in her life.

'Send some words of comfort to the Queen,' an Italian had once written to his master, 'for she needs a little loving.'

Shortly before midnight, Elizabeth, who had fallen into a stupor after receiving Extreme Unction, opened her eyes and Henry stooped to take her cold hands in his. The doctors drew back.

Struggling to raise herself and speaking with great urgency, Elizabeth whispered: 'Where one truly loves, nothing can make any difference.'

The death-rattle sounded in her throat and the doctors moved back to her side. They bent over her, then straightened, signing that the Queen was dead. Her women began to weep softly, opening the windows so that her spirit might ride free upon the night wind, and Henry continued to look down at her, his bemused mind trying to make sense of her last words. And after a long time, he came to the conclusion that she had not been speaking to him at all, but to someone beyond him, over his shoulder, whom only she was able to see.

Postlude

HENRY outlived Elizabeth by another six years.

In the August following her mother's death, Margaret Tudor at last married James the fourth of Scotland, thus making it possible, a hundred years later, for the House of Stuart to succeed to the English throne in the person of her great-grandson, James the sixth of Scotland and first of England.

Henry, a widower with only one surviving male child, became haunted by the need to preserve the Tudor dynasty, an obsession which was to colour the life of his son. In 1506, he offered himself to the widowed Juana of Spain, who had become hopelessly mad after the death of her husband, Duke Philip, but his proposal was rejected.

Juana's sister, Catherine of Aragon, was never allowed to return home to her native Spain, nor was her dowry ever refunded by Henry. Her mother died in 1504 and Catherine lived on in England in terribly straitened circumstances, until her father-in-law's death made possible her re-marriage to the new King, Henry the eighth.

Three years after Elizabeth's death, her cousin. Edmund de la Pole, was handed over to Henry by Philip of Austria. Henry imprisoned, but did not execute him, leaving that to his son who had Edmund beheaded in 1513. Henry also imprisoned his wife's step-brother, the Marquis of Dorset, and William Courtenay, the Earl of Devon's son. They were incarcerated until the King's death finally set them free.

Henry died at Richmond on April the twenty-first, 1509. On May the ninth, his funeral cortège passed along the London streets as he was carried in regal state on that last journey, to his resting place in Westminster Abbey. Few people mourned him: he had not been loved.